OTHER BOOKS BY CHARLES WILLEFORD

Proletarian Laughter
High Priest of California
Wild Wives
Pick-Up
The Black Mass of Brother Springer
The Director
The Burnt Orange Heresy
Cockfighter
The Machine in Ward Eleven
Off the Wall
Miami Blues
New Hope for the Dead
Sideswipe
Something About a Soldier
New Forms of Ugly

THE
WAY
WE DIE
NOW

THE WAY WE DIE NOW

*No one owns life.
But anyone with a frying pan owns death.*
—WILLIAM S. BURROUGHS—

A NOVEL BY

CHARLES WILLEFORD

RANDOM HOUSE NEW YORK

LIBRARY OF CONGRESS
Library of Congress Cataloging-in-Publication Data
Willeford, Charles Ray, 1919-
The way we die now : a novel / by Charles Willeford.
p.   cm.
ISBN 0-394-56525-8 : $16.95
I. Title.
PS3545.I464W3   1988
813'.54—dc19   87-27226
                     CIP

Manufactured in the United States of America
Typography and binding by J. K. Lambert
98765432
First Edition

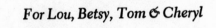

For Lou, Betsy, Tom & Cheryl

THE
WAY
WE DIE
NOW

CHAPTER 1

TINY BOCK HEAVED HIS BULK FROM THE SAND CHAIR.
He stood silently in the clearing for a moment listening, but all he could hear was the whir of insects and the scuttling of a few foraging wood rats. He folded the red-and-green webbed chair, took it to the black pickup truck and threw it into the back. He opened the cab door on the passenger's side and reached for the paper sack on the seat. There were two bologna sandwiches wrapped in oil paper and two hard-boiled eggs in the sack. He unwrapped one of the sandwiches, noticed that the lunch meat had turned green on the outer edge. He rewrapped the sandwich, put it back in the sack, took one of the hard-boiled eggs. He cracked open the egg and peeled it, but when he split the egg in two he realized that the yolk had turned purple and there was a strong smell of sulphur.

Twenty feet away a raccoon, also smelling the egg and the sulphur, rose on its hind legs and waved its forefeet, sniffing the air.

Tiny Bock noticed the raccoon and placed the two halves

of the egg on a tuft of grass. As Tiny moved to the cab of the truck the raccoon, a female, scurried forward and scooped up the two egg halves. The coon took the two halves to a muddy pool of water and rolled the egg in the water to wash it preparatory to eating. Tiny Bock, who had taken his shotgun from the cab of the truck, fired once. Eight of the twelve slugs hit the raccoon, reducing it to an unrecognizable spot of fur and blood. Bock reloaded the shotgun before replacing it on the gun rack above the seat.

Listening again, Bock could hear the airplane sound of the airboat long before he saw it. Then he spotted the boat; it was returning to the hammock from a different direction than he had expected, but Chico de las Mas was heading unerringly toward Bock and the parked truck. Skimming across the wet sawgrass of the Everglades, it resembled a giant but harmless insect.

Skidding the aluminum boat sideways, Chico stopped short of the dry brushy hammock. After Chico turned the engine off, and the whirling propeller had run down, Bock said, "What took you so long?"

"Had a hard time finding a deep enough sinkhole. But it won't matter. When the rains come this whole area'll be under a foot of water. You won't be able to drive out to the hammock here for another six months. I thought I heard a shotgun, but I wasn't sure."

Bock grinned and pointed to what was left of the raccoon. "I shot a coon."

The two men pushed the airboat into the clearing and well into the brush on the other side. Chico chained the prow of the boat to a cypress tree, and then padlocked the chain. They climbed into the cab of the truck. Chico took the wheel and drove across the dry sands, avoiding occasional puddles, toward the dirt and oolite access road, some ten minutes away. The access road had been built illegally by a group of Naples hunters almost five years ago in the Big Cypress. They had also planned to build a weekend lodge, but their plans had fallen through, so now the road, a foot above the water level, was a road to nowhere.

"There's blood on the front of your shirt," Bock said.

"I know." Chico took a bloody Baggie out of his shirt pocket and handed it to Bock.

"What's this?"

Chico laughed. "A bonus. Remember the tall one, the one they called C'est Dieu? I cut that out of his asshole."

Bock removed the soggy wad of money from the Baggie, tossed the Baggie out the window. He unfolded and counted the money. "One ten, and thirty ones. Forty bucks. Did you cut the others?"

"Didn't have to. I've been watching them close, and no one ever let old C'est Dieu out his sight. Always one or two with him. So I knew he was holding it for all of 'em."

Bock folded the bills and put them into his back pocket. "There's a couple of bologna sandwiches left in the sack if you want 'em."

"Sinking Haitians in a swamp is hard work, Mr. Bock. I thought we'd drive into Immokalee and get a decent meal at the cafeteria." Chico slowed down, ripped off his shirt and tossed it out the window.

"Why not? But you won't be able to eat in the cafeteria without a shirt."

"I'll buy a T-shirt at the sundry store. It's no big deal."

When he reached the access road, Chico got onto the raised road without any trouble using first gear. The road ran west for two miles before it met the state highway. Chico turned north and headed for Immokalee.

CHAPTER 2

COMMANDER BILL HENDERSON, HOMICIDE DIVISION EX-ecutive officer, Miami Police Department, entered Sergeant Hoke Moseley's cubicle, removed the *Miami Herald* from the chair beside the desk, tossed it toward the overflowing wastepaper basket, and sat down heavily. He looked at the sheet of paper on his clipboard and sighed.

"I'm running a little informal survey, Hoke."

"I'm busy right now, Bill. I think I've finally got a worthwhile lead on the Dr. Paul Russell killing."

Hoke's messy desk was littered with a half dozen sheets of bond typewriter paper, supplementary reports, and a red accordion file. He had been drawing diagrams on the bond paper with a ruler and a ballpoint.

"This is an important survey."

"More important than solving a cold case homicide?"

Bill pulled his lips back, exposing large gold-capped teeth that were entwined with silver wire. "Depends on whether you smoke or not. Have you quit yet?"

"Not exactly, but I'm down to about ten a day. I've tried to quit cold turkey, but the longest I've managed to go was about six hours. Now I time it and smoke a Kool every four hours, with maybe a few extra at night when I watch the tube. If I can hold it down to only ten a day, it's almost like not smoking at all."

Bill shook his head. "I switched over to cigars, but I still inhale, so I'll probably have to go back to cigarettes. After five cigars my throat's raw as a bastard, and I've been coughing up all kinds of shit in the morning."

"Is that the end of the survey?" Hoke picked up a Telectron garage opener device, the size of a king-size pack of cigarettes, and showed it to Bill Henderson. "Know what this is?"

"No, I don't, and no, I'm not finished. This really is important. I attended the new chief's weekly briefing this morning, and he's come up with a terrible plan. He wants to stop all smoking inside the police station. His idea's to set up a smoking area in the parking lot, and anytime you want to smoke you have to sign out for personal time and go out to the lot. Then, when you finish your smoke, you sign back in again and return to your desk or whatever. A lot of guys have already quit smoking, you see, and they've complained to the new chief that smoke from heavy smokers is invading their space."

"What about the men's room?"

"No smoking inside the building, period. That includes interrogation rooms, suspect lockup, everywhere except the outside parking lot."

"It won't work, Bill. Lieutenant Ramirez, in Robbery, smokes at least three packs a day. He might as well move his fucking desk out to the parking lot."

"That's what we tried to tell the new chief. But he figures if he makes it hard on smokers, they'll either cut down radically or quit."

"Does the new chief smoke? I never noticed."

"Snoose. He dips Copenhagen. He usually has a lipful of snuff, but he doesn't spit. He swallows the spit instead."

"That figures. The rule won't bother him any, so the bastard doesn't give a shit about the rest of us. But I don't think a rule that dumb can be enforced. Guys'll sneak 'em in the john or even at their desks."

"Not if they get an automatic twenty-five-dollar fine they won't."

"Jesus." Hoke took a Kool out of his pack and lighted it with his throwaway lighter. He took one drag and then butted it in his ashtray. "I lit that without thinking, and I've still got an hour to go." He returned the butt to his pack.

"That's why I'm running this survey, Hoke. If a big majority complains, he probably won't put in the rule. So I'll put you down as opposing the new rule, right?"

"Right. Now let me tell you about this little gadget—"

"Some other time. I've got to see some other guys before they go off shift." Henderson got to his feet. "One other thing—I almost forgot to tell you." Henderson snapped his fingers and turned in the doorway. At six-four and 250 pounds, his body almost filled the doorframe. "Major Brownley said to tell you to let your beard grow, and he'd call you Sunday night at home and let you know about the meeting—"

"This is only Thursday, and I work tomorrow. Does he mean that I let my beard grow out now, or do I shave tomorrow?"

"All he said was what I told you. So I suppose he means to let it grow from now till he tells you to shave."

8

"Did he say why? Perhaps I should talk to him about this first."

"You can't. He went down to the Keys and won't be back till Sunday night. He'll call you at home then and explain it to you, and also about the meeting."

"What meeting?"

"He didn't say. He's got a visitor, an old fraternity buddy he went to A and M with in Tallahassee, and they went fishing down in the Keys. Off Big Pine, I think."

"I've never grown a beard, Bill. Even if I go a day or two without shaving, it makes my neck itch. Did he give you any hint—"

"I'm only the executive officer. Major Brownley's the division chief, and he doesn't take me into his confidence on every little thing. I'm just passing along the message he gave me over the phone. He didn't come in today, and that's why I went to the new chief's meeting instead of him. If it was important for me to know, he would have told me the reason. Don't worry about it."

"Why shouldn't I worry? Wouldn't you be concerned if Willie ordered you to grow a beard?"

"I'd like to stay and talk about this with you, although it's a fruitless discussion. I say fruitless because anything we say would only be idle conjecture, based on inadequate information. But I suspect sometimes that Willie Brownley pulls shit like this once in a while just to keep us off-balance. My son Jimmy's like that. Only yesterday Jimmy asked me if he could grow a mustache."

"Jimmy's only twelve years old."

"Eleven. But I gave him permission anyway. I figure it'll take another six years before it grows out long enough to be noticed. But he was happy as hell when I told him to go ahead."

"At least Jimmy asked for permission. Sue Ellen had her hair all kinked up and then dyed it electric blue right down the middle. She didn't say anything. She just did it."

"But she's seventeen. If Jimmy was seventeen, he'd grow his mustache without asking me for permission."

"She looks terrible. She looks like the kind of girl who goes with boys who've dropped out of school."

"If she's still working at the car wash, that's the only kind of boy she's likely to meet. I'm not criticizing—at least she's got a job. But she's probably the only white girl in Miami working full-time at a car wash."

"I know. She's even picked up some black dialect. But I've discouraged her from using it around the house."

Henderson disappeared from the doorway. Hoke gathered his work sheets together and put them into the red-flagged Dr. Russell file. He locked the file, together with the supplementary reports, in his two-drawer file cabinet. He slipped into his blue poplin leisure jacket and dropped the garage door opener into the left leather-lined outside pocket before leaving his cubicle on the fourth floor of the Miami police station. Hoke always carried several loose .38-caliber tracers in the outside pocket of his jacket, and he'd had it lined with glove leather for this purpose.

Hoke rode the elevator down to the garage and climbed the ramp to the outside parking lot. He paused at the exit, inhaling the hot, humid air, and wondered where the new chief would put the smoking area in the lot. The fenced-in area would be crowded as hell if three hundred cops on each shift made trips back and forth to smoke. Not all of them smoked, however. But even one hundred and fifty cops going and coming from the building would crowd the elevator and stairways. It would take approximately twenty minutes for each cop who smoked to make his round trip and smoke a cigarette, and if each cigarette was charged to personal time, without pay, six smokes a day could mean a loss of two hours' pay for each smoker. That meant that many would be sneaking cigarettes and then get a twenty-five-dollar fine when they were caught. All this extra money coming into the department would mean that the new chief would probably meet his annual budget for the first time in the city's history.

Hoke climbed into his battered 1973 Pontiac Le Mans and lighted a cigarette for the drive home to Green Lakes. If the rule went in, despite the advice not to do it, the odds were good that it would be rescinded within three days. Tomorrow he would get together with Bill Henderson, and they could make up an office pool on how long the rule would last. After they made up the card, Hoke decided he would take number three before they sold the other slots around the office. This would be like found money. A rule that stupid couldn't possibly last for more than three days. . . .

THE GREEN LAKES SUBDIVISION, WHERE HOKE LIVED IN northwest Miami, bordered Hialeah, Dade County's second-largest city, but it was still primarily an enclave for WASPs, rednecks, and well-paid blue-collar workers who were employed, for the most part, at the Miami International Airport. There were a few Cuban families in the subdivision, but not very many, and one entire block had filled up with immigrant Pakistanis. The houses were all concrete block and stucco, three-bedroom, one-bathroom buildings, constructed during the mid-fifties. The homeowners' association had managed to stop more Pakistanis from buying houses by passing a new rule that limited the occupancy of each house to only six residents—unless a second bathroom was added to the building. The sewer system, also installed during the mid-fifties, was considered inadequate for any more added bathrooms, so no new permits for additional bathrooms were granted. This rule effectively kept out any additional Pakistanis, with their families of twelve or more —and often up to twenty-five—and it excluded large, extended Latin families as well. There was a grandfather clause, of course, so original WASP homeowners, with several children apiece, were not affected by the new ruling.

Most of the houses, but not all, backed up to a series of small square lakes—formerly rock and gravel quarries— that looked as though they were filled with green milk. The houses all were built from the same set of blueprints, but many owners, over the years, had added garages, carports, Florida rooms, and short docks for small boats. There were a few swimming pools, but not very many, and even a few gazebos. Because of drowning accidents, swimming was prohibited in the lakes. This rule wasn't enforced, and sometimes, late at night, a few bold people did some skinny-dipping. The lakes were bordered by tall Dade County pines, and the residents had planted their yards with orange, grapefruit, and mango trees, hedges of Barbados cherry and screw-leaf crotons, and several varieties of palms, including a few stately Royals. At one time coconut palms, planted by the original construction company, had lined the vertiginous streets, but when lethal yellow attacked the trees in the late seventies, they all had been removed by the Metro government. Nevertheless, the subdivision was a green oasis in the middle of a highly urbanized city, and Green Lakes, with its own Class B shopping center and mall, was considered a desirable location for white Americans to live. There was a zealous Crime Watch program, and the curving streets had large speed bumps spaced out every fifty yards and fifteen-mile-per-hour speed limit. Drivers who ignored the limit and the high, rounded speed bumps soon needed new shocks for their vehicles.

Hoke, with the windows of his car rolled down (although he had air-conditioning), observed the speed limit, easing his car over the bumps at an angle, and tried to open garage doors with the door opener whenever he passed a garage with a closed door. Not every garage had an electric door-opener; but many of them did, he knew, and he was trying to see if the late Dr. Russell's door opener would work on any of them. He tried it on at least a dozen garages before he pulled into his own driveway, but it didn't open any of them. Apparently each garage door opener had its own frequency.

Hoke's house had an open-sided carport but no garage. Ellita's Honda Civic was in the carport, and Sue Ellen's Yamaha motorcycle was chained and padlocked to the left steel roof support. Hoke parked behind the Civic and entered the house.

Pepe, Ellita's one-year-old, was crying and shrieking as Hoke came through the front door, and Hoke's two daughters, Sue Ellen, seventeen, and Aileen, fifteen, were setting the table in the dining room.

"What's the matter with Pepe?"

"He needs changing," Aileen said.

"Why don't you change him then?"

"We're setting the table now, and Ellita's in the kitchen."

Hoke lifted Pepe out of his crib in the living room and carried the screaming, writhing body into the bathroom. He removed the soiled Pamper and tossed it into the black plastic Hefty bag that was kept in the bathroom for this purpose. The bag was half-filled with dirtied Pampers, and the fetid odor permeated the small bathroom. Hoke turned on the water in the shower, adjusted the taps one-handed until it was warm, and then, holding the boy by his wrists, hosed him down with the hand-held shower head. He dried Pepe with Ellita's face towel, sprinkled the boy's bottom with Johnson's baby powder, and put on a clean Pamper.

Pepe had stopped crying now, and Hoke returned him to his crib in the living room.

Hoke went down the hall to his own small bedroom at the far end of the house and changed from his leisure suit into a pair of khaki shorts and an old gray gym T-shirt that had the arms cut off at the shoulders. He lay on his cot and looked at the cracked ceiling, holding the garage door opener in his right hand. The device was simple enough. It worked on radio waves, or something, and each garage mechanism was set a little differently. You pressed the button, aiming at the radio box in the garage ceiling through the closed door, and the door opened. If you pressed the button again, still aiming, although you didn't even have to get close to the box in the garage ceiling, the door closed. There was also a button inside the garage, usually by the door to the kitchen. If you pressed that, it also opened the door. When the door was closed, no one could open it manually from the outside, although it could be raised manually from inside the garage. An opener like this was not supposed to assist in a murder—and yet it had. Of that much, he was positive.

But he wasn't certain; he merely had an intuition, and that meant that he was getting anxious again, pressing too hard. When he was first assigned to the cold cases, together with Bill Henderson and Ellita Sánchez, they had been lucky, solving three three-year-old cases during the first ten days. Then Henderson had been promoted to commander, and Hoke and Ellita had worked alone. He had pushed, trying too hard and putting in too many hours, and had come very close to suffering a breakdown. A month's leave without pay had given him enough distance to realize that this was just a job, not a mission. After Ellita had been shot and retired on disability, he had worked alone until they gave him González, a young investigator too inexperienced to provide much help. Hoke hadn't come close to solving a cold case since he had returned from his month's leave, and now, what with the shortage of detectives in the Homicide Division, this was an assignment Major Brownley couldn't keep him on much longer. He was needed for regular duty, and so was González; but it would be rewarding to solve at least one more case before he returned to straight duty.

Hoke shook his head. It didn't pay to become obsessed with anything, especially a case as gelid as the Russell murder. If he solved it, fine; if he didn't, what difference would it make a hundred years from now? Hoke clicked the door opener several times, aiming at nothing. Then Ellita called to him that dinner was ready. He tossed the opener onto the dresser and, barefoot, padded down the hall to the dining room.

CHAPTER 3

HOKE SHARED A LEASED HOUSE WITH ELLITA SÁNCHEZ; her baby son, Pepe; and Hoke's two teenaged daughters from his broken marriage.

Patsy, Hoke's ex-wife, had kept the two girls, following their divorce, for ten years. She had then married a pinch hitter for the Dodgers, a black ballplayer named Curly Peterson, and moved to Los Angeles. Before she left Vero Beach, Florida (she had met Curly Peterson there during spring training), she had shipped the two girls down to Miami and Hoke on a Greyhound bus. Hoke had not seen or heard from the girls in ten years, when they had been six and four years old. Because there was no way he could think of to get out of the responsibility for them, he had, of course, taken them in. Ellita had moved in with him to share the expenses when her father had thrown her out of his house when she became pregnant. Hoke was not the father of Pepe Sánchez; that honor belonged to a one-night stand Ellita had picked up in Coconut Grove, but Ellita's parents suspected strongly that Hoke was the father because

Ellita had moved into the house with Hoke and his two daughters.

Then, one night, Ellita had been shot in the shoulder by an escaped holdup man. As a result of the wound, she had lost approximately twenty percent usage of her right arm, and now she stayed home full-time with Pepe. Because of the rehabilitation exercises she had had to perform to get her arm and body back into shape, she looked better now than she had before she had been wounded. She had trimmed down to 120 pounds, her pretty face was thinner, and although she was thirty-three, she could pass easily for twenty-nine.

Sue Ellen and Aileen helped Ellita with her baby, so she had ample time to shop every day and have a "standing" every Thursday at the beauty parlor. By living with Hoke and his daughters, instead of living under her father's tyrannical thumb, she had unlimited freedom and no longer had to hand over half her salary to her father. Her disability pension was more than adequate to pay her share of the expenses, and she intended to stay home with Pepe and keep house until he was old enough to go to school before she looked for a part-time job.

The girls adored the baby and were always willing to baby-sit if Ellita wanted to go out with one of her old girl-friends to lunch or dinner, or to attend mass at St. Catherine's in Hialeah. After the baby was born, Ellita's father had forgiven her and asked her to move home again, but she had refused. At thirty-three Ellita had no intention of giving up her freedom again. Ellita's mother, who sold Avon products in Little Havana, visited the house frequently, and Ellita took Pepe home occasionally (Señor Sánchez, a security guard, would not set foot in Hoke's house) to see his grandfather.

Hoke did not even pretend to be the titular head of this

household. He accepted his responsibility for the girls as their father, and he would feed and clothe them and give them a home until they reached maturity (or got married); but they were allowed to do pretty much as they pleased so long as no one else in the house was inconvenienced. Sue Ellen had dropped out of school to take a full-time job in the Green Lakes Car Wash and was allowed to keep all of her weekly paycheck and tips. She was also encouraged to buy her own clothes, now that she had a steady income, and so long as she was paying for them, Hoke didn't feel that he could tell her what to wear. She had bought a motorcycle, on time payments, without his permission, and he wasn't happy about that; but he taught her how to ride it and insisted that she wear a helmet, leather pants, and jacket every time she mounted the vehicle. If she skidded across the asphalt, he explained, in an accident (and the chances were sixty-forty that she *would* have an accident), the leather clothes would prevent the pavement from scraping her skin and flesh right down to the bone.

Sue Ellen and Aileen both were sensible girls, so even when the heat and humidity reached the nineties in Miami, Sue Ellen wore her helmet and leathers when she rode her Yamaha. Hoke had ridden a motorcycle when he had been assigned to Traffic, and he knew how dangerous it could be. He had explained the dangers, but that was as far as he went with it. He had had some narrow escapes as a motorcycle cop, and the fact that he would not ride Sue Ellen's bike, under any circumstances, had helped make her take his warnings seriously, but not enough to give up the motorcycle. The bike, she insisted, gave her a certain status at the car wash, and she needed an edge to put her on equal terms with the male black and Cuban teenagers she worked with every day.

Aileen was filling out nicely after recovery from bulimic anorexia, but at fourteen she had been so thin Ellita had nicknamed her *La Flaca* ("The Skinny One"). She now ate everything within reach at the table and snacked between meals as well. She was reconciled to being a female now, and her curly chestnut hair fell down to her shoulders in soft waves. Her pointed breasts had swelled, and because she didn't wear a brassiere, they bobbed under her T-shirt as she helped set the table. Aileen's teeth were slightly crooked, and she had a noticeable overbite; but her generous mouth provided her with a big white smile.

Sue Ellen, who toweled down wet cars under a blazing sun every day, was sunburned a deep golden brown and was almost as dark as Ellita. Her short, curly hair, clipped an inch from her skull and dyed electric blue down the middle, gave her the punk look she coveted, but she was attractive in spite of herself. She wore two pairs of plastic earrings and was considering the idea of having third holes punched into her earlobes for another pair. Both girls, when they were home, wore shorts and T-shirts and usually went barefoot around the house as well. Ellita, unless she was going out, almost always wore jeans, sensible heels, and a long-sleeved blouse. She thought her thighs were too fat to wear shorts, but the Miami heat didn't affect Ellita as much as it did Hoke and his daughters.

It was habit—not a rule—but everyone did his or her best to eat dinner at home every night, and it was the only time of the day they all were together as a family. Hoke, of course, as a homicide detective with odd hours at times, couldn't always make it home in time for dinner. But when he couldn't, he phoned, and Ellita always saw to it that he had a hot meal when he did come home. The rest of the time each family member went his or her own way, getting up at a different time and preparing personal meals other than dinner.

Hoke took care of the finances, the rent and the utilities, and Ellita purchased everything else that was needed for the house, including food, cleaning materials, or the odd plumbing job that called for a professional. At the end of each month Hoke and Ellita sat down and figured out how much each owed, and then they paid the bills.

Hoke ate and slept much better than he had when he was single and unencumbered, and he also spent more time watching television than he had when he had lived in a hotel room as a single man. Even with Pepe to care for, Ellita still managed to keep the house neat and clean, and she prepared enormous meals at night.

The major drawback to living as a family man (when the girls' stereo made too much noise, Hoke could always retreat to his small bedroom and close the door) was that Hoke couldn't very well bring a woman home with him to spend the night. He knew that Ellita wouldn't mind, but he had to set an example for his daughters. He was afraid that if he brought a woman home, they might decide to bring boys home to their room overnight. As a consequence, when Hoke managed a rare conquest, which now happened at longer intervals, he had to take the woman to a hotel or motel. Miami hotel rates are expensive, even during the off-season, and there had been times that he had dropped a promising pursuit when he knew he would have to pay at least seventy-seven dollars, plus tax, for a hotel room. Hoke was forty-three and looked every single day of it. The women he attracted, divorcées and widows he met in bars, were not, in most instances, worth that much money to him. Unhappily the divorcées and widows who were interested in sleeping with Hoke were usually in their late thirties, or older, and more often than not had teenaged children of their own; that also denied them the use of their own houses and apartments. It had been more than four years since Hoke had slept with a woman who didn't have stretch marks. But he didn't mind the stretch marks so long as she didn't complain about his middle-aged paunch.

For several months Hoke had carried on a long-distance affair with a married woman from Ocala, who would fly down to Miami once a month for a shopping trip. They would check into the Miami Airport Hotel, which had reasonable day rates, and spend the afternoon. Then she would fly back to Ocala. A few days before she flew down, she would telephone Hoke and tell him what she was shopping for, and he would buy the items and have them ready in the hotel room when she checked in. She would reimburse him for the packages, of course, and they would spend the afternoon in bed. Hoke paid for the room. Once a month was better than nothing, but Hoke didn't like to do the shopping for the woman (which cut into his off-duty hours), and after their fourth monthly liaison they had more or less run out of things to talk about. She hadn't called Hoke for several weeks, and Hoke had a hunch she had found someone else to do her Miami shopping. When he thought about it, as he did when he got horny, he discovered that he was just as happy that she hadn't called, and he wouldn't really mind if he never heard from her again.

Now that Hoke had a family again, he had all the advantages of a family man (except for a regular sex life), and few, if any, disadvantages. Ellita respected him, and he got on well with his daughters. His clothes were always clean; Ellita did his laundry and put it away for him, and on Saturday mornings Aileen shined his policeman's black, high-topped double-soled shoes. He was one of the dozen men in Miami who still wore shoes with laces. He didn't like low-cut, slip-on shoes. Ellita was a wonderful cook, and in the past year Hoke had regained the twenty pounds he had dieted away and was back to his prediet weight of 210. This was at least twenty-five pounds too much for a man of five-ten. Hoke's waist had swelled from thirty-eight to forty-two, and he had been forced to buy two new poplin leisure suits in the cut-rate Miami fashion district because his old pants couldn't be let out any farther. Every day he promised to cut down on his eating but could seldom manage to do so. He also found it difficult to hold himself down to only two cans of Old Style a night when the refrigerator was always stocked with at least a dozen cans of his favorite beer.

Hoke was also doing well professionally. He had a permanent assignment as sergeant in charge of the cold case files, which gave him almost unlimited time to work on the old and all but hopeless unsolved homicides. He had passed the examination for lieutenant and was at the head of the WASP list. Being at the top of the WASP promotion list meant that he had passed the exam with a higher score than any other candidate in the department, but it did not mean that he would be the next sergeant promoted to lieutenant. Because of affirmative action, there were three Latins and two blacks ahead of him for promotion (all with much lower scores than Hoke's), but if the department ever *did* get around to promoting a white American to lieutenant again, Hoke would get the promotion. He had a little more than five years to go for retirement, and he was positive— or almost positive—that he would be promoted before he retired. And if not, whoever said that life was fair?

When Ellita called him to dinner, Hoke broke his rule and decided to have a beer with his meal instead of waiting an hour after eating. To justify it, he decided he would drink only one more that evening and would hold off until 10:00 P.M., when the rerun of *Hill Street Blues* came on the tube.

Dinner was roast pork loin, accompanied by boiled yucca, fried candied plantains, black beans, boiled pearl rice, hard Cuban rolls, and a salad of sliced tomatoes, avocados, and iceberg lettuce, with Ellita's homemade Thousand Island dressing. There was a bottle of garlicky *criollo* sauce for the pork, a bowl of mixed green and black olives, and butter and guava jelly for the rolls. Hoke was served a baked potato instead of yucca (he didn't like yucca). After he had split and mashed the potato, he spooned black beans over it and added a jigger of sweet sherry to the mixture. Ellita and the girls took ample portions as well, but unlike Hoke, they wouldn't eat seconds. Ellita, who starved herself during the day, always felt entitled to at least one decent meal at dinnertime, so she still managed to keep her weight on a fairly even basis. Hoke took second helpings but ate only one baked potato.

After everyone was served and eating, Hoke told them about the new chief's planned no-smoking-in-the-station rules.

"Henderson was taking a survey in the division, and it could be a narrow margin. A lot of guys have quit already, and it may be a majority for the new chief. If so, I'll have to go outside every time I want a smoke."

"You've been trying to quit," Ellita said, "and if he makes the rule, it'll be that much easier for you to stop."

"That isn't the point, Ellita. Smoking's still a legal activity in this country, and cigarettes are still sold in the stores. If it's legal to buy 'em, it should be legal to smoke 'em. It's a hard habit to break, and I don't think the new chief can enforce a rule like that for very long without a rebellion

23

from the PBA. So tomorrow I'm going to get together with Bill and start a little office pool. I think, if the rule goes in, it'll last for only three days."

"I'd say five," Ellita said. "Put me down for number five in the pool. How much for each ticket?"

"I hadn't thought about it. Five dollars, do you think?"

"That's too much. Make it two dollars a ticket. I'll give you the money after dinner. Save me number five."

"I still say three."

"According to the *Miami News*," Sue Ellen said, "the army's already stopped soldiers from smoking in their vehicles and inside all government buildings."

"Where'd you see that?"

"In the paper. A few weeks ago."

"How come I didn't see it?"

"I don't know, but it was in there."

"The army won't be able to enforce that rule either. At least they wouldn't't've been able to when I was in the service, and I was an MP."

"When you were in the army," Aileen said, "they didn't know that cigarettes caused cancer. Not back in the world war."

"I wasn't in the world war. I was in the Vietnam War."

"They still didn't know, not way back then."

"They don't know now either," Hoke said. "They only suspect cigarettes cause cancer. There's no real proof."

"The surgeon general says they do," Sue Ellen said.

"Who're you going to believe?" Hoke asked. "The Tobacco Institute or the surgeon general?"

"The surgeon general," both girls said in unison; then they giggled.

Hoke grinned. "Me, too."

Hoke put two slices of white pork on his plate, cut off the fatty edges, and frowned as he looked around the table.

"Aileen," Ellita said, "please get the Tabasco sauce for your father. You didn't bring it in when you set the table."

Aileen went into the kitchen for the Tabasco. Ellita put her utensils down and looked sideways at Sue Ellen. "As a favor to me, Sue Ellen, I'd like to ask you one more time. Please dye your hair back to its natural color for Sunday, and I'll help you dye it blue again on Monday. Mama wants Sunday to be a very special party for Uncle Arnoldo, and she says it would upset him to see blue hair on a woman. Tío Arnoldo's a very conservative man, and he wouldn't understand."

Sue Ellen shook her head. "No, Ellita. If he's going to live here, he'll have to accept America as it is, and it might do him good to see blue hair. Miami isn't Cuba. We can do what we please here."

"He understands that, but he's been waiting in Costa Rica for four years for his visa, and every relative we have will be at the party Sunday. He's my father's older brother and very dignified."

"I'm conservative, too," Sue Ellen said. "But if you think the color of my hair'll bother your uncle, I'll just go to work instead. I can get more overtime in the car wash. In fact, I can work every Sunday if I want."

"I think you'll enjoy the party, and I want you to come. It's just that Mama wants everything to be nice for him. He was in prison for twenty-two years before he got to Costa Rica."

"I don't speak Spanish anyway." Sue Ellen shrugged. "I'd just as soon go to work."

"If you don't come now, Sue Ellen, Mama'll think it's her fault, and you know she loves you."

"I like your mom okay, too, but I won't dye my hair back just to go to a dumb party."

Hoke cleared his throat. "I don't think I'll be able to make it either, Ellita. I meant to tell you earlier, but it slipped my mind."

"You *have* to come, Hoke," Ellita said. "Tío Arnoldo doesn't know any Americans, and Mama's already told him that I live here with you. If you don't come, he'll think you don't approve of him."

Aileen returned from the kitchen and handed Hoke the Tabasco sauce. He unscrewed the top and sprinkled his pork liberally. "That doesn't make any sense," Hoke said. "Whether Sue Ellen or I come or not—or Aileen—makes no difference. We're not related to your uncle. He wasn't a political prisoner anyway. You told me he was sent to prison for killing a man, a man who was sleeping with his wife. He served his time and then got a visa to Costa Rica, so he's paid his debt to Cuban society. I don't hold anything against him. Now that he's here in Miami, he's just another lucky Cuban far's I'm concerned. I can't see why your family's trying to make a big hero out of him. If he was a Marielito, with his prison background, he'd probably be locked up in Atlanta, waiting for shipment back to Cuba with the rest of the criminals."

"Tio Arnoldo's not a criminal!" Ellita said. "He's a man of honor, and he's family! If you were getting out of prison and then exile after twenty-six years, we'd give a party for you, too. When you were married to Patsy, if you'd caught her sleeping with another man, wouldn't you have shot the *cabrón?*"

"Hell, no! You don't shoot a man just because he falls in love with your wife. What you do, you get a legal divorce."

"You don't understand Cuban honor."

"The Cuban judge didn't either. He sentenced your uncle

26

to life, didn't he? Even though he got out in twenty-two years. But I don't hold it against him. I intended to go to the party, but I have to stay home and wait for a call from Major Brownley. This afternoon, just before I left, Bill Henderson told me to let my beard grow and that Brownley was going to call me at home Sunday."

"What kind of message is that?" Ellita raised her eyebrows.

"It's the message Bill gave me. It's probably some special assignment. We're shorthanded in the division, and Brownley decided to give it to me. What with the suspensions and resignations, I don't think I'll be on cold cases much longer."

"What time will he call you on Sunday?"

"Bill didn't say."

"Can Major Brownley do that, Daddy?" Aileen asked.

"Do what?"

"Make you grow a beard?"

"I don't know. One thing I do know—the department can make you shave *off* a beard, and a mustache, too, if they want. That was a concession we had to make with the new PBA contract. But I don't know if they can make a man grow a beard or not. At any rate I won't shave till I talk to him. Willie Brownley's weird sometimes, but he's not frivolous."

"Why didn't he tell you himself, instead of Bill?" Ellita said.

"He's fishing down in the Keys with one of his old college buddies and won't be back till Sunday."

"He can call you at my father's house just as easily as he can here. I'll phone Mrs. Brownley, give her the number, and he can call you there. You aren't getting out of this party, and neither's Sue Ellen."

"Okay." Hoke shrugged. "Call her then. You heard that, Sue Ellen. We're all going to the party."

"In that case," Sue Ellen said, sighing, "I'll dye my hair brown again—if you'll help me, Ellita."

"I said I would, and I'll help you dye it back again next Monday night."

"You don't have to do that, Sue Ellen," Hoke said, "if you don't want to—I hope you know that."

"I know, but it'll make it easier for Ellita. Besides, all afternoon those old Cubans will be whispering about the *chica* with the *pelo azul*, and I'm liable to say something nasty."

Hoke grinned. "You've picked up a few Spanish words, haven't you?"

"I hear the Cuban dudes talking behind my back at the car wash. They make jokes about my blue pubic hair, too—but not to my face. They know what kind of temper I've got."

"If you want my opinion—" Aileen said.

"I don't."

"—I think it looks gnarly. Blue hair, I mean."

"That's enough about hair at the dinner table," Hoke said. "Let's talk about something else."

Sue Ellen glared at her sister for a moment and then doused her pork with *criollo* sauce without speaking. Pepe awoke and started to cry. Ellita got the baby from the crib, sat in her chair again, rolled up her blouse, and the baby began to suckle the left nipple.

"Which breast does Pepe like best, Ellita?" Hoke asked. "The left or the right?"

"What kind of question is that? He usually takes the left first, but that's because I hold him that way. He doesn't have any preference."

"Not according to Melanie Klein," Hoke said. "When

you took your psych course at Miami-Dade, did they ever discuss Dr. Klein's theories about babies?"

"I don't think so. Melanie Klein?"

"Dr. Klein. She was a child psychologist, like Anna Freud, one of the first to analyze children. She claimed that babies developed a love-hate relationship with breasts. Breasts are good, both of them, at first. Then, when the babies are weaned, sometime during the first two years, let's say, and the breasts are denied to them, they become bad because they're a source of frustration. Being denied means they're bad objects instead of good objects, and they look at breasts as separate from their mothers. What mothers have to do then is to get them to see the mother as a whole person and not just as a woman who's got two objects hanging off her to be loved or hated."

"What about the good breast and the bad breast?"

Hoke thought for a moment but couldn't remember. His complete knowledge of Dr. Melanie Klein was limited to a book review he had read of her biography in the *New York Times Book Review*. He had picked it up in the men's room on the fourth floor of the police station. He had read the review while he was in the can, sitting on the commode, and he remembered thinking at the time that the theories of Dr. Klein were ludicrous.

"It's very complicated, Ellita. It has something to do with transference, but I haven't read any Klein for several years, and I'm not sure exactly how it works. I do remember that Karen Horney supported Klein's theories."

"We read Karen Horney at Miami-Dade. There was a chapter from Horney's book *Self-Analysis* in our textbook. But I don't remember any mention of Melanie Klein."

"It's just a theory, I guess, like everything else in psychology. But if Pepe begins to favor one breast over the other, maybe you'd better look into it."

"I think Dr. Klein is full of shit," Ellita said.

Pepe dug his fat knuckles into Ellita's left breast, trying to increase the flow. Ellita, eating awkwardly with her right hand, dropped a forkful of lettuce saturated with Thousand Island on Pepe's head. She put down her fork and wiped the baby's head with a paper napkin. She smiled.

"Are you making all this up, Hoke?"

"As I go through life"—Hoke shook his head—"I find that when I tell people something they don't already know, they almost always think it's a lie. Dr. Klein was a famous pioneer in child psychology. Just because you never heard of her doesn't make her a nonexistent person."

"Daddy wouldn't make up a story like that," Aileen said. "He doesn't have that much imagination."

Ellita and Sue Ellen laughed.

"Thank you, sweetheart," Hoke said, "for defending your old man."

Pepe squirmed, and Ellita shifted him over to the right nipple. He suckled and gurgled. The four of them smiled at the red-faced baby's greediness.

"So much for Melanie Klein," Hoke said.

AFTER DINNER SUE ELLEN AND ELLITA CLEARED THE TABLE and retreated to the kitchen to wash the dishes. Aileen, who usually helped, had a baby-sitting job down the street, and she left the house wearing the earphones to her Sony Walkman, listening to her new Jimmy Buffett tape.

Hoke went into the bathroom, scrubbed his false teeth, and then put them into a plastic glass with water and Polident to soak overnight. He sat in his La-Z-Boy recliner, after turning on the set, and tried to change channels with the Telectron garage opener. It didn't work on the TV either, so he turned off the set. He went over his theory in his mind.

Three days before his death Dr. Paul Russell had parked in his marked space at his clinic—the clinic he owned in partnership with Dr. Leo Schwartz and Dr. Max Farris. Sometime during the day his garage door opener had been stolen from his white Mercedes. Nothing else had been taken. He missed the garage door opener when he got home because it wasn't in the glove compartment where he always kept it. He parked in the driveway and entered his house through the front door. His second garage door opener— the one Hoke held in his hand—was kept as a spare, according to his wife, Louise, on a small side table in the foyer.

For the next two days Dr. Russell had intended to get another opener but hadn't got around to it. He was a busy doctor, and he still had the second opener. However, instead of taking the spare opener with him in his car, where it might be stolen again, he opened the garage from inside, backed his car out to the driveway, got out of his car, closed the door with his opener, and then went into the house through the front door. He put the opener on the little table in the foyer again. The procedure was annoying but not onerous, and he didn't want to have the opener stolen again—not until he obtained another spare.

On the third morning, after he had backed onto his driveway and closed the door, as he crossed the lawn to the front door of his house, someone stepped out from behind an Australian pine on Dr. Russell's front lawn and shot him between the eyes with a .38-caliber revolver.

Dr. Russell had had a gallbladder operation scheduled at 7:00 A.M. at the Good Samaritan Hospital and had backed out of the garage at approximately 6:15. His dead body, still warm, had been discovered at 6:30 by the *Miami Herald* deliveryman when he threw a paper onto the lawn. He had then knocked on the front door to call the police.

Mrs. Louise Russell wasn't home. She had gone to Orlando the day before to visit her younger sister, who taught the second grade. The deliveryman had then gone next door and called the police. He waited until the police came, standing beside the body, and said he didn't touch anything. Dr. Russell had been killed instantly, and the garage door opener had fallen from his hand. His expensive gold Rolex wristwatch continued to keep accurate time on his wrist. The Russells' Mexican maid didn't get to the house until 7:30, and when she did arrive and saw the homicide team and the dead body, she became hysterical. It took Sergeant Armando Quevedo, the detective in charge of the case, several minutes to calm her down before she could tell them that Mrs. Russell was in Orlando. Sergeant Quevedo had called the clinic to inform the nurse about the murder. Dr. Farris had gone to the hospital to take out the gallbladder Dr. Russell had been scheduled to remove.

All this had happened three years before—three years and three months ago—and now the case was very cold indeed. Some of Quevedo's notes were in Spanish, but they were reminders to himself. The supplementary report was written in Quevedo's clear, easy-to-follow English. There were no leads whatsoever, except that the killing had all the earmarks of a professional hit.

Quevedo could discover no motive. Dr. Russell had no known enemies. He had been a hardworking professional, and he had put in long days. He earned more than $150,000 a year, and he also owned an eight-unit apartment house in Liberty City. The apartment house was managed for him by a company that specialized in renting properties to blacks, and the company kept fifteen percent of the rents it collected. And it always collected, or the residents were evicted immediately. Although the black people who rented the substandard apartments might have resented

Dr. Russell if they had known that he was their slumlord, they were unaware of his ownership.

Dr. Russell owned the two-story house in Belle Meade, where he lived with his wife, Louise (they had no children), and she had said that they had a limited social life because of his busy schedule. He wasn't robbed. In addition to the expensive gold Rolex, there was a gold ring set with an onyx and a diamond on his ring finger. His wallet contained eighty-seven dollars and a half dozen credit cards. It was possible, Quevedo suggested in his supplementary report, that the hit man, whoever it was, had hit the wrong man.

Hoke didn't accept that. The stolen garage door opener interested Hoke. Whoever had stolen the opener from Dr. Russell's Mercedes had had to be familiar with his habits. The man—or woman—who shot the physician must have known that he would cross the lawn at that point to get back to the front door and put the opener away before returning to his car.

Who had profited from Dr. Russell's death? Dr. Schwartz and Dr. Farris hadn't brought in a new doctor to replace Dr. Russell in their clinic. After his death they had split Dr. Russell's practice between them. They both had profited because of their partnership insurance. Also, and this is what piqued Hoke's curiosity, four months ago Dr. Leo Schwartz had married the widow, Louise Russell. He now lived with her in the Belle Meade house, a house Dr. Russell's mortgage insurance had paid off in full at his death. Dr. Schwartz now drove the white Mercedes, and Hoke wondered if Dr. Schwartz was wearing Dr. Russell's Rolex and ring as well. And why, Hoke wondered, had Louise Russell decided to visit her sister in Orlando at that particular time? The sisters were not close; the Orlando sister had never visited the Russells in Miami. All this, of course, was not known by Sergeant Quevedo.

Whoever had stolen the garage door opener from Dr. Russell's locked car at the clinic, and then relocked the car door afterward, was probably the murderer or the person who had hired the killer. Hoke suspected that that person was Dr. Leo Schwartz, or perhaps it was Dr. Schwartz *and* Dr. Max Farris—with an assist, perhaps, from Louise Russell Schwartz? All he had to do was find some proof.

The garage door opener, the spare, had been locked away as evidence, and Hoke had checked it out of the property room (it took Baldy Allen, the property man, more than two hours to find it, three years and three months being a long time for evidence to be stored away), but Hoke was convinced that the opener was the key, somehow, to the case.

Perhaps Dr. Schwartz had taken the original door opener, and if so, instead of throwing it away, he still had it? If so, and if he had also planned three years ago to marry Louise, and if they had been having an affair at that time, he was currenty using the original door opener to get into the garage now that he was married to Louise and living in her house—and driving the white Mercedes. Everything seemed logical; the killer could very well be Dr. Schwartz. Tomorrow, when he got to the office, he would see where Leo Schwartz had been when the murder was committed. There was nothing much in the report about Schwartz, except that he and his partner, Max Farris, both had attended the funeral. Sergeant Quevedo had attended Dr. Russell's funeral and had copied down the list of everyone who had signed the register. But Quevedo hadn't checked on any of these people to see where they had been during the murder. It might be a good idea to check the Belle Meade house, too. He would see if this spare opener still opened the garage. If it did, it might mean that Dr. Schwartz did indeed have the original opener—the one stolen from the

Mercedes. If the spare didn't open the garage, it could mean that a new radio signal and new openers had been ordered and that he was on the wrong track. . . .

Hoke fell asleep in the recliner. Ellita brought him a cold beer at ten o'clock and woke him in time to watch the rerun of *Hill Street Blues*.

CHAPTER 4

THE NEXT MORNING, WHEN DETECTIVE TEODORO GONZÁLEZ came into the office, Hoke handed him the garage door opener and told him to go to the late Dr. Russell's house and see if it would open the garage door. Hoke didn't tell González why. All he had was a theory, even if the opener did open the garage. If it worked, however, his suspicion would be stronger, and it would confirm that he was at least on to something.

"After I open the garage," González asked, "should I go inside, or will I need a warrant?"

"All I want you to do," Hoke said slowly, "and I want you to do it as inconspicuously as possible, is open the door —*if* it opens. Then, if it opens, push the button and close the door again. If anybody's around, don't do it. Drive past the house. Keep circling the block, and don't let anyone see you open and close the door. If you think Mrs. Schwartz is at home or see her out in the yard, just drive away. Go back later when she isn't home."

González slipped the opener into his outside jacket

pocket. He was wearing an iridescent lime green linen sports jacket, a black silk T-shirt, with pleated lemon-colored gabardine slacks, and tasseled white Gucci slip-ons.

"And take off that jacket. Your T-shirt's okay, but that jacket isn't inconspicuous, and neither are your slacks. So don't get out of your car either."

González nodded. He removed his jacket and draped it, silk lining side out, over his arm. "Don't I check and see what's in the garage after I open it? I mean, take a quick little survey, something like that? What exactly am I looking for?"

"Nothing. Just see if that gadget opens the door. Then come back and tell me. Do you know where the Belle Meade neighborhood is? How to find the address on Poinciana?"

"I know about where it is. There's a Publix market at the corner of Poinciana and Dixie, so all I have to do is turn there and follow Poinciana till I get to the address."

"Okay, then, move out. And come straight back here when you finish trying the opener."

González hadn't been promoted to detective-investigator because he had earned it. He had been promoted after only one year of patrol duty in Liberty City because he had a degree in economics from Florida International University. González had a poor sense of direction and often got lost in Miami, even though he had lived in the city for the last ten of his twenty-five years. Hoke almost always found it necessary to brief him about directions before he sent him out of the office to do legwork. On the other hand, González was excellent with figures and had saved both Ellita and Hoke money when he had prepared their income tax returns for them.

Hoke hadn't realized how much he had depended upon Ellita for detail work until she was no longer his partner.

González was barely adequate at best, if he was told exactly what to do. He had no initiative, and Hoke had already asked Brownley for a replacement for González at the earliest opportunity. But the Homicide Division was short-handed, after three recent suspensions and several resignations, and it was unlikely that González would be replaced.

After González left, Hoke took a clean yellow file folder out of the cabinet. He began to grid it with a black felt-tipped pen and a ruler to make up a pool card. There would be forty squares. At two bucks a square, if he sold them all, the winner of the revocation of the no smoking pool would win seventy-eight dollars. After he finished the card, Hoke wrote his name in number three, and Ellita's in number five and left his cubicle to look for Commander Bill Henderson.

Henderson emerged from the elevator, carrying a Styrofoam cup of coffee in his left hand and his clipboard in his right. He grinned broadly as Hoke approached him, holding up the pool card.

Henderson shook his head. "Forget it, Hoke. There's been a compromise. There'll be no smoking in vehicles, but it'll still be okay inside the building. Not out here in the bull pen, but in offices like yours it'll be okay. Men can smoke in the john, too. We finally persuaded the new chief that it would be impractical to have men going to and coming from the lot all day and all night."

"Shit. It took me twenty minutes to make up a pool card."

"Hang on to it. The new chief's really gung ho about this no smoking business and may change his mind back again."

"I don't see anything wrong about smoking in a patrol car, unless a man's partner objects."

"I don't either. But that was the compromise. Besides, it doesn't apply to you because you drive your own car. But it will apply to unmarked cars from the motor pool."

"Unmarked cars, too? That doesn't make sense."

"That's the rule. I'm going to type up the notice and post it on the bulletin board now—after I finish my coffee."

"Any other truly important news at the meeting?"

"Yeah, there is. Every division's got to appoint a crack committee. They want us to come up with something or other to help the new Crack-Cocaine Task Force. According to new statistics, Miami's got more crack houses than New York had speakeasies during Prohibition. So something drastic has to be done. You didn't shave this morning, Hoke, so you're the new chairman of our Homicide Crack Committee."

"You told me yesterday *not* to shave, you bastard!"

"I know I did. But I don't have anyone else available just now. You can pick out two more detectives for your committee, and start thinking of ways to crack down on crack abusers and crack houses."

Hoke ripped up the pool card, tossed it into a wastebasket, and went down to the basement cafeteria. He got a *cafe con leche,* dark on coffee, and sat at an empty table. He was due in court at ten-thirty, making an appearance as the investigating officer in an old case that had already been continued several times. It would, in all probability, be continued again because the defendant, who had killed his wife with an aluminum baseball bat, had fired his court-appointed lawyer and the court would have to appoint a new one.

Hoke finished his coffee and lighted a Kool, wondering what, if anything, he could come up with (as a homicide detective) to combat the use of crack in Miami. He couldn't think of anything, except to charge crack sellers with second-degree murder. Crack abusers died off eventually, if they didn't break the habit. But legislation like that was unlikely. He would select Sergeant Armando Quevedo and Detective Bob Levine for his committee. The three of them could go out for a few beers at Larry's Hideaway, kick the idea around, and then come up with a meaningless report of some kind. Hoke hadn't been out drinking with Quevedo and Levine for some months now, and this was a reasonable excuse to have a few beers and shoot the breeze with his old buddies. He was getting too housebound for his own good.

It was unfair of Bill Henderson to make him the chairman, but Hoke didn't resent the appointment. He knew that if he had been in Henderson's position, he would have appointed the first man he happened to see, too. The idea was stupid in the first place. A committee like this one was just busywork, another public relations ploy the new chief could hand out to the media to make it look as if something were being done about drug abuse. Education didn't work, Hoke thought as he stubbed out his butt in the ashtray. He knew he shouldn't smoke, and he knew he shouldn't drink, but that hadn't stopped him from smoking and drinking. So far this year thirty-six Miamians had died from smoking crack, but crack use increased daily.

Hoke returned to his office and slipped into his leisure suit jacket. He decided to drive over to the Metro Justice Building a little early because it was difficult to find a parking space over there. The phone rang.

"Hoke," Ellita said, when he picked up the phone, "you know the house across the street, the run-down place that's been for sale for the last year?"

"What about it?"

"A man moved in this morning. They unloaded a van of furniture earlier, and the guy who moved in has a little Henry J. It looks like a brand-new car."

"You must be mistaken, Ellita. They haven't made any Henry Js since the fifties."

"It's a Henry J, Hoke, and it looks like a new one. After the van left, the man brought a dining room chair out to the lawn, and he's been sitting and staring over at our house for the last hour. The grass over there's a foot high, and he looks funny, just sitting there in a chair and staring at our house."

"What about it? If he bought the house and moved in, he's entitled to sit on a chair on his front lawn, whether he mows it or not. I'm glad the house finally sold. Now someone'll have to take care of the yard."

"I don't like it, Hoke. I know he can't see me, or anything like that, because I'm here inside. But every time I go to the front window and look over at him through the curtains, he's staring directly at our house. He's wearing a dark blue suit, and it must be ninety out there in the sun. It bothers me."

"What do you expect me to do about it, Ellita? I've got to go to court this morning."

"I thought maybe you could find out who he is."

"Hell, you can do that yourself. Call the realtor and ask him. The sign out there was Paulson Realtor, wasn't it?"

"I already called the realtor, and they let me talk to a Mrs. Anderson. She's the woman who handled the sale, but she wouldn't tell me anything. She said if I was interested, the neighborly thing to do would be to go over and introduce myself. Then if he wanted to talk about himself and why he bought the house, it would be up to him."

"That seems reasonable, Ellita. Why don't you do that?"

"I don't know. It's just that he looks so weird over there. Like a sitting statue or something. Wearing a blue suit."

"Look, I've got to go to court. If you're afraid of him, take your pistol along—"

"I'm not afraid of him. It's just that it looks—Never mind. If your case is continued again, will you come home for lunch?"

"I don't know. I'll try to call you from the courthouse."

AS HOKE SUSPECTED IT WOULD BE, THE CASE WAS CONTINUED, although the angry judge said it would be the last time. The new lawyer, a young woman from the public defender's office, requested a thirty-day delay so she could prepare a defense. Hoke almost felt sorry for her. This was her first homicide case, and she would certainly lose it. The defendant, an insurance salesman and Little League baseball coach, had killed his wife with a bat because she had berated him for not letting their son pitch. His son could neither pitch nor hit, he told the desk sergeant when he turned himself in and handed the bloody bat over and confessed at the station. Hoke had prepared the supplementary reports on the simple case. If the man's signed confession was allowed as evidence, the guy would go to prison, no matter what kind of defense the attorney attempted.

Hoke called Ellita from the courthouse.

"I've been waiting for your call, Hoke—"

"Go ahead and have lunch without me. I've got too many things to do today to come home for lunch."

"I found out who that man is, Hoke. And I don't think it's a coincidence. It's Donald Hutton!"

Hoke laughed. "Hutton's a common name, Ellita. My Donald Hutton's still doing twenty-five years in Raiford. A mandatory twenty-five before he's eligible for parole."

"You're wrong, Hoke. This is *your* Donald Hutton. I went over and introduced myself. He told me he was waiting outside for the water man and the FPL to turn on his utilities. He said he just moved down here from Starke, that's where Raiford Prison is, and he's had his furniture and little Henry J in storage for the last ten years. Then he told me his name was Donald Hutton. I didn't tell him you lived in the house with me, but I've got a hunch he already knows that. That's why he bought the house—"

"Did you ask him if he was in prison?"

"That isn't something you ask a person you're meeting for the first time, Hoke. I couldn't very well say, 'Did you just get out of prison?,' could I?"

"I guess not. I'll check it out while I'm here at the courthouse."

"Call me back. I'm not going out."

"I'll call you."

Hoke recalled the Donald Hutton murder case well. This had been Hoke's second homicide investigation, and he had worked hard on it, trying to prove himself as a new detective.

Donald Hutton, and his older brother, Virgil (Virgil was five years older than Donald), had moved to Miami from Valdosta, Georgia, in the sixties. They had started a knotty pine paneling business. They already owned hundreds of acres of pinelands in Georgia, and they specialized in paneling offices and dens in new homes. During the building boom of the early seventies they had prospered in Miami. Eventually they had twenty-two employees. They lived together in an old mansion in the Bayside section of Miami, overlooking Biscayne Bay.

Virgil had married a modestly successful interior designer, a young woman named Marie Weller. She had kept her maiden name when they married, because of her established business. Her new clients were often advised to panel one or two rooms in knotty pine (she could get them a substantial discount). Then Virgil Hutton disappeared.

Donald Hutton had made a nuisance of himself at the police station, demanding that they find his big brother. Virgil had no known enemies, and according to everything Hoke could find out, he had been a "good old boy." Virgil did the selling for the two-man firm. Donald took care of the paperwork and also supervised the actual paneling that was put in by their hired craftsmen.

Donald also complained to the media, claiming that the police were not looking hard enough for his brother. How could a two-hundred-and-forty-pound man, six feet tall, disappear into the hot, moist air of Miami?

Marie Weller couldn't understand it either. She and Virgil had been married only for a year and were happy together, she claimed. In fact, they had even talked to the attorney, Randy Mendoza, about the possibility of adopting a child. At thirty-two Marie Weller was capable of bearing a child, but Virgil, forty-three and fifty pounds overweight, had a low sperm count. Virgil had disappeared without a trace. No money had been taken from his bank account, and his Cadillac was still in the three-car garage. His extensive tailored wardrobe was still intact.

One Saturday morning a photograph of Donald Hutton and Marie Weller appeared in both newspapers. Considering the possibility that Virgil might be suffering from amnesia, Marie and Donald had gone downtown and checked the skid row breadline at Camillus House, believing that Virgil, if he were having an amnesia attack, might be sleeping under an overpass at night and getting mission handouts. They had notified the newspapers of their impending trip downtown, and photographers and reporters had been there to check the breadline with them. Virgil had not been among the homeless men, of course, but some excellent human-interest photos of other bums in the line were published in both papers.

Negative PR like this put additional pressure on Hoke Moseley and the Homicide Division.

Because of their partnership agreement, Donald Hutton, in essence, now owned one hundred percent of the business. Marie Weller, naturally, continued to live with her brother-in-law in the big Bayside mansion. Donald Hutton —although he didn't have to—paid Marie Weller a fair share of the profits from the business, but until Virgil was declared officially dead—not just missing—the business was all his, not Marie Weller's. If the body was found, Marie Weller would inherit her husband's half of the firm.

Hoke discovered the body.

Before he found the corpse, Hoke had learned, during routine checks of Donald's movements in the weeks preceding Virgil's disappearance, that Donald had purchased three pounds of strychnine at the Falco-Benson Pharmaceutical Company, in Hialeah, ostensibly to get rid of rats at his house. Inasmuch as the Huttons had a live-in cook, a daytime maid, and a gardener who spent two days a week taking care of their yard, why would a busy executive like Donald Hutton decide to kill the rats himself? Wouldn't he hire an exterminator, or else tell the regular exterminator who visited the house every month, to take care of the rats? It wasn't much to go on, but the third judge Hoke talked to signed a second search warrant. Hoke discovered the body buried under the garage floor beneath Virgil's parked 1974 El Dorado. The house had been searched briefly earlier, when a two-man detective team looked about for evidence in the disappearance, but they hadn't moved the

Cadillac during this first, and rather perfunctory, search. Donald Hutton was arrested when the autopsy revealed traces of strychnine in his body. Marie Weller had been in North Carolina attending a furniture convention when Virgil disappeared, so she was not a suspect.

The evidence was largely circumstantial, and perhaps a good criminal lawyer could have obtained a not guilty verdict for Donald Hutton, but Donald had retained Randy Mendoza, and Mendoza, a corporation lawyer without criminal law experience, made the mistake of putting his client on the stand. The prosecutor had managed to make Hutton lie, after accusing him of sleeping with Marie Weller, his brother's wife, during a long weekend in Key West. After Hutton had denied the allegation, the prosecutor produced a photocopy of the hotel registration card (obtained by Hoke during his investigation). He also put another witness on the stand, a hotel maid, who claimed that the two of them were in bed together on the morning she entered their room (at their request) to clear away their breakfast dishes. Marie Weller was then put on the stand. She admitted sharing the bed in Key West with her brother-in-law but said that she did so only because all the other rooms were booked up. They had slept together, she said, but they "hadn't done anything."

The jury found Donald Hutton guilty of first-degree murder but recommended life imprisonment. The magistrate accepted the jury's recommendation. Life, on a murder one conviction, meant twenty-five mandatory years in prison before Hutton would be eligible for a parole. Technically Donald Hutton should still have fifteen years to serve. . . .

Judge Hathorne was not in his chambers, but his law clerk informed Hoke that Hutton's case, on a third appeal, had been granted a new trial by the state supreme court.

Hutton's attorney, they concluded, had prepared an inadequate, incompetent defense. Mendoza should not have put Hutton on the stand, and he should have accepted a plea bargain of guilty for the reduction of the charge to second-degree murder. If Hutton had pleaded guilty to second-degree murder, he would have been eligible for parole in only eight years. Rather than retry the case (now that Hutton had served ten years), the state attorney had gone along with the recommendation to release Hutton for "time served." And so Hoke learned that Ellita was right. *His* Donald Hutton, a man who had promised to "get him" someday, a threat Hoke had considered empty at the time, was back on the street, or, more specifically, living in a house directly across the street from Hoke's house.

Hutton had money, lots of money, and if he had let it grow at ten percent interest or more in the bank, while he was serving ten years, he was a lot richer now than when he had been sentenced. Of course, the appeals had cost him considerable sums, but Marie Weller had paid him a good price for his half of the paneling business.

As Hoke drove back to the police station, he concluded—as Ellita had—that Donald Hutton's purchase of the house across the street was not a random coincidence. Perhaps Hutton's threat to "get him" someday was no longer empty. Hoke was not fearful of Hutton, but the circumstances made him a little uneasy.

When he got back to his cubicle, Hoke called Blackie Wheeler, Hutton's parole officer and a man he had known for several years, and asked Wheeler about Donald Hutton's parole status.

"I've talked to him only once, Hoke," Blackie said on the phone. "He has to report to me once a month. He'll have to come in person for the first two or three months, but after that I'll probably just let him call in by phone. He's not exactly a criminal, or wasn't when he went up to Raiford, and he shouldn't give me any problems. In fact, I wish I had a few more like him in my load. He has independent means, so I don't have to see that he has a job and check with his employer, and he has no ex-criminal buddies to associate with. He told me that he intended to start a small business of some kind, once he got settled, just to have something to do."

"I can tell you where he lives right now," Hoke said. "He lives across the street from me in Green Lakes."

"I've got his address—"

"When he was found guilty, Blackie, he threatened to kill me someday, after he got out of prison. So I don't think it's any coincidence that he moved into that house."

"He isn't a professional criminal, Hoke. And he's entitled to live anywhere in the city he wants. Of course, if you're afraid of him, we might be able to get a restraining order to keep him off your property. But I'm not so sure a judge'll even do that much. After all, the threat was made ten years ago, and the guy was understandably sore at the time. But I don't think Hutton would relish doing any more time. Even with all his dough, it was still rough on him in prison. Keep in touch, though, and if he does anything funny, let me know. Meanwhile, if you want me to ask him why he bought in Green Lakes, I will. It might be that it's just a nice neighborhood. He's already forbidden to contact Ms. Weller. She doesn't want anything to do with him, naturally. I've talked with her on the phone, and she's planning to get married again—to the guy who owns the Cathay Towers over in Miami Beach. I've got his name written down here somewhere—"

"That's okay, Blackie," Hoke broke in. "I'm not worried about Weller or Hutton, I just wanted to check with you, is all. She's not dumb enough to take up with him again. It would be bad for her business. But I still don't think it's just a coincidence that he moved in across from me."

"It could be."

"Not if you saw the house. The previous owner let it go to hell, and it's been vacant for more than a year. He's gonna have to spend a lot of dough just to get it back into livable shape."

"He's *got* a lot of dough, Hoke. Look, I've got two guys waiting here to see me. . . ."

"Thanks, Blackie. I'll keep in touch."

A few minutes later González came into the office. He handed the garage opener to Hoke.

"It opened the door okay," he said. "But when I pressed it again, and I was parked right there in front of the driveway, it wouldn't close again."

"If it opened the door, it should've closed it."

"What can I tell you?" González shrugged.

"Did anybody see you?"

"Nobody was around. It's a quiet neighborhood. But I felt bad driving off leaving the door open. Somebody could come along and steal the riding mower that's parked inside the garage."

"That's Robbery's problem, not ours. Take the opener back down to Property, and turn it in. Bring back the receipt, and I'll put it in the file."

Hoke hid his disappointment from González. At least he had been half right.

Until Ellita had phoned him, Hoke had forgotten all about the Donald Hutton case, but there were some interesting parallels between the Hutton case and the Dr. Russell case. When he had more time, maybe he would dig out the old Hutton file and compare the two to see if he could discover anything else that was similar. He needed a fresh idea.

But that was the trouble with cold cases. They were cold because everything, or practically everything, had been checked out already before they were abandoned and filed away in pending. That's why they were called cold cases.

Hoke decided to go out and eat lunch before González came back from Property. He had to work with González, but if he timed it right, he didn't have to eat with him.

CHAPTER 5

*A*FTER LUNCH HOKE TYPED HIS NOTES ABOUT THE OPENER, his speculations, and put them into the Russell file, together with the receipt González brought back from Property. He slid the accordion file back into his pending drawer. He would let his subconscious mind work on the case for a couple of days before he took the file out and looked at it again.

Hoke and González sat across from each other at a glass-covered double desk in their small two-man cubicle. They shared a phone and a typewriter. A two-drawer file cabinet with a combination lock held the cases they were currently investigating. The other cold case they had been studying for the past week was equally baffling. Instead of two accidental deaths, or suicides, it had turned out to be two homicides, and there were no discernible leads.

Miami has termites, just like every other city, but they breed quickly and eat a lot of wood in the subtropical climate. Once they are discovered in a house, a "tent job" is the only way to get rid of them. It isn't unusual for a homeowner, once termites have been discovered, to have a new tent job every two or three years. Termite swarms have an uncanny knack for finding their way back to an edible house, and exterminators in South Florida thrive on repeat business. The house is put under canvas, and the tenants must stay away for from thirty-six to seventy-two hours while the Vikane gas kills the termites and other insects inside the house. Food and other perishables are placed in plastic bags during the tenting, and homeowners either stay with friends or put up in a motel until it's safe to return home. Burglaries of tented houses occur frequently, and three or four times a year, and sometimes more often than that, dead burglars, overcome by the Vikane gas, are discovered together with the dead insects when the owners return home. Vikane is a powerful poison, and it kills people as easily as it does termites. Burglars who specialize in tent job invasions wear gas masks and get in and out quickly with their loot. But amateurs who hold dampened handkerchiefs over their mouths and stay too long looking for valuables can be overcome by the fumes and drop dead to the floor like the roaches and termites. Usually, dead burglars are teenagers, high school dropouts with low IQs, but occasionally they are mature men who should know better. Warning signs are posted on all four sides of the tented house, in English and Spanish, but more than thirty percent of the Miami burglars are illiterate in both languages and cannot read signs. At one time the exterminator used to post a guard in front of the house. But the insurance rates went up considerably. The insurance companies told the exterminators that the fact that they did have guards meant that they could be sued by a dead burglar's family for failing to keep the man out. While a guard was sitting in his car out front, smoking and listening to a rock station on his radio, a house prowler could sneak under the tent through a back entrance. After this decision exterminators no longer posted guards and merely put up warning signs. Exterminators were not responsible for illiterate burglars because high school principals were not responsible for graduating illiterate students.

No female burglar, teenage girl or mature woman, has ever been found dead from Vikane gas in a tented house. Females, Hoke reflected, taught by their moms about the danger of household cleaners, wouldn't be caught dead going into a tented house.

Two dead black men, well bloated by the heat, were discovered in the foyer of their home, after a tent job, by Mr. and Mrs. James Magers. The Magerses, during the tenting, had made a holiday out of it and had taken the Friday evening to Monday morning cruise to Nassau on the *Emerald Seas.* When they cleared customs and drove home, it was almost 11:00 A.M., and the canvas had already been removed by the exterminating company. The windows had been opened, and the Vikane gas had blown away. The exterminator was still there, however, and so were two uniformed policemen, who had been called by the exterminator when he reopened the house. The Magerses couldn't identify the two dead men, and they had been removed to the morgue. Except for crude tattoos on the backs of their hands—stars, circles, and two inverted V's— there was no other identification on the two men. It was apparent that nothing in the house had been taken. There were no valuables in their pockets, and the house hadn't been ransacked. After checking, the Magerses said nothing was missing. Mr. Magers had left his World War II Memorial .45-caliber semiautomatic pistol (a highly pilfer- able item) in the house, and it was still safe in its glass display case. Mrs. Magers had prudently taken her jewelry with her on the cruise, and the purser had kept it locked in his safe when she went ashore in Nassau.

The two men, or someone, had jimmied the front door open, after slipping under the canvas, and dropped dead in the foyer. Death was caused by the Vikane gas. The medical examiner then discovered bruises on the backs of both skulls, indicating that the men had been sapped and then tossed, still alive but unconscious, into the foyer. Also, the killer(s) knew that the bodies would be safely hidden inside the house for at least seventy-two hours, allowing ample time for a getaway. Hoke's problem, and González's, was to discover the identity of the two men. The case was now two years old, and Hoke had no leads. The original investigator, a detective who was no longer on the force, had given up on the case after three fruitless months of checking. The homemade tattoos on the backs of their wrists indicated that they had once been in a Cuban prison or perhaps in some other Latin American prison, and that was all Hoke had to go on. Latin prisoners, in many cases, tattooed the backs of their hands with their crime specialty —burglar, arsonist, holdup man, and so on. But the stars, circles, and V's were not listed on the tattoo ID sheets Hoke had requested from Atlanta, where a thousand Mariel prisoners awaited shipment back to Cuba someday—if Dr. Castro ever decided to take them back.

If the two men had arrived during the 1980 Mariel boat-lift, they would have been fingerprinted. But there was no record of their fingerprints in Atlanta or in the FBI files in Washington. There were several Mariel prisoners at the Krome Detention Center in Miami. These men had served their sentences for crimes committed in America and were waiting deportation to Cuba, although they would probably remain incarcerated in Krome until Dr. Castro died before they could be returned.

"I'll tell you what, Teddy," Hoke said. "Take these Polaroid mug shots and the tattoo photos out to Krome, and talk to some of the Cuban detainees. Even if we can't get an ID, they might know what the tattoos represent. We haven't got anything else. They're black men, but most of the Marielitos were black Cubans."

"Will they cooperate with me at Krome?" González asked. "The INS, I mean."

"The INS, yes. But the Cubans may not. They're bitter, you know. They've served their sentences in Atlanta and want to be released to their families here. But you speak Spanish, and you can talk to them. After all, these poor bastards are in limbo here, with nothing else to do. They might cooperate, just to be doing something, or else think that if they help you, you might help them later by putting a good word in their files."

"Is it okay to promise them that? That I'll write a favorable report for their files if they help me?"

"Why not? A promise means nothing. They aren't going back to Cuba till Castro says they can, no matter what you tell them. See what you can find out about the tattoos."

"How do I get out to Krome? I've never been out there."

"First, drive west on Calle Ocho until you reach Krome Avenue. Turn left, or south, and look for the sign. Then talk your way in, and see if they'll let you interrogate some of the black Marielitos. Be sure to wear your jacket. It'll impress the Marielitos with its sincerity."

"What's wrong with this jacket? This is a Perry Ellis jacket."

"Nothing. It's perfect for this job, kid. If I had one like it, I'd wear it out to Krome myself. Take your own car, instead of one from the pool, and go on home when you're finished. I'll see you Monday morning."

After González left, Hoke wrote redline memos to Quevedo and Levine, appointing them to his crack committee. He placed the memos in their mailboxes. They both were on the night shift, and he would be gone before they read the memos and cursed him for giving them this opportunity to serve their division and community.

WHEN HOKE PULLED INTO HIS DRIVEWAY AND PARKED BEHIND Ellita's car, Donald Hutton, wearing a dark blue suit, was still sitting in a dining room chair on his front lawn. Hoke got out of his car without rolling up the windows first, slammed the car door, and crossed the street. He stopped on the sidewalk, not wanting to trespass on the man's property.

"Why are you sitting there, staring at my house?"

Hutton, who had been a tall, spare man to begin with, unlike his dead brother, Virgil, had lost more weight in prison. He unfolded his long arms, which had been crossed over his chest, and placed his spatulate fingers on his bony knees. Unlike Hoke, he had retained all his hair, and it had been teased into ringlets. A fringe of black curls obscured the hairline on his high forehead. His long nose hooked slightly to the left. His deep-set dark eyes were more violet than blue, and he had long black eyelashes. As he widened his eyes, Hoke could see the outline of the full optic circle. A half-smile made Hutton's full lips curl on the right side only, and there was a tiny square of dentist's gold on his right front tooth. He had been a handsome man at the trial, ten years ago, and he had worn a different suit and tie every day. Now that he had a few craggy lines around his eyes and at the corners of his mouth, he was even more handsome. Or craggy. Yes, that's the word for him, Hoke thought: *craggy.*

Hutton pointed a forefinger at Hoke. "I think I know you, sir. Aren't you Detective Moseley?"

"Sergeant Moseley."

Hutton nodded. "I thought you looked familiar, but you've lost a little hair. And you live over there?" Hutton moved his finger slightly to the right, so it was no longer pointing directly at Hoke. "Then we must be neighbors. What do you do, Sergeant—congratulations on your promotion, by the way—rent a room from Mrs. Sánchez?"

"That's Ms. Sánchez, and she lives in my house."

"You aren't married then? That isn't your baby?"

"No, that's Ms. Sánchez's son. My two daughters also live with me."

"I saw them earlier. Nice-looking girls. How old are they?"

"What are you doing out here, staring at my house?"

"There's not much else to look at. But sitting out in the sun has been a rare privilege for me in recent years. I occasionally look down the street because I'm watching for the FPL man to turn on my electricity. The water man came already; but the FPL promised faithfully to send out a man today, and I don't want to miss him."

"How come you bought this house? This particular house, right across from mine?"

"Oh, I didn't buy it, Sergeant. I leased it for a year at a very attractive rate, with an option to buy at the end of the year. But I don't think that's any of your business. How much did you pay for your house?"

"I'm leasing it."

"At least your house is on the lake, and mine isn't. D'you ever swim in the lake?"

"Swimming's forbidden. It was a pretty deep quarry, and some kids drowned."

"A nice breeze comes off the water, though, doesn't it?"

"A hot breeze. But you haven't answered my question."

"I thought I did. I got an attractive deal, and I've always thought that Green Lakes was a quiet part of Miami to live. It's not quite as nice as I remember it, but it's convenient for shopping. The new shopping center's only five blocks away."

"You threatened my life, Hutton. D'you remember that, too?"

"Yes, I did, didn't I?" Hutton smiled crookedly. "But I was upset at the time. After all, I was an innocent man and was sentenced for a crime I didn't commit."

"You killed your brother, all right. That was proven to the satisfaction of the jury."

"A new trial would bring a different verdict. But I was denied a new trial. I took the deal, anyway, to get out of prison. But I still didn't kill my brother. Did you ever ask yourself how I, a man fifty pounds lighter than my brother, managed to get him to eat two spoonfuls of rat poison?"

"Many times. How did you persuade him? There were traces even in the roots of his hair, so he took it over a long period of time."

"I didn't put it in his shampoo either, Sergeant. I loved my brother and wished him no harm. I only hope that someday you people will catch the real killer. But it's written off now, isn't it? I don't hold a grudge against you or the system. I think now you were only doing your job, as they say, so I don't hold a grudge against you. You may disregard my old threat, Sergeant, if you haven't already. I hope we can be good neighbors."

"We'll never be good neighbors, Hutton."

Hoke was perspiring freely. It was only 6:00 P.M., and

with DST there would be another two and a half hours of sunlight. Hoke took off his jacket. The heat had no apparent effect on Hutton, despite his heavy blue serge suit.

"The only way we'll ever be good neighbors, Hutton, is if you stay on your side of the street and I stay on mine. And keep away from my family." Hoke turned on his heel and crossed the street. He imagined that he could feel Hutton's violet eyes boring into his back. He rolled up the windows in his car and went into the house without looking over at Hutton. Hoke realized he had come out badly in the little confrontation. He should have ignored the man altogether, but it was too late now.

Hoke showered and wished that he could shave. The dark gray stubble on his chin and cheeks, and the thick mixture of black and red hairs on his upper lip, made him feel seedy and unclean, even after his shower. He put on a pair of khaki shorts and a clean white T-shirt and sat on the edge of his army cot in his small bedroom.

He was angry about Hutton, but there didn't seem to be anything he could do about it. Ten years was a long time for a man to hold a grudge. Either a man would forget about it altogether, or he would nurse it, hugging it to his chest, and let it become an integral part of his being. Donald Hutton was an educated man, with a degree in agriculture from Valdosta State College. He still had a trace of Georgia accent in his voice, but not very much. Voices flattened out, and accents—except for Latins—eventually disappeared after a man had lived in Miami for a few years. Even Hoke called the city "Miami" now instead of "Mi-am-ah," as he had when he first moved down here from Riviera Beach, Florida.

How *did* Donald persuade his brother to take strychnine? This was a point that Hoke had never been able to clear up, although it hadn't mattered too much at the time.

Hoke's part in the process was to find enough evidence to go to trial, and he had. What the state's attorney and the jury and the judge did with the evidence was not important to Hoke. Cases where the evidence had been very strong indeed had been lost by the state; other cases, with little or weak evidence, had obtained convictions. But if Hoke worried about lenient judges and juries letting people off, he would be (as some of his fellow detectives were) in a constant state of rage. In Hutton's case the man was surely guilty. Hoke was certain of that, although it hadn't mattered to him whether or not Hutton was convicted and put away. That part of the process was not his job, and Hoke was objective about the outcome of most murder trials, including the ones he had worked on. Hutton, of course, hadn't shared his objectivity. Perhaps now, with the knowledge he had gained at Raiford, Hutton had mellowed out. What did he say? "You were just doing your job." Right. By the time Aileen came back to his room to call him to dinner, Hoke had decided that Hutton was not an immediate threat to him or his family. The girls didn't know anything about the Hutton case, but he would remind Ellita to keep the threat a secret from the girls. There was no need to alarm the girls unless there was a need to alert them.

Hoke went into the kitchen and told Ellita to say nothing about Hutton's ten-year-old threat.

"You don't have to tell me that," she said. "I'd never tell them anything without talking it over with you first."

"I realize that. But I don't want anything to slip out. We don't want the neighbors to find out who he is either. Otherwise, they'll be taking walks every night to take a gander at him out of morbid curiosity."

Hoke took the platter holding the turkey breast out to the table and began to carve it into even quarter-inch-thick slices. There was Stove Top corn bread dressing, mashed potatoes and gravy, and boiled rutabagas. There were avocado halves filled with shrimp salad as appetizers. Ellita had always laughed at the TV commercials of the housewife tests for Stove Top dressing. "Did the husbands prefer Stove Top dressing to mashed potatoes?" The husbands invariably wanted the Stove Top dressing, instead of the mashed potatoes, but Ellita knew that most men would want both—not one or the other.

There was a dish of jalapeños for Hoke, black and green olives, and a bowl of jellied cranberry sauce. Hoke distributed slices of turkey and then sat in his chair as Ellita passed around the other plates of food.

There was a knock on the front door. Ellita got up. "I'll get it."

"If it's anyone for the girls," Hoke said as he chopped a jalapeño over his turkey slices, "tell them we're eating now and to come back in an hour."

"Ellita," Sue Ellen said, "says that little car across the street's a Henry J. How much would a little car like that be worth today, Daddy? I've never even seen one before, and we get just about everything through the car wash."

"I don't know, sweetie. Back in the fifties you could pick up a secondhand Henry J for about a hundred bucks. A used one, I mean. But after twenty years a car in Florida becomes a classic, so it would all depend on how much a collector would be willing to pay for it."

"D'you think I could talk the owner into a Simoniz job? I could do it Sunday and give him a better price than he could get down at the car wash."

"We're going to the Sánchezes' Sunday afternoon. Remember?"

"If I can make thirty-eight bucks on a wax job, I'll skip the party. I'm not all that thrilled about—"

Ellita entered the dining room with Donald Hutton. He was carrying a small aluminum coffeepot in his right hand.

"This is our neighbor from across the street," Ellita said, "Mr. Hutton. You already know Sergeant Moseley, but these are his daughters, Sue Ellen and Aileen."

The girls nodded and smiled. Hutton shifted the coffeepot to his left hand and shook hands awkwardly with the two seated girls. He cleared his throat and lifted one corner of his mouth in a lopsided smile. "I, ah, was only asking Ms. Sánchez here for a pot of hot water, thinking I'd brew up some instant coffee. My electricity hasn't been turned on yet, and I don't want to go out for anything because the man could show up at any time. I certainly didn't invite myself to dinner." He looked at Hoke, who said nothing in return.

"I invited you," Ellita said, gesturing to Aileen. Aileen got up and brought a chair in from the kitchen and placed it next to her seat. Sue Ellen went into the kitchen for silverware and another plate. Ellita took the plate from Sue Ellen and filled it. Hutton sat in the chair Aileen brought to the table, shifting the empty pot from one hand to the other; then he placed it on the floor between his feet.

"Dig in, Mr. Hutton," Hoke said. "None of us cares for dark meat, so Ellita usually cooks a turkey breast instead of the whole bird, except when she fixes *mole* sauce."

Hoke passed Hutton the dressing and the gravy boat. His fingers trembled slightly from rage, although his voice hadn't betrayed him. What he wanted to do was kick Ellita squarely in her big fat ass! What in the hell was the matter with her, inviting this bastard to the table?

"This really looks good," Hutton said. "It's been a long time since I've had a home-cooked meal."

"Did your wife die, Mr. Hutton?" Sue Ellen said.

"That's a personal question, Sue Ellen," Hoke said.

"Oh, that's quite all right," Hutton said, smiling as he spread a heaping tablespoonful of cranberry sauce on his turkey. "I've never been married. I came close a couple of times, but somehow I just never got around to it. I'm forty-five now, and it's a little too late to start a family, I guess."

"We were talking earlier about your Henry J," Sue Ellen said. "How much is it worth, a little antique car like that?"

"It isn't for sale. It's the only car I've got left. At one time I collected classic cars, but I kept the little Henry J. It's only got twenty-seven thousand miles on it, and I'll just use it for transportation."

"Would you like a beer, Mr. Hutton?" Ellita asked.

"I'm not allowed to drink." Hutton shot a quick glance at Hoke. "Doctor's orders," he added.

What a bastard, Hoke thought; did Hutton think he would turn him in to his parole officer for drinking a lousy beer?

"I wouldn't mind some coffee, though," Hutton said, smiling at Ellita.

"We usually have coffee later, with dessert. Cuban coffee. And we're having *Tres Leches* for dessert."

"Three milks?"

"It's a homemade custard. I haven't started the coffee yet, but—" Ellita started to get up.

"Sit down, please. I'm in no hurry for coffee."

Ellita sat down, and Aileen jumped up. "Let me make it, Ellita. I know he wants his coffee now, or he wouldn't've brought his pot over."

"Please—" Hutton held up his right hand.

Aileen went into the kitchen.

"I work at the Green Lakes Car Wash," Sue Ellen said. "But I can do wax jobs for people on my own time. I could do a nice Simoniz job on that Henry J for you at a bargain price. Thirty-eight dollars. It'll cost you fifty at the car wash. I can't do it this Sunday because we're going to a party. But I can do it next Sunday."

"That sounds fair to me." Hutton nodded. "I don't have a garage or a carport, so it might be a good idea. If it's going to sit out in the sun all day, that might be the thing to do."

"Sunday week, then, Mr. Hutton. I'll also bring along a can of new car spray, and you can keep it in your car. It'll look like a new car when I finish, so you'll want it to smell like one, too."

"Sure. Why not? This turkey's wonderful, Ms. Sánchez."

Aileen came back from the kitchen. "There's a van over in front of your house, Mr. Hutton."

"That's probably the FPL man." He started to get up.

"I'll go," Hoke said. He got up and placed a hand on Hutton's shoulder. "I know where your meter is. Finish your dinner." Hoke left the house and went across the street. He hadn't been able to take another bite after Hutton had sat at the table.

After the Florida Power electrician had turned on the electricity, Hoke signed "D. Hutton" and the time on the man's clipboard. He finished his cigarette before he went back to his house. He had calmed down by this time and was half amused by his former anger. He decided to say nothing to Ellita. It was as much her house as it was his, and if she wanted to invite the killer to dinner, she was entitled to feed him.

When Hoke took his place at the head of the table again, Ellita was nursing Pepe. She had folded her T-shirt back, exposing her large alabaster breasts, with faint tiny blue veins. Hutton, a little bug-eyed, was trying to keep his violet eyes off them but couldn't quite manage it. He stared at his plate, and then cut his eyes over, and then shifted back to his plate again, obviously discomfited.

Hoke was able to eat now. He finished quickly so the others could get to their desserts and coffee. Hoke enjoyed Hutton's uneasiness. Hoke hadn't paid that much attention to Ellita's breasts before, but he saw them with new eyes, thanks to Hutton. Ellita was a D cup before she began nursing, but her breasts were much larger now. Pepe, red-faced, nursed audibly.

Hutton refused a second cup of coffee, finished his custard, thanked Ellita again, and left the house. Aileen walked him to the front door and then came back, hesitating in the archway between the living and dining room. Aileen looked at her sister and giggled.

"Did you notice his eyelashes?"

"Did I?" Sue Ellen rolled her brown eyes. "I'd give my left ovary for eyelashes like that."

"His eyes are violet, not blue," Ellita said. "Just like Elizabeth Taylor's."

"Jesus Christ," Hoke said, and he threw his napkin down on the table. He left the table and went into the living room to catch the last half of the *Kojak* rerun on Channel 33. The women cleared the table, and he could still hear them talking and laughing in the kitchen over the cacophony of the New York traffic coming from the television set.

CHAPTER 6

SATURDAY MORNING AFTER BREAKFAST HOKE MOWED THE lawn. The lawn mower was old, and the blades needed sharpening; but Hoke enjoyed the exercise. The activity, he felt, was good for him, but he wanted to finish before the sun got too hot. It had been eighty degrees at six-thirty, with humidity to match, when he went out to get the newspaper. The paper stated that the highs would probably be in the low nineties. The Henry J was gone, so Hutton, thankfully, was off somewhere. Hoke was pleased about that. He hadn't relished the thought that Hutton might sit out in his front yard and watch him work for two hours.

At ten-thirty, when Hoke had finished the front lawn and was sweeping grass cuttings off the sidewalk, Ellita called him in to answer the telephone. It was Teodoro González.

"Hello, Teddy," Hoke said into the phone. "How'd you make out?"

"They let me talk to four Cuban guys wearing orange

jumpsuits out in the yard. What they told me doesn't mean much, but they got my Omega."

"Your wristwatch?"

"Yeah. One of the bastards took it, but when we shook 'em down later, nobody had it on him. I didn't miss it, you see, until I was leaving and picking up my pistol and cuffs at the main gate. We went right back, but by then whoever took the watch had a chance to ditch it. Security said they'd shake down the barracks this morning and let me know if it shows up. But I'll never see it again, and I paid a hundred and eighty-five bucks for that watch."

"You should've checked it with your pistol at the gate."

"Tell me about it."

"What about the tattoos?"

"They said they weren't prisoner tattoos. Those stars and circles were new to them, and they thought the little V's might be initials. The dead men could be cane cutters, they said, Jamaicans or Haitians, but whatever they are, they aren't Cubans."

"What made them so certain?"

"Because the tattoos don't mean anything. And only cane cutters would be dumb enough to make meaningless tattoos. I don't see how any of this'll help. There's no cane in Miami to cut, so when I told 'em how the men were killed, they said they were probably *droguistas*."

"It's more than we had before."

"I had my watch before, too."

"You don't need a watch. You notice I don't wear one. If you need to know the time, there's always some asshole around to tell you."

"Well, don't ask this asshole again because I no longer have a watch."

"Maybe it'll turn up in the shakedown, Teddy."

"I don't think so."

"I don't either. Buy yourself a nineteen-dollar Timex."

"I'll do that, Hoke." González laughed. "Soon's I make my last two payments on my Omega. They all shook hands with me when I left, so one of those slick bastards must've slipped it off then. Far's I'm concerned, those Marielitos can rot out there in Krome."

"Write up your notes, and put 'em in the file. We might as well bury it in old cases now and give up on it. If they're alien Haitians or Jamaicans, we'll never find out who they were. Unless we get some new leads, it can't be solved till we get some positive ID. But you did well, Teddy. See you Monday morning."

HOKE SHOWERED AND THEN TOOK ELLITA GROCERY SHOPPING at the Green Lakes Supermarket. Aileen stayed home to give Pepe a sunbath and then a sponge bath. Sue Ellen had gone to work at the car wash. Saturday was the busiest day of her six-day week.

While Ellita fixed Hoke a turkey sandwich for lunch, Hoke tried to phone Quevedo and Levine to arrange a committee meeting. Mrs. Quevedo said she didn't know where her son was or when he would be back. Myra Levine said her husband had gone to the races at Calder, and she had no idea when she could expect him home. Hoke thought both women were lying, but he couldn't do anything about it if they were. He'd have to set up a meeting later on next week, when he could corner the two elusive detectives at the station.

Feeling restless, Hoke drove Aileen to the Cutler Ridge Mall, bought her a pair of Wrangler's jeans, and then they went to the early bird movie at Multitheater No. 5 and watched *Friday the 13th: Jason Returns*. Aileen spent most of the movie with her face buried in Hoke's right armpit.

Afterward she told him that this was the best version of the Jason story she had seen so far.

"That's because Jason killed mostly cops this time, as well as yuppies," Hoke explained. "People hate cops and yuppies, and old Jason keeps up with the trends in each new movie."

"You always told us that policemen are our friends."

"We are, and most people know that, sweetheart. But everybody feels guilty about something or other, and cops in uniform remind them of their guilt."

"Why do people hate yuppies? I don't hate yuppies."

"Americans hate anyone who's more successful than they are."

"I don't know a yuppie from anyone else. How can you tell one? I dress well, but I'm not a yuppie."

"Ask who they voted for. If they like Ronnie and Nancy Reagan, they're yuppies. It's a simple but effective test."

"But you voted for Reagan."

"My vote doesn't count. I didn't vote for Reagan, I voted against Carter. Carter let all those Marielitos in and ruined Miami as a decent place to live. You were still living up in Vero Beach with your mom then, so you don't remember what a pleasant place Miami used to be before they let in all that scum."

"Maria, my friend at school, is a Marielito, and she isn't scum. She's very nice—"

"I'm not an absolutist, baby. Some of them are all right, I suppose. But crime's gone up twenty-five percent because of the Marielitos since they got here. I was talking to my partner, Teddy González, this morning. I sent him out to Krome yesterday to talk to some Marielitos, and while he was talking to them, one of them stole his wristwatch."

"Right off his wrist?"

"Right off his wrist, and he never noticed it."

"But he already knew that the Cubans at Krome were criminals. He should've checked his valuables at the gate before he talked to them."

"That's right. When you grow up, I'd like to have you as my partner."

"When I grow up, I'm gonna marry a rich yuppie, buy a penthouse condo on Grove Isle, and tool around town in a red Ferrari."

Hoke sighed. "My daughter's a yuppie. Where did I go wrong?"

Aileen giggled and took his arm. They went out to find his Pontiac in the parking lot.

HOKE PULLED INTO HIS DRIVEWAY AT FIVE-THIRTY. TWO LATIN gardeners were finishing their work on Hutton's yard across the street. They had cut the grass, trimmed the Barbados cherry hedges, and lopped off some of the lower limbs of the smelly melaleuca tree in the front yard. A formidable pile of cuttings was stacked on the grass verge at the curb. The yard looks nice, Hoke thought. If he gives the house a new paint job, at least it will improve the appearance of the neighborhood. But he wasn't going to suggest the idea; the less he had to do with Donald Hutton, the better.

Ellita met them in the dining room. She had rolled up her long black hair in empty Minute Maid orange juice cans. Ellita had an abundance of hair, and she had used eight cans. Her face was flushed, and her nails, freshly varnished, were the color of arterial blood. Her fingers were spread wide, to allow her nails to dry.

"Can you baby-sit tonight, Aileen?" Ellita held up her hands, palms outward, fingers spread.

"I'm supposed to sit for the DeMarcoses tonight."

"Can't you take Pepe along with you? I've already fed and changed him and prepared a bottle of water and another of orange juice. If he wakes later, you can give him one or the other or both."

"You and Rosalinda going out?" Hoke asked.

"Rosalinda got engaged a month ago, Hoke. I told you all about that." Ellita blushed and turned her head away. "I've got a date."

"You've got a date?" Hoke asked.

"I'll take care of Pepe," Aileen said. "But I'd better call Mrs. DeMarcos and ask her if it's all right to bring him."

"I already called her. She doesn't mind. And Sue Ellen will be home later, if you run into any problems."

"You've got a date?" Hoke asked again.

"For dinner and a movie. But we're going to the movie first and then out to dinner. *Los Olvidados*, at the Trail. It's an old Buñuel movie he made in Mexico about slum children. And I've never seen it."

"*Los Olvidados?*"

" 'The Lost Ones.' It's supposed to have a lot of sur-realistic symbolism, but I've never seen it."

"Who're you going with, if not Rosalinda?"

"I have a date. What do you care?"

"I don't care. I think it's nice. It's just that you haven't had a date, since, hell, I don't know—"

"In almost two years. And I don't want you to get all upset about it."

"I'm not upset. I'm pleased. Why should I get upset?"

"Good. You'll have to get your own dinner. But there's turkey in the fridge, and you can make sandwiches. There's still enough *Tres Leches* for dessert, and there's ice cream, too. Heath Bar Crunch, the kind you like. Can you help me, Aileen?"

"Sure."

They left for Ellita's bedroom (Ellita and Pepe shared the master bedroom), and Hoke got a can of Old Style out of the refrigerator. He didn't recall being told about Rosalinda, Ellita's best friend, getting engaged. If she had told him, he would have remembered. She hadn't told him; she only thought she had told him.

Sue Ellen roared into the yard on her motorcycle. She stripped off her leathers in the living room. She wore denim cutoffs and a Green Lakes Car Wash T-shirt under her leathers. She tossed the garments and her helmet on the couch and sat on the bean bag next to Hoke's La-Z-Boy recliner. Sue Ellen's nose, prominent to begin with, looked larger because it was plastered with white Noskote.

"I'm really tired, Daddy. Can I have a sip of your beer?"

Hoke handed her the can. She took a sip and returned it. "It's good and cold, but I still don't like the taste of beer."

"Sit there. I'll get you a Diet Coke."

Hoke brought her a Diet Coke and sat in his La-Z-Boy again. "I think six days a week is too much for you, Sue Ellen, especially out in the sun all day. Why don't you work five days and rest on weekends?"

"On Saturday I get double time. And I usually don't mind because we trade off jobs. But today I was drying all day and never got a job in the shade. Drying's easier than vacuuming, but when you vacuum, you can sometimes talk the driver into a pine spray, and you get ten percent off the spray job. But Arturo hogged the vacuum all day and wouldn't trade off with anyone."

"Why not take Sunday and Monday off then?"

"Because if you don't work five days, the sixth day isn't a double-time day. You know that. But I'm so tired I'm going to take a shower and go to bed right after dinner."

"I'm making sandwiches tonight. Ellita, apparently, is going out."

"Ellita's going out?"

"That's what I said. She's got a date."

"Where is she now?"

"In her bedroom. Aileen's helping her dress, I guess."

"Why didn't you tell me before?"

Sue Ellen struggled out of the bean bag and ran down the hall toward Ellita's bedroom. Hoke went into the kitchen and began to fix a platter of turkey sandwiches. There was pork, so he made some pork sandwiches, too. He used mustard on the pork sandwiches and mayonnaise on the turkey sandwiches. He put out another plate of sliced tomatoes, in case someone wanted to add them to a sandwich. He set the table and put the platter of sandwiches in the center. The table looked bare, so he opened a jar of pickles and a jar of olives, put some into bowls, and added the bowls to the table. He put glasses at the girls' plates. There was a quart jar of iced tea in the refrigerator, Diet Cokes, and milk. Hoke was hungry, but he waited to eat with the girls. He sat in his La-Z-Boy and lighted a Kool.

Ellita, when she appeared in the living room, flanked by the two grinning teenagers, was transformed. A vision, Hoke thought. She wore a white organdy dress with a full circle skirt, and it fell just below her knees. She wore a pair of five-inch spike-heeled silver slippers, and a thin silver chain belt engirdled her narrow waist. Some cleavage showed in the V-necked dress, but not too much, and her golden skin seemed to glow. She had combed out her hair, and it hung in black curls to her bare brown shoulders. She wore coral lipstick and had touched her high cheekbones with traces of coral blusher as well. She had also used too much Shalimar perfume and had then added musk to that. Shalimar and musk filled the entire living room.

"Wow," Hoke said, grinning. "You really look nice, Ellita."

"Not nice, Daddy," Aileen said, "beautiful."

"What time is it? Is it six-thirty yet?" Ellita said.

"Six thirty-five," Sue Ellen said. "Let him wait another five minutes. He'll wait."

"Where's my purse? The movie starts at seven."

"I'll get it," Aileen said. "It's in the dining room." Aileen brought the purse, a large patent leather bag. The shoulder strap had been broken and had been tied instead of mended.

"Your old bag spoils the effect," Aileen said. "What you need is a little silver evening bag to go with that dress."

Ellita shrugged. "No, I need my big bag. I'm just happy I could get into this dress again. Well, I guess I'd better go."

"Isn't he coming to pick you up?" Hoke asked.

"No." Ellita lifted her chin. "He lives right across the street."

Aileen and Sue Ellen giggled. Ellita looked at Hoke and smiled, but she blushed.

"You don't mean you're going out with Hutton?"

Ellita shrugged. "Donald came over this afternoon and asked me, so why not? He told me about the Buñuel movie, I haven't seen it, so I said I'd go."

"Have you got your pistol?"

"In my bag." Ellita patted her purse.

"Good luck then," Hoke said, "and have a good time."

"I intend to." Ellita left, and the girls, watching through the screen door, looked at her as she crossed the street.

"The table's set," Hoke said. "And I fixed sandwiches."

They moved into the dining room and sat down.

"Isn't Mr. Hutton a little old for Ellita, Daddy?" Sue Ellen asked.

"He's only forty-five, and she's thirty-three. Men like to go out with younger women, as a rule."

"That doesn't mean you have to go out with them." Sue Ellen frowned. "I was propositioned last week by an old man—he must've been sixty-five—driving a Datsun. I told him to grow up!"

"I'd better take a look at Pepe for a sec," Aileen said, getting up from the table.

"Don't worry about Pepe," Hoke said. "Let him sleep. He knows how to yell when he wants something. Get something to drink from the kitchen. I didn't pour you anything because I didn't know what you wanted."

"Don't get anything for me, Sis," Sue Ellen said. "Did Ellita tell you where they were going for dinner, Daddy?"

"No, she didn't."

"The Biltmore, in Coral Gables. He made a reservation and everything, for ten o'clock."

"When I came to Miami, the Biltmore was a VA hospital—"

"Ellita said he told the man on the phone to have the wine opened and burping on the table when they got there. Isn't that funny?"

"Yeah," Hoke said, biting viciously into a pork sandwich. "That's funnier than a son of a bitch. I only wish I'd been here to hear him say it."

CHAPTER 7

*T*HEY TOOK BOTH CARS TO THE PARTY FOR TÍO ARNOLDO
Sánchez. All of his Miami relatives were there. Except for
Ellita's parents, Hoke didn't know any of them. There
were cousins and cousins-in-law by marriage and a few old
men who had known Arnoldo back in Havana thirty years
earlier.

Señor Sánchez (Ellita's father) ignored Hoke, as was his
wont, and because everyone at the party was speaking
Spanish, Hoke didn't try to mingle—nor did he want to
mingle. The girls, both a little shy in this Latin gathering,
stayed close to Ellita, taking turns holding Pepe so Ellita
could talk unencumbered to her friends and relatives. Pepe
began to cry, and Señora Sánchez, Ellita's mother, filled his
bottle with two ounces of *jus* from the roast beef platter.
He enjoyed this greasy treat and stopped crying immediately. Hoke, with a plateful of pig's feet and a long-necked
bottle of Bud, shared a yellow velvet couch with two
middle-aged, obese Cuban women who had no English
whatsoever.

Hoke wanted desperately for Major Brownley to call him soon. No matter what Brownley told him on the phone, it would give him a chance to bug out early. This is why he had insisted on taking both cars, even though his Pontiac had ample room for the five of them, including Pepe's paraphernalia.

Hoke, when they first arrived, had shaken hands with Tío Arnoldo and welcomed him to America. The old Cuban—who wasn't really all that old in years but had been broken in prison and looked as ancient as God—had wept. He looked a little dazed and confused as well. He cried and smiled at the same time, exposing some snaggled teeth in his purple gums, and said something to Hoke in Spanish in a gargling voice.

This was a very emotional family, Hoke concluded—all of them. They laughed and cried at the same time as they talked rapidly and stuffed enormous quantities of food into their mouths.

Tío Arnoldo, Ellita informed Hoke, was the last one left in her father's family, and now there were no more relatives to get out of Cuba. It had cost her father more than thirty thousand dollars to buy Tío Arnoldo a visa in Cuba and to support the old man in Costa Rica until his entry visa to the United States came through. But everyone in the family had chipped in something or other, even if it was only a food package mailed to the old man during his four-year wait in Costa Rica.

Hoke admired the Sánchez family loyalty but didn't think that the old man would contribute much, if anything, to America. Mr. Sánchez would support him, but within a few days Tío Arnoldo would be signed up for SSI and Medicaid and would be hospitalized eventually, free, of course, because he didn't have a dime and was obviously going to die within a few months—certainly within the year. He

77

was brown skin and frail bones, and the last job he had held—twenty-six years ago in Cuba—was that of a file clerk in an Havana bank. As a matter of "honor," Ellita had said, Tío Arnoldo had refused to do any work in Castro's prisons, and the wardens had been hard on him.

On the table the pig's feet had looked appetizing, but now that Hoke had them on his plate he couldn't eat them. They weren't prepared the way he was used to eating pig's feet (pickled, and from a jar), but had been fried in bacon grease saturated with garlic. He couldn't cut the thick skin with the white plastic fork he had taken from the table, and the feet were so slippery with hot grease he couldn't pick them up with his fingers either. Hoke returned the uneaten plate of pig's feet to the table casually and went out on the porch to smoke a cigarette.

He finished his beer and put the empty bottle on the porch rail. There was a shrine to Santa Barbara in the front yard. It was surrounded by a well-tended bed of geraniums, and someone had placed a bouquet of roses in front of the three-quarter-size saint inside the concrete brick and stucco shrine. Hoke wondered if Señor Sánchez practiced *Santería* and if he had sacrificed a goat or a chicken in honor of Tío Arnoldo's arrival. He wouldn't put it past him, but he hoped that Ellita was too civilized for such practices. He didn't know for sure. He had thought he knew her very well, after working with her in the division and living with her for more than a year, but apparently he didn't know her as well as he had thought. He still couldn't get over the astonishment that she would actually go out on a date with Donald Hutton, a man who had murdered his own brother.

Hoke had fixed his own breakfast that morning and had heard Ellita and the girls talking in Ellita's bedroom while he ate his Grape-Nuts and toast in the dining room. When

Ellita came out to fix her own breakfast, she hadn't said a word about her date. It was none of his business, and he hadn't asked. But his curiosity was high. If she didn't volunteer any information, there was nothing he could do to find out. He could always ask Aileen, who would tell him anything he wanted to know, but he wouldn't take advantage of his daughter's desire to please him.

Hoke flipped his cigarette butt into the shrine and wondered if he had been at the party long enough to leave without hurting the Sánchezes' feelings. He could drive Ellita's Honda home and leave the keys to the Pontiac so she could bring the girls and Pepe home later. Then Ellita appeared on the porch, holding a bowl of mixed rice and beans (*moros y cristianos*) and a plastic spoon.

"I saw you sneak those pig's feet back on the table," she said, smiling, "so I brought you something you could eat."

"You didn't have to do that." Hoke took the bowl and spoon. "There're plenty of things on the table I could eat. But those pig's feet are gross."

"Major Brownley hasn't called yet, Hoke. But I told my mom I'm expecting him to call, and she's been listening for the phone."

"There've been about a dozen calls already."

"It's always that way. At a party like this it rings off the hook. People who can't come want to talk to Tío Arnoldo anyway, and people who're coming later want to know what to bring, or they say they'll be late—you know—Cuban time."

Hoke nodded. "I didn't hear you come in last night. I watched the news but didn't stay up for *Saturday Night Live* because I was too sleepy."

This wasn't the whole truth. Hoke had gone to bed earlier than he had wanted to because he didn't want

Ellita to think that he was waiting up for her to come home. There was nothing physical between Hoke and Ellita—no sexual sparks—and he had always considered her asexual. But as he had watched the eleven o'clock news, he had considered the possibility that Donald Hutton, after ten years in prison, had looked at Ellita as a desirable sex object and was probably trying to get his hand up under her dress as he sat beside her in the Trail Theater watching the old Buñuel film. And Ellita, being a mature woman, might very well open her legs and encourage such explorations. Why not? She was entitled, and it was none of his business what she did.

"*Los Olvidados* was a good movie, Hoke. It was in Spanish, with English subtitles, but whoever wrote the titles really didn't understand the street idioms. So I had to explain a lot of them to Donnie during dinner."

"Donnie?"

Ellita nodded. "He likes to be called Donnie instead of Don or Donald. His mother always called him that, he said."

"Jesus Christ, the man's forty-five years old! Isn't that a little old for the diminutive?"

"What about Ronnie Reagan? He's thirty years older than Donnie."

"But Reagan's primarily an actor, like Swoosie Kurtz."

"Donnie did some acting in prison, he said. They had a little theater group there for a while."

"I'll bet he did. He did plenty of acting at the trial, too, but it didn't help him any."

"He told me he was innocent, Hoke."

"You don't believe him, do you? Monday, if you like, I'll dig out the old files and bring them home so you can take a look at the evidence."

"I'm not a fool, Hoke," Ellita said with a little laugh.

"I was a cop for nine years, remember? They *all* say they're innocent. I told Donnie he should try to put it out of his mind. Innocent or guilty, it didn't make any difference to me. He was free now, I told him, and he could start a new life. All of that was behind him."

"What did he say to that?"

"That he was trying. But inasmuch as he hasn't been given a new trial, and he accepted the parole, his name will never be cleared now. So when he thinks about it, it still galls him."

"We proved conclusively that he was fucking his brother's wife." Hoke put the untouched bowl of rice and beans on the porch rail next to the empty beer bottle.

Ellita nodded and smiled. "He explained all that to me at dinner. His brother wasn't altogether infertile, he just had a low sperm count, that's all. Marie Weller and Virgil had a regular sex life, but she was impossible for him to impregnate. So Donnie was doing his brother a favor, he said, because Virgil wanted a son. She really wanted a baby, too, and was planning to adopt one. So Donnie said he would impregnate her instead, and Virgil would then think it was his, you see. Being they were brothers, the baby would even look something like Virgil and Donnie, and Virgil would think it was his. Virgil and Donnie even had the same blood type—AB. But Donnie said he couldn't get her pregnant either, and he really tried."

"What a crock of shit! Jesus Christ, Ellita—"

"Isn't it?" Ellita threw her head back and laughed. "But he was wonderful, Hoke. He told me all this shit with such a solemn face and was so earnest about it. I could just picture him working on Marie Weller with this proposition. She did go to bed with him, you know. Not only in Key West that weekend, as they proved at the trial, thanks to you, but he met her several times at the Airport Hotel.

They have reasonable day rates at the Airport Hotel, he said."

Hoke cleared his throat. "That's what I heard, too. Look, Ellita, give me your Honda keys, and you drive my Pontiac home." He handed her his car keys, which were attached to his old army dogtags with a small chain. "I'd better go home and wait for Brownley's call there. I've met your uncle and put in my appearance, so your folks'll understand if I have to leave for police work."

"There's going to be a cake later and—"

"Fuck the cake."

"I'll bring you a piece when I come home."

Ellita took Hoke's car keys and left to look for her purse and the Honda keys.

MAJOR WILLIE BROWNLEY CALLED HOKE AT SEVEN-THIRTY. By then Hoke had finished three beers, and he suppressed a belch when he picked up the phone.

"Good!" Brownley said when Hoke answered. "I'm glad I tried your house first before I called the Sánchezes. It's always hard to get through to a Latin house. When they hear you speaking English, they think it's the wrong number and hang up on you."

"We do the same, Willie. When I get an answer in Spanish, I hang up, too."

"I never thought about that, but I do, too, now that you mention it."

"I went to the party, Willie, but bugged out as soon as I could. It's a madhouse over there. And just as I was leaving, a neighborhood group of kids was setting up to play salsa. The phone was tied up most of the time anyway. Besides, I was getting eager to hear from you so I can shave off this damned stubble."

"You haven't shaved, have you?"

"Not yet. I've let my beard grow since Thursday, such as it is, and my neck itches. If this is some kind of joke on your part, Willie—"

"It's not a joke. Here's what I want you to do. Wear some old clothes tomorrow."

"All my clothes are old."

"I mean some old jeans, maybe a blue work shirt, if you've got one. An old pair of shoes. And meet me at seven-thirty at Monroe Station."

"Out on the Tamiami Trail?"

"That's right. It's about forty miles out, maybe a few miles more, on the other side of the Miccosukee Trading Post."

"What's this all about, Willie? Are we going hunting?"

"Something like that. Have you got a hat, a straw hat?"

"I haven't got any hats. You've never seen me wear a hat."

"Okay, I'll bring you one. What's your hat size?"

"In the army I wore a seven and an eighth."

"With a straw, I guess it doesn't make that much difference. I'll see what I can find."

"What's this meeting all about?"

"I don't want to talk about it on the phone, Hoke. And don't tell Ellita about it either. I'll explain everything tomorrow morning. Now when you get out to Monroe Station, don't go inside. You can park out front where the trucks and dune buggies are, but then you take a little dirt trail on the right of the restaurant, the other side of the gas pumps. That's west of the building. There's a small clearing in the scrub palmettos and pines there called the wedding grotto. The restaurant owner's a notary public, and sometimes he marries people in the little grotto. You'll see the sign. I'll meet you there, in the grotto. The owner uses that clearing as a marriage chapel."

"Should I bring a present?"

"A present? What do you mean?"

"If I'm going to a wedding, I thought maybe I should bring a wedding present."

"Don't try to be funny, Hoke. I'm not up to it. I got badly sunburned down in the Keys. And when a black man gets burnt, it's a lot worse than when a white man does. My neck and shoulders are on fire. It seemed cool out on the water, and I took my shirt off. Anyway, that's it. Seven-thirty A.M. In the wedding grotto at Monroe Station. Got it?"

"I've got it. Did you catch anything?"

"We were fishing for permit, so even when you catch one, you still haven't got anything, if you know what I mean. In the morning then."

Without a good-bye Brownley hung up the phone. Hoke listened to the dial tone for a moment and then racked the phone himself. Willie Brownley was not a secretive man, and this mysterious business was out of character for him. Well, he would just have to wait and see.

Without the girls around, it was lonely in the house. Hoke went out to the White Shark on Flagler Street. He played bottle pool with a detective he knew from Robbery until ten-thirty, drank four more beers during their games, and then went home.

CHAPTER 8

HOKE LEFT THE HOUSE EARLY, STOPPED FOR BREAKFAST at a truck stop at Krome and the Trail, and then drove cautiously down the two-lane Everglades highway toward Monroe Station. The Tamiami Trail was an extension of Eighth Street, renamed *Calle Ocho* by the Cubans, but was still referred to by the old-time Miamians as the "Trail." When the two-lane highway had been built from Naples to Miami, road crews had worked toward each other from both sides of the state. Monroe Station had been a supply camp then for workers and had found its way onto the state map.

As ordered, Hoke wore an old pair of blue jeans and a plaid, almost threadbare, long-sleeved sport shirt. Remembering the fierce mosquitoes, he wanted sleeves that rolled down to the wrists. He wore his regulation, high-topped policemen's shoes, figuring they were old enough. Although the temperature was in the eighties, he drove with the car windows rolled down, and it was cool enough with the wind coming through. Except for a few trucks, the traffic was relatively light this early in the morning. On weekends, with cars bunched up in clusters, all waiting for an opportunity to leapfrog along the ninety-six-mile stretch to Naples, the Tamiami Trail was a dangerous highway. Head-on crashes were not infrequent. The Miccosukees and the Seminoles who lived in reservation villages at intervals along the Trail had special licenses and rarely drove more than fifteen miles an hour. The Indians were never in a hurry, and sometimes there would be a string of twenty or thirty cars behind an Indian, all waiting for a chance to pass him.

Although Monroe Station is still on the state map, there are just a two-story building and a few sheds on the property. Behind the restaurant, on the ground floor of the wooden building, two hundred yards south on the old loop road, there's an abandoned forest ranger station and a shaky, unoccupied lookout tower. Now that the Big Cypress National Preserve is all government property, the restaurant is merely "grandfathered" in. When the current owners die, it will be razed, and only the sign on the Tamiami Trail, MONROE STATION, will be left. At one time a good many people lived on the loop road that wends through the Everglades, and Al Capone once owned a hunting lodge in the area. But that's gone, and most of the shacks and trailers that loners and pensioners lived in out on the loop road have been destroyed, too.

Hoke had been out to the Big Cypress Preserve a couple of times on wild pig and wild turkey hunts, but that had been four or five years ago. It had been fun for the first hour or so to ride in a dune buggy; but the hordes of lancing mosquitoes had always spoiled the day for him, and he had never managed to shoot either a turkey or a wild pig. Now, except for the Indians and a few men with special permis-

86

sion, dune buggies and airboats have been outlawed in the preserve.

Hoke parked beside a rusty Toyota pickup in front of the Monroe Station restaurant and glanced at the home-made signs plastered onto the building as he got out of his car.

STOP AND EAT HERE BEFORE WE BOTH STARVE
COUNTRY HAM BREAKFAST WITH GRITS RED EYE GRAVY
AND HOT BISCUITS
NOTARY PUBLIC—MARRIAGES, BUT
NO DIVORCES . . .

Near the gas pump, on the side of a whitewashed generator shed, a fading blue and white poster proclaimed THIS IS WALLACE COUNTRY. George Wallace, when he ran for president, had racked up a sizable vote in rural Florida, and Hoke had all but forgotten the Wallace frenzy. Hoke found the narrow path to the grotto and brushed away some dew-laden cobwebs before he reached the small clearing in the hammock of pines and scrub palmettos. He sat on a wooden bench, lit a cigarette, and slapped some of the gnats away from his eyes.

At seven thirty-five Major Brownley and another black man joined Hoke in the clearing. The major, a squat man in his early fifties, with skin the color of a ripe eggplant, was wearing a pink T-shirt, with "Pig Bowl" printed on it in cherry red letters. He wore faded jeans and unlaced Reebok running shoes. The other black man, who was about the same age, was at least a foot taller than Brownley. He wore khaki trousers and a shirt with the creases sewn in, and he had pulled a snap-brim fedora well down on his forehead. His skin was the color of a dirty basketball, and mirrored sunglasses hid his eyes. His Wellington boots, rough side out, had seen hard wear. Brownley was carrying two unopened cans of beer and a new straw hat. He handed the hat and one of the beers to Hoke.

"Try this for size."

Hoke put on the hat and pulled down the brim. "It fits okay." He popped the top of his beer and took a long pull.

"This is Mel Peoples, Hoke. Mel, Sergeant Hoke Moseley." Hoke shook the tall man's hand. Instead of a beer, Peoples was drinking a Diet Pepsi, and his spidery fingers were damp and cold.

"Let's sit down," Brownley said. Peoples and Hoke sat on the bench, but Brownley remained standing. His short, kinky hair, with shiny black sidewalls, resembled bleached steel wool, and he scratched his scalp with his right forefinger. There was a razor-blade part on the right side of his head. "I guess you're wondering what this is all about."

"Not at all," Hoke said. He put his beer on the bench and lighted a Kool. "It's pleasant to meet in the Glades like this instead of in your air-conditioned office, although I imagine it'll be pretty hot out here along about noon."

"It won't take that long. Mel and me go back a long way, Hoke. We were roommates at A and M for two years, and we majored in business administration. We were even in business together for a while, scalping tickets to the FSU games."

Mel chuckled. "But it didn't last the full season."

"You got caught?" Hoke said.

"No." Mel shook his head. "Our source at FSU was expelled. He never got caught for the football tickets, but he stole the final exams from the social science department."

"I thought it was the history department—"

"This is interesting," Hoke said impatiently. "Should I tell you now about my year at Palm Beach Junior College?"

"Sorry, Hoke," Brownley said. "Mel's a field agent for the State Agricultural Commission. A kind of trouble-shooter. Isn't that right, Mel?"

"Something like that, and a little more. For six years I was investigating complaints statewide, concentrating on migrant workers. But for the last two years I've been in Collier County on a permanent basis. In the last few years lots of things have changed. What with unemployment insurance, food stamps, and welfare, a lot of former migrants have quit migratin'. After the harvest season, instead of moving on the way they used to, they stay put and pick up unemployment or go on welfare. Then, too, we've got us a large illegal Haitian population, and they ain't movin' either. They've got a language problem, and they wouldn't have no one to talk to if they moved on up to Georgia, say—"

Hoke nodded. "So now you stay in Collier County because you've got enough migrant problems without moving around the state?"

"That's the size of it. I check growers' complaints as well as migrants'. Haitians are good people, but they're used to tiny one-man farms back in Haiti, so they can't understand teamwork. This makes for discipline problems, and we've tried to get some training programs started. But that takes money, and the legislature ain't going to give us money for people who've entered the country illegally. Technically they ain't even here. But they *are* here."

"Discipline? You're punishing Haitians because they don't understand teamwork?"

"No, not at all. Say you've got ten Haitians, and you assign each one to a row of tomatoes. They all start out okay, and then one guy gets a little ahead and sees a nice tomato in the next row. He goes over and picks it. Then he spots another, three rows over, even bigger, so he gets that one, too. The other Haitians do the same, and the first fucking thing you know Haitians are scattered all over the field. And half their assigned rows are unpicked."

Hoke laughed. "The bigger the tomatoes, the sooner a man gets a full basket, right?"

"Right. But the growers have to use 'em 'cause, like I said, the old-time fruit tramps have quit pickin' and migratin'. They either sit tight on welfare or find other jobs. Then they put their kids in school and register to vote. We've still got a trickle of illegal Mexicans and lots of Haitians, but our old reliable source has dried up. To get harvests in on time, the big growers've been hiring tougher crew bosses."

"I still don't see where this is leading," Hoke said, looking pointedly at Brownley. "I'm working on the old Russell case right now, and I've got a fairly good lead—"

"Finish your beer, Hoke. Let Mel tell you the rest of it."

"The thing is, Sergeant," Mel continued, "you could put Delaware in Collier County and never notice it was there, and I'm only one man. I had me a clerk, but she quit last month because she can make more money puttin' pickle slices on burgers at McDonald's." Mel crushed his Pepsi can and placed it on the bench.

"I still don't know what you expect me to do about that."

"You speak any Creole, Hoke?" Brownley said, taking a sip of his beer.

Hoke grinned. "I just know their worst swearword. *Guette mama!* I was called it once in Little Haiti, so I checked it out."

"*Guette mama?*"

"Yeah. That's Creole for *linguette mama*, or 'your mama's little tongue.' At one time, in Africa and Haiti, they used to cut off a woman's clitoris when she got married. It was called the little tongue, a useless thing to be thrown away."

"My wife wouldn't agree on that," Brownley said. "Why would they cut off a woman's clit?"

"Without a clit, a man's wife's less likely to fool around, Willie. They don't do it in Haiti any longer. But it has a nice sound to it as a swearword, doesn't it?" Hoke lowered his voice and growled: *"Guette mama!"*

Brownley frowned at Mel. "Tell him, Mel."

Peoples nodded, and sucked his teeth. "Haitian farm workers've been disappearing, Sergeant Moseley. We didn't notice it for some time because they stay to themselves. Because of the AIDS scare, American black men don't even go after their women, you see. And Haitians don't complain about things 'cause they're afraid of being sent back to Haiti. But word gradually gets around. A family man'll disappear, and his woman'll ask if anyone's seen him. Then someone'll say, 'I think he went over to Belle Glade to work.' But a Haitian won't leave his wife without sending her money. And they all send money back to Haiti. They're Catholics and family-oriented. But once one of these Haitians disappears that's the end of him. He ain't in Belle Glade or anywhere else. And we don't know how many are missing altogether."

"When you say 'we,'" Hoke said, "are you talking about you and Willie here, or you and the clerk who went to work for McDonald's?"

Mel shook his head. "Me and Sheriff Boggis, in Collier County. I also had a dialogue with a deputy over in Lee County, but he said he wished they all were missing, so I didn't talk with him again. But what happened, we finally found a body."

"You and Sheriff Boggis?"

"No, a truck driver from Miles's Produce, over in Tice. He picked up a load of melons in Immokalee and then stopped on the highway, a couple of miles past the Corkscrew Sanctuary cutoff, to take himself a leak. He went behind the billboard there, the one that advertises the Bonita Springs dog track, and found some toes stickin' up. It had been raining, the ground was marshy, and the foot had worked its way up. He dug around a little with a stick, enough to see it was a foot, and then phoned Sheriff Boggis when he got to Bonita Springs. Boggis took a look, and then he called me out there to see if it was a missin' Haitian. And it was."

"How'd you know? Not just because he was black."

"He had a tattoo on the back of his left hand. *Le Chat*, with a couple of pointed ears below the words. The tattoo had been carved in, probably with a razor blade. Haitians, as you probably know, eat cats."

"No, I didn't know. These so-called ears, could they be little V's?"

"I guess you could say that. Why?"

"Nothing. I was thinking about another case. Go ahead."

"They eat cats because they think it'll make 'em invisible. It's a folk myth, because no one's ever become invisible by eatin' a cat. But they hear about it, believe it, and then get a cat and try it, you see. If you go to Port-au-Prince, you won't see any cats at all. Dogs, yes, but no cats. Man owns himself a cat he locks it up inside his house, or someone'll grab it and eat it. This Haitian cat eater had this tattoo on his arm to prove it. The little ears were put there to show that the rest of the cat was invisible and inside the man.

"So he was a Haitian, Sergeant. Afro-Americans don't tattoo French words on their hands. Besides, his feet and hands were calloused, and he'd been a field worker all his life."

"How was he killed?"

"The ME wasn't positive. He'd been badly beaten around his head, and the ME didn't know whether he was dead or just unconscious when he was buried, so he marked it down as 'Death by Misadventure.' "

"That's pretty damned vague, especially if the man was buried alive."

"The ME couldn't say for sure. He'd been in the ground too long."

Hoke nodded. "So all you have to do now is find the man—or woman—who buried him and see if he's buried a few more somewhere."

"Yeah," Brownley said. "That's what we want you to do."

"Me?" Hoke shook his head. "Collier County's a little far out of our jurisdiction, isn't it, Willie? We can't—"

"I know, but this is a special case, Hoke. I told Mel I'd help him out. And we've got something to go on. It's something you could check out in a couple of days. The ME dug some dirt out from under the corpse's fingernails and toenails, and it didn't match the loam where he was buried. It matched the dirt in a grower's farmyard this side of Immokalee. A man named Harold Bock, nicknamed Tiny Bock. That name ring a bell? Tiny Bock?"

Hoke shook his head. "I don't know the name."

"There was a feature article on him a few years back in the *Miami News*. He was an old-time alligator poacher, born in Chokoloskee. Then, when the state cracked down on poachers, and they couldn't sell the skins up North any longer, he bought up farmland in Lee and Collier counties and became a grower. His property's scattered, but he's got about two thousand acres, all in two- and three-hundred-acre parcels. He usually runs three or four gangs of workers, and he grows all kinds of shit. But the farmhouse he lives in is on the Immokalee road between Carnestown and Immokalee. Mel got this sample of soil from his farmyard, and it matched the dirt under the dead man's nails. I had it checked out at the University of Miami by Dr. Fred Cussler, the forensic geologist."

"I met Dr. Cussler once," Hoke said. "White-haired guy, supposedly the world's authority on oolite. But most of the soil in South Florida's about the same, isn't it?"

"In a way—coquina stone, shale, gravel, sand, oolite. But you give Cussler a sample, and he'll tell you where it came from in Dade County. Besides, this Tiny Bock beat a slavery rap three years ago, you see. He had a bunch of winos living in a trailer and was charging 'em more for their food and rent than he was paying 'em. He wouldn't let anyone leave until they paid what they owed, and they couldn't get even. He also gave 'em free wine."

"So how'd he beat the rap?"

"One of the winos escaped and told the sheriff about the other men out there. Sheriff Boggis went out there and turned 'em loose, but there was no case. Bock had books proving that all these winos owed him money. He was charging three bucks for a plate of beans and a chunk of corn bread and ten bucks a night for a straw mat in the trailer. So there was no case."

"They do this in Dade County, too, Willie," Hoke said.

"But this is different. Because of this incident with Bock, a workers' co-op got started in Immokalee, and the growers blame Bock. Half the migrants' wages must be paid to the co-op each week, and then the co-op gives that money, less expenses, to the workers when they finish the job."

"What you're telling me is that Bock is disliked by the other growers—" Hoke started to say.

"Hated is more like it," Mel broke in. "Because of Bock they all have a lot of paperwork to do now, and they can't hide any income from the IRS. Not very well they can't."

"So anything that happens, the other growers'll all say it's probably Tiny Bock?"

"That's true," Mel agreed. "But Bock's the only suspect we have, and the dirt did match at his farmhouse yard. Him and his foreman live alone, 'cept for a couple of pit bulls he keeps in the yard. I was a little nervous the night I went down there to get the soil samples."

"I still don't see what you expect me to do about it," Hoke said. "I don't know shit about farming. I wouldn't even know how to begin to investigate something like this. What did Sheriff Boggis say when you told him you were bringing me in, Willie?"

"Mel and I didn't tell Boggis anything about you, Hoke. Mel tried to get Boggis to assign a deputy in plain clothes, but Boggis said his deputies are too well known in the county to do any undercover work. Any deputy wearing civvies nosing around would be recognized in no time. But Mel and me talked this over, and naturally I thought about you—"

"I'm not right for this," Hoke protested. "You need a Department of Law Enforcement man, some stranger from Tallahassee. I don't have any jurisdiction in Collier County. If the sheriff found me nosing around, my ass would be buttermilk, for Christ's sake."

"That's the whole idea," Brownley said. "You won't be official. You'll just be a private citizen. If you find out anything, just get word to Mel here. He'll get in touch with Boggis if there's something concrete to go on. I'm asking you to do this as a favor to me because I owe a big favor to Mel."

"Okay, let me get this straight, Willie. You want me to

visit Tiny Bock's farm, sneak past a couple of vicious dogs, and then dig around the farm to see if I can find a few more dead bodies. That it?"

"Not exactly, Hoke," Brownley said. "Bock's advertised for crew chiefs in the *Immokalee Ledger*, but no one wants to work for him. Only someone desperate for money'll work for the son of a bitch. Lately Bock and his foreman, a Mexican named Cicatriz, have had to drive over to Miami to find Haitian laborers. They soon quit and drift back to Miami.

"So when you go out to the farm and ask for a crew chief's job, he'll hire you. Once you're living there, you'll be able to check around with no sweat."

"It won't work, Willie." Hoke shook his head. "He'll ask me some questions about farming, and he'll know immediately that I don't know the difference between my dick and a cucumber."

"You won't be picking cucumbers or nothing yourself. If he hires you, you'll be supervising pickers, and they know what to do. You should be able to supervise a gang of Mexicans, Haitians, and winos—"

"What about my cases in Miami?"

"González can handle things till you get back. After all, they're all cold cases anyway. A couple of days won't matter. I'll have him report daily to Bill Henderson."

"What I was going to have González do today was to check to see if Dr. Schwartz is wearing the late Dr. Russell's Rolex and diamond ring. But González isn't subtle, and I have to tell him how to go about it."

"I'll explain it to him. Is this important?"

"Might be. Schwartz married Russell's widow and drives his Mercedes, so it might be worthwhile to know whether he's wearing his watch and ring as well."

"Don't worry. I'll tell Gonzáles how to go about it."

"How?"

"I'll just have him make an appointment. Then, when he goes in, he can take a look when Schwartz examines him."

"Examines him for what? What's supposed to be wrong with González?"

"What kind of doctor is Schwartz?"

"Internal medicine."

"Okay, I'll tell González to say he's got a bellyache."

"No." Hoke shook his head. "Ulcer. Two hours before his appointment, make a peanut butter ball, the size of a marble. Let it dry a little, and then have González swallow it without chewing it. In two hours it'll spread out a little in his stomach and look like an ulcer on an X ray."

"You sure?"

"A lot of guys beat the draft that way during Vietnam. And it'll work on Dr. Schwartz. I don't want him to suspect anything, so Teddy'll have to get his story straight."

"I understand that. Anything else?"

"Several things. What're you going to tell Ellita and my daughters? I can't just disappear for a few days without a word—"

"I'll tell Ellita you're on a special assignment when I drive your car back. As an ex-cop she'll understand that."

"You're taking my car, too?"

"You won't need it. And don't write or call Ellita either."

"There's one other thing, Willie. It might be important, and it might not. But Donald Hutton got paroled—"

"The man who poisoned his brother? You must be wrong. He got a mandatory twenty-five."

"I know. But he was awarded a new trial on his last appeal. The state attorney didn't want to retry the case, so he's out on a time-served. It isn't all that unusual."

"You don't think he's still out to get you, do you? After all, it's been ten years."

"I don't think so, no. But he bought the house right across from me in Green Lakes. If I'm out of town, he might try to get back at me through one of my daughters or even Ellita. I'm not really worried about it, but this is a bad time for me to be away for a few days."

Melvin Peoples got up, and shoved his hands into his pockets. "I don't know what this is all about, Willie, but if Sergeant Moseley's family's in any danger, we'd better forget about this idea or postpone it. This investigation could take three or four days or more—"

"Take it easy, Mel," Brownley said. "I can handle this. I've got to drive Hoke's car back anyway, so I'll stop by and talk to Hutton myself. The threat he made ten years ago doesn't mean much. But I'll talk to him, and if I don't like what he says, I'll make him move."

"I already checked with his parole officer, Willie," Hoke said. "He told me Hutton can live anywhere he wants, and there's nothing we can do."

"He can't do anything, but I can."

"It's not that important, Willie, but I thought you ought to know about it."

"I'll check him out. Now empty your pockets and put everything on the bench here."

"What for?"

"I've got a new ID for you. If Bock finds your gun and badge on you, he won't believe you're a crew chief so down on your luck you're asking him for work. Gun first."

Hoke took his gun and holster from his belt in back and placed it on the bench.

"Cuffs, too."

"They're in the car—glove compartment—together with my sap." Hoke put his badge and ID case on the bench. He removed his money from his wallet—eight dollars— and put the wallet beside his ID case.

"What else you got in your pockets?"

"Cigarettes, about a half pack. This Bic lighter, some Kleenex, some change. Car keys and fingernail clipper. That's it."

"Okay. Keep the lighter and cigarettes, and put your money in this wallet. It's your new ID." Brownley handed Hoke a well-worn cowhide wallet that was torn on one side. There was a yellow business card, advertising Goulds' Packers, Goulds, Florida, with an address and telephone number. There was a letter on lined stationery that had been folded and refolded. Hoke took the letter out of the envelope, addressed to Adam Jinks, General Delivery, Florida City, FL, and read it:

Dear Adam,

I got your money order for ten dollars the one from Farm Stores, but how long do you think ten dollars will last not long when I still have rent to pay and Lissies been sick with the croop and needs to see a doctor. I can't find no work here in Lake City where I can take Lissie with me and I been sick myself. So if you can send another MO soon I won't bother you soon again.

All my love EVIE.

"I guess," Hoke said, "when I get paid I'd better send my 'wife' some more money up in Lake City."

"If you do, it'll be a shock to Evie. Adam Jinks was killed in a knife fight in Florida City last Friday night. By now she knows it, but no one else down here does. I kept his wallet. They brought Jinks up to Jackson, and he died there. I got his effects, such as they are. And because it happened down in the Redland, it didn't make the Miami papers."

Hoke nodded and looked at the rest of the wallet's contents. There was an unused condom wrapped in a piece of tinfoil, a photo of a freckled young woman with a little girl on her lap, a fourteen-cent stamp with Sinclair Lewis's face on it, and a coupon torn from a newspaper that would entitle the owner to a free Coke at Arby's if he also bought a roast beef sandwich.

"Is this all?" Hoke asked. "There's no money."

"Jinks was fired from the Goulds packinghouse, and he was broke. He got knifed trying to steal a man's change off the bar in Florida City. Put your own money in the wallet, and there's your ID. Adam Jinks is an easy name to remember."

"There should be a Social Security card."

"He probably knew his number and lost the card. Hell, I lost my card ten years ago and never asked for another. I know my number."

"All right," Hoke said. "If I'm asked, I'll use mine."

"Give me your teeth, too, Hoke." Brownley held out his hand. "Jinks didn't have any teeth, so you can't either."

"He had false teeth, didn't he?"

"Not when he was knifed, he didn't. He probably pawned 'em, but there wasn't any pawn ticket with his effects. Hand 'em over."

Hoke removed his upper and lower dentures, wrapped them in a tissue, and placed them in Brownley's hand. Brownley dropped the teeth into his right front pocket. "I'll take good care of these, Hoke. Soon's I get home I'll put 'em in water with some Polident."

"How'm I supposed to eat? Without my fucking teeth?"

"Stick to soft stuff for a while, but your gums ought to be pretty tough by now."

"Without my teeth I look a hundred years old, 'specially with this gray beard, for Christ's sake!"

"You just look down-and-out, Hoke, and that's the look you'll need to get a crew chief's job with Mr. Bock."

"On the road to Immokalee," Mel Peoples said, "you'll pass by Tiny Bock's farmhouse. It's on the east side of the road. Don't stop. Go on into Immokalee and talk to some of the migrants in town before you do anything else. It's unlikely that Jinks would know anything about Bock's hiring problem down in Goulds or Florida City, so you'll have to pick up that information in town before going out to his farm."

"I understand that," Hoke said, nodding.

"Tom Noseworthy's the man to contact in Immokalee if you find out anything. Contact him, and he'll call me, and then you can go back to Miami. When you get to Immokalee, go down the main drag. Go straight instead of taking the dogleg to Bonita Springs, and continue down the street for two more blocks. You'll pass a drugstore and a Sixty-six station, and then you'll see the sign for Noseworthy's Guesthouse. It's a two-story building with gingerbread trim, a bed and breakfast place. Noseworthy's a Bahamian from Abaco. He isn't doing too well with this bed and breakfast place because not many tourists spend any time in Immokalee. But it's a nice place if you can afford it. Sixty bucks a day, with a free breakfast. It's too steep for hot-bed traffic, so at least he gets legitimate guests. Anyway, Tom knows how to get ahold of me, but don't go near him till you're ready to leave."

"I'll need some money to eat on," Hoke said. "Eight bucks and change won't go far."

"That's plenty," Brownley said. "In fact, it's almost too much. You've got to play the part of Adam Jinks, and he's got to be broke enough to actually hit Tiny Bock up for a job."

"All right, Willie, I'll play it your way this time. But after this you're going to owe me a big one."

Mel shook hands with Hoke. "Good luck, Sergeant. I've

got to get moving. I'm due back in Naples before noon."
Mel turned and started up the path.

"Just stay here for about twenty minutes," Brownley said,
"and then go out and hitch a ride on the Trail." He turned
to leave.

"Just a second, Willie. Is this some kind of test or what?"

"In a way maybe, but don't worry about it. Just look at
this as another routine investigation." Brownley trotted
up the path to catch up with Peoples.

Hoke sat on the bench and lighted another cigarette.
With cigarettes selling for a buck and a half a pack, he
would have to go easy on them for a while—at least until
he got some more money. Why didn't he tell Brownley to
go fuck himself? The story about the dirt at Bock's farm
matching the dead Haitian's toenails and fingernails was
thinner than his hair, for Christ's sake. There must be
dozens of farms in the Immokalee area with the same kind
of dirt. For some reason they wanted to get something on
Tiny Bock. He didn't have to take this weird assignment.
He was on his own now—without a badge, gun, or authority—and he didn't know exactly what he was supposed to be
looking for—except those little V's nagged at him a bit—
and neither did Peoples and Brownley. Well, he would find
out soon enough. Some branches broke up the path, and
Hoke got to his feet.

Brownley came back into the clearing. He wiped his
sweaty forehead with the back of his hand. "Those dogs,
Hoke, the pit bulls. D'you know what to do if one of 'em
attacks you?"

"Sure. I run like a striped-ass ape."

"No, that isn't the way. He'll catch you. When one of
'em jumps for your throat, he tucks his front legs up a little,
like this, see?" Brownley held up his wrists in front of his
chest and let his hands dangle. "What you do then, you

grab these forelegs, drop onto your back, and flip the dog over at the same time. Hang on to his legs. This'll break both of his front legs, you see, and then he can't chase after you again. That's all you have to do."

"No shit? That's all I have to do, huh? Just hang on to his legs. Suppose both dogs jump for my throat at the same time?"

"You'll have to dodge one when you get the other one. But I wanted to be sure you knew what to do in case you got attacked, that's all."

"You ever do this, Willie?"

"Not with a real dog, no. But when I was at Fort Gordon, Georgia, during the Korean War, we practiced how to do this with a sack of sand. The sergeant would throw the sack at us, and it had two little legs dangling off it. We practiced grabbing 'em, and it wasn't too hard once you got the hang of it."

"A sand dog and a pit dog aren't the same, Willie."

"Sure they are. The principle's the same. You'll catch on in time. I just wanted to make sure you knew how to do it, that's all. Good luck, Hoke."

Brownley waved and disappeared up the path.

CHAPTER 9

WHEN HOKE EMERGED FROM THE SHADY GROTTO TO stand on the north side of the trail, his Pontiac was gone. Perhaps he should have argued with Brownley to keep the car, but it wouldn't have done any good. A toothless migrant like Adam Jinks could hardly explain how he came to own a 1973 Pontiac with a new engine and a police radio. The rusty Toyota was still there. A tourist family had parked beside the pickup and was disembarking for breakfast (a middle-aged man in green canvas shorts, two teenage children, and an obese woman—the wife, no doubt, carrying a sleepy two-year-old on her hip). Hoke wanted to follow them into the restaurant and drink another beer, but Brownley had told him not to go inside. Besides, he had to guard his eight bucks and change until, somehow, he managed to obtain some more money.

It was another twenty miles to the hamlet of Ochopee, and then seven or eight more to Carnestown, the crossroads where he would have to take the state road north to Immokalee. The Tamiami Trail continued southwest into

Naples at Carnestown, and south of Carnestown, two or three miles, was Everglades City, the major port for marijuana coming into South Florida.

The traffic was thinly spaced, and no cars slowed to his raised thumb. Why would they? Without his teeth, and with the stubble of gray beard on his long face, he looked like a wilderness wino. The sun toasted his back through his threadbare shirt, and he was grateful now for the new straw farmer's hat with its green plastic brim. It protected his balding dome from the direct rays. Sweat dribbled down his sides, and his shirt was wet. His balls were damp in his Jockey shorts. There were fewer mosquitoes out on the highway than there had been in the dusty clearing, but there were still clouds of gnats nibbling at the moisture about his eyes and lips. Two hundred yards up the road, across from Monroe Station, was a small Seminole village. There were a half dozen chickees behind the peeled pole palisade, and he could see the tops of the thatched roofs of the chickees. At the gate, on the other side of the canal, across the small bridge, there was a small clapboard store selling Indian artifacts. A pipe rack outside the store displayed multi-colored Seminole jackets and aprons.

Hoke walked down to the village parking lot and stood under the shade of an Australian pine. There were no tourists as yet, parked in the gravel lot, but he would wait for one and then ask the driver for a ride as far as Carnestown. It would be much more difficult for a man to refuse his direct request than it would be to ignore his thumb from passing cars.

There were buses on the Tamiami Trail, Trailways and Greyhound, but they went straight through to Naples and didn't stop for passengers on the Trail. If a man lived out here in the Glades, he either owned his own vehicle or had to cadge a ride with a friend. The migrant camps had buses and trucks, and if one came by, Hoke might be able to get a ride in one or the other; but his best bet, he thought, was a sympathetic tourist.

Monday morning was not, apparently, a good day for tourists of any kind. An Indian kid, black as tar and with a heavy black braid down his back, came out of the village and crossed the road. Hoke watched the boy go into the Monroe Station restaurant and then come out a couple of minutes later eating a Mounds bar. He nibbled the bar as he walked back and then tossed the candy wrapper into the canal before crossing the little bridge into the village again. Ah, Hoke thought, Indian culture at first hand. The Seminoles and Miccosukees both, in Hoke's opinion, were a surly lot. If you bought gas at their Shark Valley reservation station, near their restaurant, the attendant would merely look at you without expression until you told him what you wanted. After he had filled your car, he would take your credit card without saying anything and walk away. You got no thanks or any other acknowledgment from the pump jockey when he returned with your card or change. It was as if the Indian were doing you a big favor by selling you gas, gas that was ten or fifteen cents more per gallon than you could buy it for in Miami. If you asked the jockey to check under your hood, he didn't hear you. He went back inside his office and waited until you drove away, frustrated and angered by his attitude.

The Indian kid with the Mounds bar had not looked at Hoke either going to or coming from the Monroe Station restaurant when he crossed the highway. It was nice to know that officially the United States and the Seminole Indian nation had not, as yet, signed a peace treaty and that the two nations were still at war. This was a mere technicality to the United States, but perhaps the Indians took it more

seriously and therefore refused to fraternize with the enemy
—except to take American money.

An hour later the sun was hotter yet, but Hoke discovered that if he walked back and forth on the lot instead of standing still, he could discourage some of the lazier gnats. Smoking also helped keep them away, but he was now down to only six cigarettes in his crumpled pack. No more cigarettes, he promised himself, until he got a ride.

The stillness in the Everglades was appalling. There were six chickees inside the compound, but no noise or talking came from inside. The woman inside the open door to the little shop didn't come out to take a look at him. Indians never offered any help or suggestions and merely grunted the price of something if you asked. There was no dickering either. Except for the striped, multicolored Seminole jackets fluttering on the pipe rack, all the other Indian artifacts they sold were made by other Indian tribes—not by the untalented Seminoles or Miccosukees. The turquoise jewelry came from New Mexico, and the rubber tomahawks were imported from Taiwan. But the Seminoles were getting rich anyway. They sold taxless cigarettes and ran bingo games on their reservation in Broward County, and the federal government couldn't do anything about it— so long as they stayed on their reservation. But Hoke wouldn't live out here in the Glades if he made two hundred thousand dollars a year. Hell, it would take more than three hours to get a Domino pizza delivered from West Miami!

What *was* he doing out here anyway? No driver's license, no weapon, no teeth, and no ID except for a handwritten identification card in his beat-up wallet—the kind that comes with a cheap wallet when you buy it. Not even a Social Security card for the unmourned Adam Jinks, stretched out now on a gurney in the Miami morgue with the top of his skull sawed off. He shouldn't have let Brownley take his teeth. Even if Adam Jinks was also toothless, he must have had a set of choppers stashed somewhere. The more Hoke thought about it, the more absurd the mission seemed to be. What was he supposed to do? Exactly. Get hired somehow by Tiny Bock or perhaps by his honcho, Cicatriz, and then poke around on the farm to see if he could discover a few more buried Haitians? Cicatriz . . . Cicatriz? The name sounded familiar. Of course. *Cicatriz*, in Spanish, means "scar," so that couldn't be the Mexican foreman's real name. He would have a scar, and it would be a lulu of a scar if he used it as his moniker. Jesus, what was he getting into, and why should he do it?

Hoke lighted another cigarette and decided to return to Miami. He could cross the road to Monroe Station, buy a fresh pack of Kools, and then pay someone—sooner or later—five bucks to give him a ride back to Miami. This was not a legitimate assignment for a Miami homicide detective, and there wasn't a damned thing Brownley could do about it.

A huge Mack sixteen-wheeler slowed slightly as Hoke held out his thumb and pulled to a wavering stop some two hundred yards past the Indian Village. Hoke ran toward the truck but slowed after the first hundred yards, panting for breath. He was almost out of wind by the time he reached the cab. He climbed the three steep steps, opened the door, and collapsed on the sheepskin seat in the air-conditioned comfort of the monstrous cab.

"Sorry," the young driver said, grinning, "I didn't stop a little sooner, but I was afraid she'd jackknife on me."

Hoke nodded, gasping. "That's okay."

"I don't know how to back her very good neither. To go one way, you see, you gotta turn the wheel the other way,

and even then it don't always back straight. I'm still learnin'
how to drive her. You may not believe it, but this baby's
got seven shifts forward and three shifts in reverse."

"Sure, I believe it. But you'd better move it on out 'cause
you're still on the road, and someone might ram into you."

"Right. I'll just take a quick look at this little diagram
on the dashboard here. It's got all the shifts on it and stuff.
I don't know what all this shit means yet on the dash.
What's the tack-o-meter for? When I get her rolling past
fifty, that needle spins around like crazy. So I slow her back
down to forty-five."

"It just measures the engine's revolutions per minute,
that's all. Ignore it. But forty-five's a nice speed for a rig
this size. What're you hauling, fish?"

"Smells like it, don't it? But I don't think it's fish. The
back's all sealed up, but the guy on the loading dock had
him a couple of cartons marked 'lobster tails,' so I think
that's what I'm carryin'."

"Didn't he tell you?"

"No, but it don't matter none to me. For two hundred
bucks I'd haul a load of dead babies, wouldn't you?"

The driver, with a long chestnut mane, a silver stud in
his right earlobe, and smudgy traces of sparse brown hairs
on his upper lip, was about nineteen, Hoke thought. He
wore tight, faded jeans, running shoes with red racing
stripes, and a rose-colored T-shirt with a white sailboat
printed on it. A CAT gimme cap rested lightly on the back
of his head. He bit his lower lip with concentration as he
studied the gear diagram bolted to the dash and then took
the lever noisily through five gears as he accelerated. He
didn't double-shift, and the truck jerked at each progression.

"I usually skip four and five," he said, sitting back, "and
it don't seem to make no difference."

"It probably won't hurt anything on a flat road like the

Trail. There's only a one-foot drop in elevation between Miami and Naples."

"That's where I'm goin'. Naples. You got a driver's license?"

"Yeah, but not on me. I left it back in Miami."

"Me neither. That's too bad, pops. The main reason I picked you up was because I thought you might have a license. I don't mean I'd let you drive or nothin', but I wanted to tell a trooper, in case he stopped me, that you were the driver and you was givin' me lessons drivin' across the Trail. See what I mean?"

"Not exactly. Who're you driving for? What company?"

"He didn't say. I was drinkin' a Miami Nice Slurpee and readin' *Auto Trader* outside the Seven-eleven on Bird Road when these two guys drove up in a brown Volvo. Black guys. I guess I must've looked at 'em a little funny, you know. I never seen a black man drive a Volvo before, have you?"

"Never."

"Anyway, the driver got out and asked me if I knew how to drive a truck. I told him I sometimes drove my dad's pickup, and then he asked me if I wanted to make two hundred big ones. 'Sure,' I said, and got into their Volvo. We went to this warehouse over in Hialeah, and this here's the truck they give me to drive. He paid me a hundred in advance, and when I get to Naples, to the warehouse there, I get the second hundred."

"In that case," Hoke looked out the window, and peered at the rearview mirror on his side, "we should have a brown Volvo riding shotgun right behind us."

"I did, for a while. But they had them a flat tire back at Frog City. I suppose they'll catch up, though, 'cause I've been holdin' her down to forty-five."

"What you've got here, son, is a load of hijacked lobster tails."

"I think so, too. But I didn't steal 'em. I'm just a driver, and I was paid to drive a truck to a Naples warehouse for two hundred bucks. So even if I'm stopped, the worst they can do to me is get me for not havin' no license."

"They're robbing you."

"What do you mean?"

"This load's worth at least two hundred thousand bucks, maybe more, and you're only getting two hundred dollars. If I were you, I'd ditch this truck somewhere in Naples and then call the bastards and ask for more money before delivering the load."

"Do you think I should?"

"I would. You can do as you please. But now that nobody's trailing you, you could take the cutoff into Everglades City when we hit Carnestown, hide out overnight, and then make your call tomorrow. By then they'll be ready to dicker. Either that, or they'll find and kill you."

"I think I'll just take her on in to Naples."

"Suit yourself. But you can get another thousand, easy."

"Or a bullet."

"Or even a burst of bullets. Two hundred grand is a lot of bread."

"It don't take all that long to fix a flat. They might be right behind me already, just hangin' back a little."

"They might."

"But it's sure temptin', what you said."

"What else you do, son, besides hang around the Seven-eleven?"

"Well, I worked at Burger King for a while. But I don't really see myself as a fast-food man, not on a regular basis. I been thinkin' about joinin' the army."

"When?"

"When my two hundred bucks runs out!" The kid laughed. "I ain't in no all-fired hurry to join no army."

They passed through Ochopee—a gas station, the world's smallest post office, a grocery store, an abandoned motel, and a restaurant that also offered dune buggy and airboat rides to tourists—and then continued on to Carnestown without talking. Hoke got out of the truck, and thanked the driver for the ride, wished him good luck in the army— that made the kid laugh—and walked across the highway to the ranger station, thinking that he could have made a nice arrest of a hijacked truck. But he was confused by mixed feelings. It still wasn't too late. An anonymous telephone call to Sheriff Boggis in Naples would take care of it. On the other hand, the kid had been good enough to give him a ride, and he had liked the boy. Besides, at the moment, he wasn't Sergeant Moseley. He was Adam Jinks, itinerant fruit tramp. Fuck Brownley, and fuck the law; he didn't even have his badge or weapon.

THE GRAY-HAIRED LADY BEHIND THE COUNTER HANDED HOKE a partially filled four-ounce cup of grapefruit juice. Hoke tossed it down and asked for another.

She set her lips in a prim line and shook her head. "Sorry, only one cup to a visitor."

"Two ounces isn't much grapefruit juice."

"T'aint s'posed to be. It's just a sample, that's all. We get tourists in here who'd drink it all day, just 'cause it's free."

Hoke left the counter and studied the large relief map of Florida on the wall. Carnestown was just a crossroads, and no one lived here. Most travelers would stay on the Tamiami Trail into Naples, but sometimes tourists, to avoid traffic in downtown Naples, took the state road north to Immokalee. From Immokalee, they could take the dog-leg road west again to Bonita Springs and then get on the Tamiami Trail again north of Naples and miss all the stoplights downtown. Hoke hoped that some of them would take the longer road into Immokalee today. Hoke walked back to the crossroads and waited in the sun for a ride to Immokalee. An hour later an old black man driving a half-ton Ford truck loaded with watermelons stopped. Hoke opened the door, and the black man shook his head. He pulled his lips back and squinted his eyes. "In the back! If this was your truck, would you let me ride up front?"

"Sure. Why not?"

"You want a ride, you get in back!" He jerked his thumb.

Hoke slammed the door, climbed into the back, and found a narrow space for his feet on the truck bed. He didn't sit on the melons. He bent forward awkwardly to hold on to the front part of the bed, and the truck lurched away. The load was too heavy for the pickup, and the driver never got above forty all the way into Immokalee. When the old man backed into a loading platform of a packinghouse off the main road, Hoke climbed down stiffly. Both his feet had gone to sleep, and he pounded them awake, stamping on the asphalt lot. His back was sore from holding the scrunched-over position, and he hadn't seen any mailbox with a "Bock" on it when he had passed the widely spaced farms. As Hoke straightened, his back made little cricking noises. The black driver disappeared inside the warehouse before Hoke had a chance to thank him for the ride.

IT HAD BEEN AT LEAST EIGHT YEARS SINCE HOKE HAD BEEN in Immokalee, driving through without stopping on a trip to Fort Myers, but he didn't think the little town had changed much. There was a fresh coat of oil on the main drag, and he didn't remember the stoplight's being there at the dogleg into Bonita Springs. But the buildings were just as ancient, and there was a fine layer of dust over everything. Hoke walked to the nearest gas station and asked the attendant, a teenager wearing a white "Mr. Goodwrench" shirt, for the key to the men's room.

"Hell, you know better'n that," the kid said. "You're s'posed to use the place down by the pepper tree. Get outa here! My john's for customers."

The rejection astonished Hoke at first, and for a moment he considered taking the key off the doorjamb, where it was hanging, wired to a railroad spike, and using the toilet anyway. But the moment passed. His cover was working; he looked like a tramp, and he was being treated like one.

Hoke looked down the highway and spotted the tall, dusty pepper tree. It was on the edge of a hard-dirt parking lot next to a building painted a dull lamp-black. CHEAP CHEAP GROCERIES had been painted in white letters above the door of the black building. There were seven or eight Mexicans near or under the spreading branches of the pepper tree. One sat in a rubber tire that had been attached to a limb by a rope; three men sat together on a discarded, cushionless davenport; and the others merely stood there, talking and smoking. This was obviously a work pickup spot, but they were all Mexicans here. If someone needed a man for an hour or an all-day job of some kind, he drove to the pepper tree and picked up a worker. Pay for the job would be negotiated, and off the man, or two or three men, would go. There were several of these unofficial pickup stations in Miami, in Coral Gables, Liberty City, Coconut Grove, South Miami, but those were reserved for unemployed blacks. There were no black men here under this tree. Hoke walked across the lot and looked beyond the tree. Behind the tree was a row of dusty waist-high bushes, and behind them a wooden rail was balanced across a sluggish irrigation ditch. This was the open-air john, and the bushes screened it from the road. Clumps of wadded newspaper littered the ground. Hoke took a leak, returned to the shade of the tree. Across the street was a long row of one-room concrete blockhouses. Each house had been painted either pink or pastel green, but most of them were pink. There were several blacks in each house, and he could see them inside through the shadeless windows. A good many children played in the dusty yards. Three skinny black kids were kicking a sock-ball with their feet, passing it to one another without letting it touch the ground. There was no laughter. Not letting the sock-ball touch the ground was a serious matter to these Haitian boys.

Two Mexicans looked at Hoke incuriously when he joined them under the tree. One was tall; the other was much shorter and had a gold tooth. Hoke offered them cigarettes, but they were already smoking, so they shook their heads.

"How's the job situation?" Hoke asked.

"Picky spanee?" the tallest Mexican said.

"A *poco*."

"*Malo*." The tall man field-stripped his cigarette and began to roll another with Bull Durhan and wheatstraw paper. Hoke offered his pack again, but the man ignored it.

"You ever hear of Tiny Bock?" Hoke asked.

The shorter Mexican smiled, flashing his gold tooth. "*El Despótico!*"

The taller Mexican lighted his fresh cigarette with a kitchen match and shook his head. "*El Fálico! Buena suerte.*"

The two men moved away from Hoke as he lit his Kool.

Hoke went into the Cheap Cheap Grocery Store. It was more than just a grocery, although there were plenty of canned goods and a small produce section. There were also farm implements, rope and hoses, and bins of hardware items. Tables were piled high with blue jeans, bib overalls, khaki and denim work shirts, and rolls of colored cloth. There was a strong smell of vinegar, coffee, tobacco, and disinfectant. A pasty-faced white man stood behind a narrow counter next to a chrome cash register. There was a heavy mesh screen in front of the counter, with a pass-through window blocked by a piece of polished cedar.

"Let me have a pack of king-size Kools," Hoke said.

The man reached behind him and put the pack on the counter. He slid the piece of wood to one side. "Dollar seventy-five."

"In Miami they're a buck and a quarter."

The man put the cigarettes back and pointed east with his meaty arm. "Miami's that way."

"Give me a sack of Golden Grain and some white papers."

"No Golden Grain."

"A can of Prince Albert, then, and a pack of Zig Zag. White."

Hoke paid for the tobacco and papers and rolled a thick cigarette. He lighted it and inhaled deeply. He hadn't rolled a cigarette in several years, and he had forgotten how good Prince Albert tobacco smelled and tasted. He would be able to roll at least forty cigarettes out of a can of tobacco, too.

"Does Mr. Bock ever trade here with you?" Hoke asked.

"Is a bear Catholic?"

"I heard he was hiring."

"My hearing's bad. But you can hear almost anything down at the Cafeteria."

"What's the name of it, the cafeteria?"

"The Cafeteria. I just told you. Cross the road and down two blocks. You'll see the Dumpster in the parking lot."

"Thanks."

"What for?" The proprietor moved the block of wood back into place.

There were at least a dozen men in the parking lot, most of them in the near vicinity of an overflowing Dumpster, and a few cars were parked on the perimeter. Some of the men were hunkered down, Texas-style, squatting on their heels. Others were in small groups, and a few sat on wooden boxes. There were no Mexicans. Three bearded white men, middle-aged or older, were sharing a bottle of peach Riunite. The front glass window of the cafeteria, lettered THE CAFE-TERIA in black capitals and painted on the inside of the glass, had a handwritten menu taped to it beside the entrance. Hoke examined the menu, checking the prices.

With one meat, either roast pork or roast beef, a diner could have all the vegetables he could eat for $3.95. Soup was fifty cents a bowl, or a person could order a bowl of vegetables for thirty-five cents. Bread pudding, with white sauce, was fifty cents. Coffee or iced tea was a quarter. Corn bread was eight cents a slab, and margarine was two cents a pat. At these prices most of the tables inside were filled with customers. Tables were shared, and none of the chairs matched; but the diners were eating seriously. Little talk was going on, and they were going and coming from the line, serving themselves from large square pans at the steam table.

There was a heavyset black woman working the stoves and refilling pans at the steam table. Several large pots simmered on the stove. A brown-skinned man with a hooked nose, mottled skin, and glittering black eyes worked the cash register at the end of the line. He also checked the tickets on all of the diners who came back for refills. A person with a $3.95 check could have more vegetables—all he wanted—but the man had to make sure that someone with a thirty-five-cent check didn't get another refill without paying another thirty-five cents.

Hoke got a tray, a bowl of thick lentil soup, and two slabs of corn bread, without the margarine. He paid and sat at a small table for two against the wall. Hoke thought this was the best lentil soup he had ever tasted. The soup was flavored with fatback, diced carrots, onions, barley, summer squash, beef stock, garlic, peppercorns, and just the right amount of salt. Condiments were in a tin rack on the table. Hoke shook a few squirts of Tabasco sauce into his soup and began to spoon it into his mouth. A meal like this in Miami, he thought, if a man could find one like it, would cost at least five bucks. Little wonder the place was so crowded.

An Oriental woman nodded and bobbed her head and then slid silently into the empty chair across from Hoke. She had a large bowl of stewed okra and tomatoes and a piece of corn bread on her tray. Hoke stopped eating for a moment, to see if she was going to attack her gooey bowl with chopsticks, but she began to eat with a soup spoon.

The bank digital temperature gauge down the street had registered ninety degrees. Hoke knew that Florida bank clocks were correct, but they always set their temperature gauges lower to avoid upsetting passing tourists, so it was at least ten degrees higher inside the unair-conditioned cafeteria. All the burners on the kitchen stove were lit, the oven was baking more corn bread, and the body heat from the sweaty diners added to the humidity. By the time Hoke finished his hot lentil soup, he was perspiring freely from every pore. He wiped his forehead and eyes with a paper napkin and returned to the line for a glass of iced tea. For a quarter he received a vase-size glass of overly sweetened tea, filled to the brim with chopped ice. He returned to his table, rolled a cigarette, and sipped his tea. Between sips he nibbled on chips of ice and inhaled deeply, savoring the taste of the aromatic tobacco.

The woman across from him giggled. "Smoking no good for you."

"Tell me about it."

"You make me one. Smoking no good for me, too." She giggled again.

Hoke rolled a cigarette, licked the paper, and handed it over. He lit her cigarette with his lighter. As soon as she had it going, she reversed the cigarette and put the fire side inside her mouth, holding it between her lips, and allowing the smoke to escape through her broad, flat nose. She removed the cigarette and smiled. "My way, Filipino way, no waste smoke."

"Don't you burn your tongue?"

She shrugged. "Sometimes." She replaced the fire side inside her mouth and puffed away.

"D'you live around here?" Hoke asked.

"Why? You want to fuck?" She removed the cigarette from her lips and spooned up the last of her tomato and okra stew. Chewing slowly, she looked into Hoke's eyes.

Hoke looked at her a little differently now. He didn't know whether she was a good-looking woman or not, nor could he guess her age. It had always seemed to Hoke that Oriental women looked about eighteen for many years, then suddenly turned forty overnight. There were a few crow's-feet around her slightly slanted eyes, but her thick hair was so black it had tints of blue in it when the light caught it. Her skin, the color of used sandpaper, was smooth, however, and she wasn't wearing makeup, not even lipstick. She wore a pale blue elastic tube top, and her breasts were barely discernible beneath the stretchy material. Her arms were as thin as a British rock musician's but were more wiry than skinny. On the ring finger of her left hand she wore an aluminum skull-and-crossbones ring, with tiny red glass eyes. Hoke remembered having had one just like it in junior high school. All the guys wore them then; they sold these rings in Kress's for a quarter. The teachers had hated the rings for some reason, making them even more popular.

"To answer your invitation, miss, that's just about the last thing I have on my mind right now. D'you know what *peristalsis* means?"

"You show me. I try it."

"No, it's something I have to do all by myself. After this load of lentils I have to go down to the pepper tree to take a crap."

"Pepper tree's for Mexicans." She pursed her lips and lifted her chin, pointing to the cash register. The proprietor was examining a dwarf's check before allowing him to fill up his bowl again with collards. "You are white man. He'll let you use his john."

"Okay," Hoke said, getting to his feet, "I'll ask him."

"You ask Mr. Sileo. I wait. I save table for us."

"You don't have to wait for me."

"I wait."

"I'd like to use your john, Mr. Sileo," Hoke said when he reached the register.

"It's for employees only."

"And the pepper tree's for Mexicans, right? Where do white men go? I don't have a car, so I can't use the gas station."

"You want a job?"

"Sure. I'm looking for work."

"Okay, then." Sileo took a key out of his front pocket and handed it to Hoke. "The door next to the storeroom back there. Wash your hands when you get through, and start on the pots and pans. Marilyn'll need more pans soon, and then get going on the dishes."

When Hoke came out of the john, there were a half dozen dirty pots and pans in the sink. He turned on the hot water and went to work. His cuffs got wet, and he removed his shirt, which was already soaked through with perspiration. He hung it on a nail beside the storeroom door. When he finished a pan and dried it, he placed it on the counter. Marilyn, the fat black cook, would immediately start chopping vegetables into it. She chopped zucchinis, summer squash, onions, and potatoes with equal rapidity. The potatoes, Hoke noted, weren't peeled, nor were they entirely clean. But Marilyn knew exactly what she was doing, and she had several pots working on the stove. Hoke began on the dishes. He washed them in soapy water, rinsed them in clear hot water, and then carried the still-damp stacks of dishes to the counter beside the steam table. His job reminded him of the KPs he had pulled during basic training at Fort Hood, back in the Vietnam War, except that he was the only kitchen policeman here and soon found out that he was the dining room orderly as well. When he got caught up on the dishes, Mr. Sileo sent him out to clear and wipe the tables. The diners were supposed to bring their own trays and plates to the pass-through to the sink. Most of them did; but some didn't, and those who didn't left the messiest tables. Hoke got into the rhythm of the work and forgot all about the Filipino woman. Later, when he was mopping the kitchen floor, he remembered her, but by that time she was gone.

The cafeteria was open from six to six, but at five-thirty Mr. Sileo locked the front door. He let the diners inside finish but didn't allow any more in.

Marilyn took all of the leftover vegetables from the steam

table (but not the meat) and poured them all—mixed as they were—into a twenty-gallon pot. She held open the back door for him, and Hoke carried the heavy pot out to a tree stump that had been cut across the top to form a flat surface. The men in the lot were already lined up at the stump and were more orderly than he would have expected them to be. They came by with coffee cans, tin cups, and other receptacles (one guy had a cardboard box, lined with Reynolds Wrap foil), to dip out of the pot. When the pot was empty, Hoke brought it inside and washed it. He swept and mopped the dining room floor and carried out two cans full of garbage to the Dumpster. The lot was empty. After eating, the al fresco diners had disappeared.

Mr. Sileo handed Hoke a five-dollar bill. "Want to work tomorrow?"

"Not for only five bucks I don't, no."

"You only worked a half day. All day you get ten, plus you eat free."

"Hell, that isn't even a buck an hour."

"Sure it is, if you count what you eat."

"I don't know, Mr. Sileo. I'll have to sleep on it. What kind of retirement plan have you got?"

Marilyn laughed, throwing her head back. Her body, including her massive buttocks, shook all over.

"What's so funny?" Sileo turned on Marilyn. "No man ever stays more'n three or four days! I'd be crazy to set up any kind of retirement plan." He turned back to Hoke, a little calmer. "You want to work tomorrow, old-timer, be here at five-thirty. Otherwise, forget it."

Marilyn had eight slices of bread on the worktable, and she made four roast beef sandwiches. She sliced the beef into quarter-inch slices, and each sandwich had two layers of sliced meat. She put two sandwiches into a brown paper bag for Hoke and wrapped her two in waxed paper. She had a vinyl shopping bag, and it was half filled with canned goods, mostly pork and beans and canned pineapple slices. She added her wrapped sandwiches to the bag.

"I got carryin' privileges," she said, smiling at Hoke. "But I been here for almos' six months now."

"I noticed," Hoke said.

Mr. Sileo padlocked the walk-in freezer, the refrigerator, and the storeroom. He hit the No Sale key on the antique cash register, placed a twenty-dollar bill in the till, and left the drawer open. There was no other money in the till, but Hoke hadn't seen him remove it. Either it was in his pockets, or he had locked it away in the freezer while Hoke watched Marilyn make the sandwiches.

Sileo frowned at Hoke. "Somebody breaks in and don't find any money, he gets mad and breaks things up. So I always leave a twenty, just in case. It's cheaper'n buying new tables and equipment."

"Have you had many break-ins?"

Sileo shook his head. "Not since I been feedin' the homeless any leftovers. They kind of watch out for me now."

"I heard down at the pepper tree that Mr. Bock's been looking for a crew chief. That's what I do, you know. I haven't worked in a kitchen for years."

"You did a good job here. Mr. Bock's always lookin' for help, but you'll have a much easier life workin' here for me."

"I need at least forty bucks a day, Mr. Sileo. I've got a sick wife up in Lake City to support."

"You'll make that much with Bock, but you'll earn it—that is, if you've got the belly for it."

"What d'you mean by that?"

"He works Haitians, that's why. And he specks to get as much out of them as Mexicans. So his crew chiefs have to produce, that's all I mean. I don't hold nothin' against Mr.

Bock. He eats in here sometimes. You're big enough to run a crew, but I didn't figure you for a hard man."

"How do I get to his farm?"

"You don't want to go out there tonight. He'll be down at the farmers' market in the morning around five. I'll be there too, buying produce, and I'll point him out. I think once you talk to him or his foreman you'll come back here with me."

"I'll be there."

Marilyn and Hoke went out the back door, and Sileo barred it from the inside. Sileo left by the front door and double-locked it. Hoke said good-bye to Marilyn in the parking lot. She squeezed her body into a fenderless whale-shaped VW Beetle with oversize tires and drove away. The sun was down, but there would be at least another hour of daylight. The western sky was a mass of purple clouds, each of them edged in gold, and there was a slight breeze from the Glades.

The Filipino woman Hoke had eaten lunch with rose from a wooden crate beside the Dumpster. She came over and plucked at Hoke's arm.

"You come home with me now?"

"Sure. In fact, if you've got a beer at home, I'll even share my sandwiches with you."

CHAPTER 10

MRS. ELENA OSBORNE, NÉE ELENA ESPENIDA, LIVED IN
the Lucky Star Trailer Park with her son, Warren, about
nine sparsely settled blocks away from the cafeteria. As
they walked together, Elena told Hoke a few things about
her life. She was from San Fernando, Luzon, in the Philip-
pine Islands, and had married a retired army staff sergeant.
One of her friends in San Fernando had obtained a copy
of a magazine called *Asian Roses*. The magazine was published and edited in Portland, Oregon. The subscribers
were Americans, Australians, and New Zealanders who
wanted to marry Asian women. Girls and women from
Hong Kong, the Philippines, Japan, and Hawaii sent in
their photographs, short biographies, and five dollars and
were listed in the magazine. She and her girlfriend both had
sent in snapshots, biographies, and five-dollar money orders.
Her girlfriend had received three letters, and Elena had
received only two. Her girlfriend was too timid to answer
her letters, but Elena had answered one of hers. She hadn't
answered the other because it came from a seventy-one-

year-old man who had recently lost his wife, and he had merely wanted a young woman to keep him warm at night. But the other letter, from Sergeant Warren Osborne, was very persuasive. He was a very handsome man who wanted a mother for his children and a companion to share his life in Immokalee, Florida. He had been retired from the army for two years, owned his own mobile home in the Lucky Star Trailer Park, and worked as a checker for Sunshine Packers. He also owned a Toyota pickup, only two years old, and he had never been married before. His mother had lived with him in the mobile home, but she had been dead for more than a year, and he was very lonely. He also felt, now that he was forty, that it was time to get married and have a son to carry on his name. He had told the truth about Immokalee, explaining that the town was in a rural area, with the same climate as the Philippines and that there were cities nearby—Naples and Fort Myers—where they could go and shop on weekends and see first-run movies and major-league baseball games during spring training.

They had corresponded, and after a few airmail letters back and forth, and discussions with her mother, Elena had agreed to marry him. She was twenty-one years old, and although she had an eighth-grade diploma and could read and write English very well, her opportunities to find a husband in San Fernando as well-off as Sergeant Osborne were nonexistent. When she agreed, he made all the arrangements for her visa through a lawyer in Fort Myers and sent her two hundred dollars and her airplane ticket from Manila to Fort Myers, Florida. She had given her mother one hundred dollars of the two, packed a suitcase, and made the long flight, changing planes in San Francisco. He met the plane in Fort Myers, and they were married three days later in Immokalee. Her son, Warren, Junior, was born ten months later. Her husband began to drink then, after her son was born, and, after three or four months, was fired from his job at Sunshine Packers. After he lost his job, he drank even more than he had before, and when he got drunk, he would sit at the little table in their trailer and cry.

One morning he went to the bank, drew out all his savings, and gave her five hundred dollars. He was going to drive upstate, he told her, and look for work. When he found a job, he would come back for her, Warren, Junior, and the trailer. No one in Immokalee, he told her, would hire him now, so they had to move away. That was almost three years ago, and she hadn't heard from him since. His army retirement checks were no longer deposited electronically in the bank, and the teller at the bank didn't know his new address.

When her money was exhausted, she had applied for welfare, and she got an extra allowance because of Warren, Junior. She also got food stamps, but there was very little cash left to live on after she paid her mobile home space rent and utilities. To make extra money, which she needed for Warren, Junior, she occasionally turned a trick.

Hoke was puzzled mildly by her story. But not for long.

There were twelve trailer homes in the dusty park. A barbed-wire fence surrounded the lot, which had a single entrance gate. Only residents had a key to the gate, and those residents who owned cars parked them outside the fence in a graveled lot. The manager lived in the first trailer beside the gate, and when Elena opened the gate with her key, he poked his grizzled head out of his front door to see who it was and then slammed his door again when he recognized Elena.

Elena's trailer was small, with one bedroom and a double bed, a combination living room and galley, and a short corridor to the bedroom. There was a bathroom off one side of the corridor and an alcove closet across from the bathroom door. The furniture was mobile home standard, with an eating nook and cushioned seats. A window air-conditioner labored away above the table. A thirteen-inch black-and-white TV set was bolted to the wall beside the entrance door, and Elena switched it off when she ushered Hoke inside. There was a nose-tingling odor of urine and feces, but the trailer was clean. A framed black-and-white photo of Warren Osborne in his uniform was on the wall. The man was handsome enough, Hoke noted, but the photo of the soldier had been taken when he was nineteen or twenty years old.

Warren, Junior, was in a quilted box in the closet alcove, and Elena pulled the box out so Hoke could take a good look at him. The boy was wearing a Pamper, but nothing else. He moved his thin arms feebly within the box. His tiny legs had atrophied. He had thick, curly red hair, bulging green eyes, and a protruding forehead. The head was much too large for his short body, and he was obviously retarded. His mouth was full of overlapping teeth, and the harsh sounds he made in his throat resembled the caw of an aging crow. The retarded child, Hoke figured, undoubtedly explained the serious drinking and the disappearance of Sergeant Osborne. As Hoke looked at the boy, he wanted a drink himself.

Elena took a two-liter bottle of Diet Coke out of her refrigerator, filled a baby bottle, added a nipple to it, and gave the bottle to Warren, Junior. She poured two glasses of Diet Coke and joined Hoke at the table. Hoke gave her one of his roast beef sandwiches, and she brought two plates to the table from the rack beside the sink. She cut her sandwich in half and then cut up one of the halves into small squares. She fed the bite-size pieces to Warren, who chewed greedily and sucked at the nippled bottle between bites. Hoke took her knife and cut his sandwich into bite-size chunks as well, and gummed them as well as he could before swallowing. When Elena finished feeding Warren, she sat across from Hoke and began to eat her own half sandwich. Hoke got up from the table. With his foot, he pushed the box containing Warren back into the alcove out of sight. He was no longer hungry, and looking at this deformed kid gave him a sick feeling in the pit of his stomach.

"How long will he live? Warren, I mean?"

Elena shrugged. "I don't know. We are all children of God, and God decides how long we will live."

"That's one way of looking at it. If I don't get a job with Mr. Bock tomorrow, I'll be going back to Miami. If you want me to, I can find out where your husband went. I don't think he'll come back to you, but there're ways to make him send you child support."

"No." She shook her head and smiled. "When Warren finds a job, he will send for me." She crossed herself. "But sometimes, I think, maybe he is dead."

"He isn't dead, Elena. When he dies, you'll be told, and the government'll give you a VA pension and an American flag to hang on the wall beside his picture. I can find him easily enough, if you want me to."

"You are a good man, I think. I change Warren's Pamper, then we fuck, okay?"

Hoke went outside to roll and smoke another cigarette while Elena changed the helpless boy. He had never changed the diapers on his daughters (there had been no Pampers then) and had always gone out into the yard when his wife changed them. He didn't mind changing Pepe, however, so he thought he had gotten over this hang-up. He could not understand why, but he knew he wouldn't be able to watch Elena change her three-year-old without getting sick.

Hoke's initial problem had been solved, however. If Tiny Bock asked him how he knew about the job opening for crew chief, he could tell him that a Mexican at the pepper tree had told him about it, and also Mr. Sileo. He would talk to Bock at the farmers' market, and then, when he was turned down, as he would surely be, he could return to Miami. On the other hand, if Bock and his foreman came to the market every morning, it might be possible to visit Bock's farm and look around while they were at the market. That would mean staying over another day or two, but then he could at least tell Brownley that he had nosed around and found nothing.

Elena opened the door, and Hoke took one more drag before stripping his cigarette and going back inside. Elena had taken off her elastic top and denim skirt and was removing her panties and bra when Hoke sat at the little table to finish his Diet Coke. Without her high heels she was much shorter—about four-nine—and despite her small breasts, she had long dark brown nipples. Her short legs were noticeably bowed. She had an abundance of pubic hair; but it hung straight down, like a lamp fringe, and there wasn't a single kinky hair. Hoke had never seen straight pubic hair before, and he found it exotic but not erotic. That was all he needed, he thought, a case of AIDS to take back to Miami with him.

Hoke took out Adam Jinks's wallet, removed the five-dollar bill Mr. Sileo had given him and put it on the table. He weighted it with the catsup bottle so the breeze from the air-conditioner wouldn't blow it away.

"I'd like to fuck you, Elena," Hoke said, "but I'm a married man. I've got a sick wife up in Lake City. Are you a Catholic?"

She nodded.

"Then you understand why I can't make love to you. But I'll give you this five if you let me take a shower in your bathroom and sleep here tonight. This table pushes up and the cushions make into a bed, right?"

She nodded again. "But bed is too short for you. You take back bed, and I'll sleep here." She went to the alcove closet and pulled out a gray-and-white seersucker wrapper. "You go ahead. Shower. I'll stay up and watch TV." She slipped into the wrapper and tied the sash into a bow. "No hot water in shower, but it's not too cold."

Hoke took off his shirt and went into the bathroom. The zinc-lined bathroom was cramped, and so was the narrow shower, and the water came out in a drizzling trickle. There was a brown bar of Fels Naptha soap in the dish, and he soaped his body and his hair. Elena opened the door and came in.

"You want a slow hand job in shower? Hand job not the same as adultery."

"No, thanks, Elena. If I wanted a hand job, I could do it myself. Women don't know how to do it right anyway."

"I know how. You like?"

"No, but thanks anyway."

The lukewarm water felt good on his body, and Hoke took his time rinsing away the thick suds. After drying with Elena's clean pink bath towel, Hoke took his clothes to the bedroom and lay down on top of the bed. There was a sheet on the bed but no covers. None was needed. The chilly air from the air-conditioner didn't reach this far back in the trailer, and he was soon perspiring again. Hoke set his mental alarm for 4:00 A.M. and fell asleep immediately on the rubber mattress.

HOKE AWOKE WITH A START IN THE DARK, FEELING UNEASY, not knowing where he was for a moment, and then he sat up and dressed. As he pulled on his white socks, he regretted not washing them when he showered. The toes were sticky, and they were still stiff with sweat. The living room-kitchen overhead light was on, and Elena got up from the couch when she heard Hoke open the sliding door to the bathroom. When Hoke came out of the bathroom, she was stirring a pot of oatmeal on the tiny two-burner stove. She put two slices of white bread into the toaster.

"What time is it?"

"Four-fifteen," she said. "It's too early to get up."

"I've got to find the farmers' market, and I'm not sure where it is."

"In the big lot behind Golden Packinghouse. You'll see all the lights."

Hoke rearranged the seats in the eating nook, pulled down the Samsonite tabletop, and locked it in place. He had slept well, but he was still sleepy. He rolled a cigarette. "Aren't you going to make coffee?"

"No coffee." She poured a glass of Diet Coke and brought it to the table. She then served Hoke a bowl of oatmeal and handed him a spoon. Apparently she was out of milk as well. Hoke crumbled his toast into the hot oatmeal. Cawing sounds came from the closet, and Elena gave Warren a nippled bottle of Diet Coke. The caws stopped, and she filled a smaller bowl with oatmeal for Warren and placed it on the counter to cool. She sat across from Hoke and watched him eat.

"You want to shave? I'll boil some hot water for you."

"No. Yes, I want to shave, but I'm trying to see how I'll look with a beard. Aren't you going to eat anything?"

"Too early for me. I'm going back to bed."

"I'm sorry I took your bed, but there was room enough if you wanted to sleep with me."

"You said you no like me."

"I didn't say that. I said I didn't want to fuck you, that's all, and I explained why."

She shrugged and made a face.

"Have you got a social worker? D'you take Warren to a clinic for checkups?"

"Sometimes. You want more oatmeal? Toast?"

"No, but thanks for breakfast."

Elena got up from the table and picked up the small bowl of oatmeal and a teaspoon. Hoke didn't want to watch Elena feed Warren or even take a final look at the kid in his box. He patted Elena on the head, said good-bye, and left the trailer. There was a buzzer on a post that opened the gate from inside. Hoke pressed it and walked down the street. The city was dark, except for a brightly lighted area down by the tracks. Hoke headed for the lighted area.

THE FARMERS' MARKET WAS WELL LIGHTED, AND THERE WAS a great deal of activity in the large lot. Stalls were set up, and there were overhead strings of light bulbs crisscrossing the area. The larger hotels and restaurants from Naples, Fort Myers, and Marco Island sent cooks to buy produce in the market, and small farmers had regular booths. The buyers prodded and squeezed produce, and there were excellent bargains. Cantaloupes that sold for $1.39 apiece in supermarkets could be purchased here for thirty-five cents apiece. There were lugs of lettuce, tomatoes, turnips, and other vegetables that sold for only a fraction of the prices they sold for in supermarkets, Hoke noticed. Eight cents' worth of broccoli could be transformed by a Naples *nouvelle* chef into a $5.95 side dish. An old lady was selling doughnuts and coffee in a booth, and Hoke bought a twenty-fivecent Styrofoam cup of coffee. Carrying his cup, he strolled slowly through the lot, looking for Mr. Sileo. He found him in the parking lot. Mr. Sileo was hefting a fifty-pound sack of potatoes into the back of his Impala station wagon. The back was already loaded with vegetables. There was a dead naked child on the passenger side of the front seat. Startled, Hoke took a closer look and recognized that the body was the carcass of a dressed lamb.

"Good morning, Mr. Sileo."

"You ready for a good day's work?"

"I'm always ready to work, Mr. Sileo. But I haven't had a chance to talk to Mr. Bock yet. You told me you'd point him out."

"Anyone here could do that."

"There's a lot of people here. I didn't expect to see so many."

"If you get here early, you get the best shit. And if you come late, you get what's left a hell of a lot cheaper. See that fucker sleeping in the back of the Ford pickup?" Sileo pointed. "He drives all the way down here from Sarasota once a week, waits until nine or ten, and then loads up on what's left at rock-bottom prices. He has his own little grocery store up there in Sarasota, and he cleans up. I could buy the same way, 'cause I'm right here in town, but I'd rather be successful selling good food at reasonable prices."

"Sure," Hoke said, remembering that he had worked for less than a dollar an hour for this cheap Levantine bastard. "How do I find Mr. Bock?"

"He's in a tent on the other side near the coffee stall. He'll have a half dozen Haitians with him probably. I'll wait here for you, and you can ride back to the cafeteria with me."

"Don't wait. If Bock doesn't hire me, I'll work for someone else. I can't work for ten bucks a day."

"I'll pay you twelve."

"Give Marilyn my love."

Hoke got another cup of coffee before he went to the tent that the coffee lady pointed out as Mr. Bock's. Hoke realized that he was acting much too arrogantly for a man who was supposed to be a mendicant fruit tramp. He looked the part, but he still didn't feel like a migrant worker. After all, he was a detective-sergeant earning thirty-six thousand dollars a year. The farmers here were living marginally, and except, perhaps, for a few chefs from the better hotels in Naples and Marco Island, who were buying produce, Hoke probably had a higher annual income than anyone else in Immokalee.

The tent was a pyramidal army surplus top. All four sides were rolled up to waist level. Tiny Bock sat inside at a card table on a folding metal chair. He had a clipboard and a stack of vouchers on the table, the latter weighted down with a small chunk of brain coral. Bock wore a Red Man gimme cap, a blue work shirt with the sleeves cut off at the shoulders, creaseless corduroy trousers, and lace-up work shoes. His bare arms were muscular, and there was a blue rose tattooed on his left wrist. The forefinger of his left hand was missing down to the second knuckle. His thick eyebrows were gray and black and formed an almost straight line above his dark brown eyes. His tanned face was crisscrossed with hundreds of tiny fine lines. There was a sun cancer the size of a half-dollar on his right cheek, bordered by a quarter-inch hedge of gray stubble. He had a slight paunch, but it looked hard. He was probably a few years older than he looked, but he could pass for fifty-five.

Hoke rapped the doorway post but didn't enter the tent. "Mr. Bock?"

"The load's been sold," Bock said, without looking up.

"I'm not buying, sir. I'm looking for work, and I was told you needed a crew chief."

"Who told you that?" Bock looked at Hoke but raised his eyes without lifting his head.

"Mr. Sileo told me, down at the Cafeteria. I was a crew chief down in the Redland, working tomatoes."

"Why'd you leave? There's plenty of tomatoes left down there in South Dade."

"I was fired. I got into a little fight in Florida City."

"What happened to your teeth?"

"I had a set, but they were lost during the fight. When I got out of jail, I went back to the bar, but nobody'd seen them. Somebody probably found and pawned 'em, I guess."

"Follow me."

When he got to his feet, Bock was a much bigger man than Hoke had thought he was when he had been sitting. His thighs were so large they stretched his corduroys tightly, and Hoke figured that he was at least two hundred and forty pounds. Hoke followed Bock to the far edge of the lot, where five black men were unloading a semitrailer of watermelons and loading them onto another trailer. The two trailers were about fifteen or twenty feet apart. There was a man on each truck, and three men were on the ground passing the melons. The men were talking in Creole, and one man was laughing. But as Bock and Hoke approached, they fell silent. The pace of the work did not speed up, however.

"What's wrong with this picture?" Bock said, looking at Hoke with narrowed eyes.

Hoke scratched his neck. A rash had developed at the bottom of his beard, and scratching and perspiration had made his neck a little raw.

"The three men on the ground are all facing us," Hoke said. "If the guy in the middle turned around the other way, it would be easier to pass the melons. But that's not all that's wrong. If the trailers were backed up bed to bed, you wouldn't need anyone on the ground. Two men could transfer the melons instead of five."

"Then what would you do with the other three men? Have them stand around with their fingers up their ass?"

"I'd give 'em some other work to do."

"You're talking logic, but what we're dealing with here is Haitians. Two Mexicans could do it your way, but two Haitians would take all day to do it. If I made the man in the middle turn around, the other two would think he had an easier job than they did, and they'd squabble about taking turns in the middle. That would add at least another half hour to unloading the truck. D'you see what I mean?"

"Not exactly."

"Neither does the State Agricultural Commission. Two white men, or two Mexicans, can outwork five Haitians. And that's why I pay these five bastards only as much as I would pay two Mexicans. Besides that, Mexicans wouldn't break melons accidentally on purpose so they could eat one."

"What's the right answer then?" Hoke said.

"There isn't any right answer, and there ain't gonna be. Things are gonna get worse, not better. With the new immigration law, the supply of illegal Mexicans will dry up to a trickle. These Haitians will become legal residents, and they'll demand a minimum wage. If I don't pay it, the Labor Board'll fine my ass. If I hire the few illegal Mexicans who sneak through the net, I'll be fined or sent to jail. So next year my watermelons'll probably rot in the fields. Over in Miami fine restaurants put a three-inch slice of watermelon on a plate with a hamburger, and then they can charge six ninety-five for a dollar-and-a-half burger. But I can't get three bucks for a thirty-pound melon. I need a man who knows how to work Haitians. You ever hear of Emperor Henri Christophe?"

"In Haiti? Yes, sir, I've heard the name, but I don't know much of anything about him."

"He's the man who built the citadel on the mountaintop above Cap Haitien. Big square stones weighing hundreds of pounds were pushed by hand up the mountain trail. When fifty men couldn't move one of them big stones, Christophe would remove ten men and kill them. The remaining forty then found out that they could push the stone with no trouble at all. See what I mean?"

"Yes, sir. I see what you mean. But Florida ain't Haiti."

"That's right, and that's too fucking bad. My foreman does the hiring, not me. If you want to talk to him, you can ride back to my farm when the truck's unloaded. You can either help 'em unload now or stand around and watch 'em. I don't give a shit what you do."

Tiny Bock returned to his tent. Hoke watched the Haitians work, not knowing what else to do. The man in the middle dropped a melon, and it broke into three large pieces. The two men in the trailers jumped down. The Haitians divided the broken melon. One of them offered Hoke a small piece.

"*Guette mama!*" Hoke said, grinning.

All five of the men laughed, and they ate their pieces of watermelon. When the melon was gone, they tossed the rinds aside and went back to work. Hoke found that it was boring to stand there and watch, so he went back to the coffee stall for another cup of coffee. He sat on an overturned crate where he could see the two trailers. When the job was finished, about forty-five minutes later, the sun was coming up across the Everglades, and the cloudless sky was the color of steel.

When Bock left the tent, Hoke joined him at the truck.

"Get in the back," Bock said.

Hoke climbed into the back of the trailer with the five Haitians, and Bock drove away from the market.

Bock's farm was about ten miles away. After Bock crossed the wooden bridge over the canal, he drove down a twisting gravel road for almost a mile before he pulled into the farmyard. A sagging barbed-wire fence surrounded the vast yard. Beyond the fence, a field of skeletons, with little round knobs on the ends of the stems, stretched out for a hundred yards or more to the Glades. Brussels sprouts—as ugly in their natural state as they were in a bowl, Hoke thought.

There was a one-story concrete brick house with a wooden veranda in front, a barn, three rusting trailer homes behind the barn, and a dented yellow school bus. A few oaks, twenty feet tall, shaded the bus and trailers. A black Ford pickup was parked on the right side of the house. Instead of a license plate, a piece of cardboard, with "Lost Tag" written on it in black ink, was Scotch-taped to the rear window. This was an old trick. In Miami, unless a man got stopped for a violation, he could drive around with a homemade "Lost Tag" sign for years without buying a license tag.

Two pit dogs, with clipped ears and tails, were chained to a column of the veranda. Their chains were long enough to reach the porch and the doorway. The dogs stared

stupidly at the semi, but they didn't bark. There were three
loose goats in the yard. A black-and-white nanny bleated as
she came over to Tiny Bock and rubbed against his leg
when he climbed down from the cab of the truck. The
Haitians jumped down, went over to the trailers behind
the barn, and entered the one in the middle. Hoke dis-
mounted and rolled a cigarette. He lighted it and joined
Bock. Bock patted the nanny goat on the head. She bleated
again and then trotted over to a wooden box and climbed
on top of it. Her udder was full, and she wanted to be
milked, Hoke thought; but he didn't see any kids around
the yard.

A man came out of the house and crossed toward them.
He said something to the dogs, and they both went under
the veranda and crouched on their bellies in the dirt. The
man was almost as big as Bock, with long black hair that
reached his shoulders. He wore a yellow bandanna headband, a white Orioles baseball shirt, low-slung jeans, and
pointed cowboy boots. His hand-tooled leather belt had a
silver buckle in the shape of a horseshoe. There was a wide
scar on the left side of his face that went through his
eyebrow and ended at his chin. His left eye was missing,
and the skin had been gathered and sewn over the socket,
leaving a star-shaped scar. His face was slightly darker
than his brown arms, but he looked more like an Indian
than he did a Mexican, Hoke thought.

"Chico," Bock said, "this fucker here told me he wanted
to be a crew chief. If you look at his hands, you can see he's
never worked a day in his life. He was willing to ride in
back with the niggers instead of joinin' me in the cab. Find
out who he is and what he wants."

The Mexican nodded and hit Hoke in the solar plexus
with a right jab that didn't travel more than eight inches.
Hoke doubled over and fell to his knees. The cigarette flew

from his lips, and Tiny Bock stepped on the cigarette before he crossed the yard to the house without looking back.

Hoke clutched his stomach with both hands and tried to regain his breath. The griping pain went all the way through to his spine. The Mexican kicked Hoke in the right side, and Hoke heard his ribs crack. A sharp, searing jab inside his gut made him yelp—just as his breath returned—and he felt as if his side had been pierced with a spear as the Mexican kicked him a second time in the same place. Hoke vomited then and his breakfast came up—coffee, Diet Coke, oatmeal, and bread chunks. Hoke was kneeling, with both hands on the ground supporting his upper body, and trying not to breathe. Even a shallow breath increased the pain in his side. The Mexican went behind Hoke and kicked him in the buttocks. Hoke's arms gave way, and he sprawled in the dirt, his face in the pool of vomit. The Mexican then picked up Hoke's feet and dragged him, face down, arms trailing, across the yard and into the barn.

On the near verge of passing out, Hoke thought: This son of a bitch is in trouble now, because I'm going to kill him!

CHAPTER 11

THE MEXICAN BOCK HAD CALLED CHICO—NOT CICATRIZ— threw Hoke face down on a musty bale of alfalfa. The alfalfa was black with rot. It had been rained on, dried, rained on, and dried again and was so black and crumbly it looked as if it had been charred. The moldy dust made Hoke sneeze, and he felt as if knives were being jabbed into his side. Hoke rolled to his left to relieve the pressure on his right side. He couldn't think clearly; everything had happened too fast. He knew that his ribs were either cracked or broken, and if they were broken, a jagged splinter could pierce his lungs. His arms dangled helplessly over the bale, and he was afraid to move. Hoke suppressed his desire to cough and took shallow breaths through his open mouth.

Chico removed Hoke's belt and pulled his pants and Jockey shorts down to his ankles. Then he fastened the belt around Hoke's ankles and made a couple of tight loops to hold it in place. He took Hoke's wallet out of his trousers and went over to the dusty window a few feet away to examine the contents. In addition to the window, the barn had stabs of sunlight coming through cracks and holes in the roof.

Out of the corner of his left eye Hoke watched the Mexican read the letter from the wallet. His thick lips moved as he read.

"What's your name?"

For a long moment Hoke couldn't remember his assumed name. Before he could recall and say it, Chico, using his right fist as a club, brought his clenched fist down on the back of Hoke's neck. A loose rusty wire on the bale of alfalfa pierced Hoke's chin, and he began to bleed.

"Adam Jinks!" Hoke said, bracing for another rabbit punch. The pain from his bruised neck extended to his eyes, as if there were needles inside his head.

Chico dropped the wallet on the dirt floor, circled behind Hoke, bent down, and spread the cheeks of Hoke's buttocks. "Jesus Marie!" Chico said. "You got the ugliest asshole I ever seen! I'll have to pump it to get hard enough to fuck you." He laughed and unbuckled his belt.

Hoke's sphincter tightened, and he groaned. His scrotum tightened, and his balls became as hard as a classical Greek statue's. The knowledge that this Mexican intended to cornhole him sent a surge of adrenaline through his body. With his right hand, Hoke broke off the piece of wire that had pierced his chin. It was about six inches in length. He bent it into the shape of a long U and placed it on his right middle finger with the prongs sticking out. He closed his fist. He had nothing else to work with, and he would have only one chance. Hoke pushed himself up from the bale and got shakily to his feet. He tottered, but he didn't fall. He jumped up, with both feet together and turned in the air. Chico had unbuckled his belt and had pushed his jeans down well past his hips. He wasn't wearing any underwear, and his dangling flaccid penis was much darker than the rest of his body. Chico held his waistband with his left hand and raised his right fist to club Hoke down again with a sidearm blow. When Chico was within striking range, Hoke jabbed the Mexican in his good eye with the stiff prongs of the wire and dodged the sidearm blow. In dodging, Hoke fell again. As fluid squirted onto his knuckles, Hoke knew that he had got him. Hoke got to his feet. The Mexican was screaming in a high, almost feminine voice and cupped his blinded eye with both hands. Hoke hopped to the opposite wall of the barn before bending down to unloosen the belt from his ankles. He kicked free of his pants and Jockey shorts.

Chico was moaning now, a harsh, strangling sound, and was staggering about in tight circles. His jeans had slipped below his knees or the circles would have been wider. The animal noises the Mexican was making would soon bring Tiny Bock out to the barn, Hoke thought, but then he thought differently. Tiny Bock—that son of a bitch—would think the sounds of pain were coming from him, not Chico.

The barn hadn't been used as a barn for some time. There were four stalls on one side, but no horses or mules. Dusty harnesses, which hadn't been used in years, hung from wooden racks on the wall beside the stalls. There was no wagon inside the barn, and Hoke hadn't seen a wagon in the yard. There was a stack of loose boards near the barn door. The wide double doors were open. Hoke couldn't let Chico stumble outside, where Bock might see him from the house. Hoke selected a two-by-four to use as a club and circled behind the Mexican. He didn't want to get too close to Chico. If the man got his big hands on him, or even one hand, he knew it would be all over. Holding his breath, Hoke hit the Mexican on his right kneecap, swinging the two-by-four as hard as he could. The knee snapped, and Chico fell over sideways. He didn't remove his hands from his face but screamed again as he fell. Hoke hit him squarely on the head, and the scream stopped abruptly. There was a whooshing sound as the breath left his throat. Hoke pounded the man's head again, and the two-by-four splintered and broke. Hoke's hands were punctured with tiny splinters from the piece of wood. Blood and gray matter oozed from the dead Mexican's head. Blood poured from his nose and ears, and the dislodged yellow headband was saturated.

Hoke's arms were weary, and he gasped with pain. The pain in his side had increased with the effort he had put into clubbing the man to death, and Hoke bent over double to obtain some relief as he limped back to the bale of alfalfa and sat down. His tailbone hurt from being kicked. Bending forward helped him breathe, a little, but not much. When he regained his breath, gradually, Hoke crossed to the other wall again and retrieved his pants and belt. He folded his jeans into a square pad, placed the pad against his injured ribs, and pulled the belt tight around his waist to hold the pad in place. He removed a nail from one of the loose boards and made a small puncture in his belt and fastened the buckle. He could breathe a little more easily now, so long as he took shallow breaths, and the pain was not as severe. His ribs, Hoke concluded, were only cracked, not broken. He hocked and spit into the palm of his hand. It hurt to cough, but there was no blood in the spit. If his ribs had been broken, after all his activity, he would be spewing blood by now. Blood from his cut chin had dribbled onto the front of his shirt, and both sleeves were ripped at the shoulder. Hoke removed his shirt and dabbed at the blood on his chin. The puncture was deep; it went through the fleshy part of his chin all the way to the bone.

It would only be a matter of time before Bock called for

the Mexican to come to the house or came over to the barn himself to investigate the silence. Bock would have a gun. He would have several guns in the house, in all probability—a pistol or two, a rifle, and perhaps a shotgun. If the man owned three thousand acres of land in two counties, he would hunt them as well as farm them. When he found the dead Mexican, he would either shoot Hoke or call the sheriff, but Hoke didn't believe Bock would call the law. Obviously Bock didn't want any lawmen prowling around his property.

Hoke picked up his wallet, where it had fallen by the window, refolded the letter, and placed it inside. He wedged the wallet under his belt. With his thumb Hoke scraped a small circle in the dusty, cobwebby window and looked toward the veranda. Both pit dogs were on their feet, looking toward the barn. The moaning and the screams had made them curious, and the silence even more so. Hoke cupped his hands to his mouth and moaned. The bitch didn't move, but the smaller dog, a male, and probably her son, wagged his stump of a tail and strained at the end of his chain. The nanny goat came into the barn, bleated several times, and leaped up onto the bale of alfalfa.

Hoke had never milked a goat or a cow, but he had seen animals milked in movies. He grabbed both teats and began to strip them, letting the milk squirt onto the bale. Milking was slow work, and he didn't have the time for this, but he milked her long enough to give her some relief before he stopped. Milking the goat had not stopped him from thinking about what to do next.

Why hadn't the Haitians come out of their trailer when they heard the screaming? Perhaps they were used to the idea of the Mexican using the barn as a place to discipline workers? Maybe they weren't allowed to leave their trailer until they were told they could? At any rate, none of them had come to his rescue, even though he had been sent to see what had been happening to them or to their fellow countrymen. But then, they didn't know that; besides, Hoke didn't know how their minds worked. If a few of them, or a lot of them, had disappeared, why did the rest stay? Weren't they suspicious? Didn't they suspect that they might disappear as well?

He would have to get some answers from Tiny Bock.

Hoke selected a fresh two-by-four from the lumber pile and went to the back of the barn. There was a normal-size door, but it had been boarded over and nailed shut. Hoke pried the boards away and opened the door. Two game-cocks were staked out behind the barn, well separated from each other, of course, and three gamehens scratched list-lessly in the yard. If he could get as far as the semi, about twenty yards away, without being seen from the house, he would be screened. Then he could circle around the back, giving the pit dogs a wide berth. There might be—in all probability there would be—a woman in the kitchen. Hoke doubted that Bock and the Mexican would do their own cooking, although they might. He would soon find out. Crouching low, he made a lumbering run to the side of the parked truck and trailer. The hot sunlight on his naked body was a shock, and his exposed genitalia made him feel, somehow, more vulnerable. Even though he had pissed his shorts when he had been thrown across the alfalfa bale, he wished now that he had put them on again.

The toolbox on the fender was closed, and a wire instead of a lock had been twisted through the hasp. Hoke un-twisted the wire and raised the lid. There weren't many tools in the box. Except for a well-oiled jack, the other tools were rusty. Hoke took a monkey wrench out of the box and hefted it. It was fourteen inches long and had a good weight to it. It wouldn't be as effective as the two-by-four had been, but he could throw the wrench if he had to, and that was an advantage. Well screened from the front door of the house, Hoke crouched and duck walked to a small utility shed about thirty yards away. It hurt too much to run. The venetian blinds on this side of the house were closed. The dogs could still see him, and they looked at him without barking. If Bock turned them loose and sicced them on him, his situation could change radically. The only time a pit dog lets go is to get a better bite.

From the utility shed Hoke walked directly to the side of the house. To see him now, crushing the geranium and fern beds that surrounded the house, Bock would have to raise a window and look straight down at him. Hoke edged along the wall to the back and looked through the screened porch that led into the kitchen. There was a masonite-topped table and four padded aluminum-legged chairs on the porch. A deal table was flush against the wall, and it held a small hibachi for barbecuing. There was also an aged Kelvinator refrigerator against the wall, and it was dotted with rust. There was probably a new refrigerator in the kitchen, and this old one was used for extra storage for ice and drinks. The screen door was unlatched, and Hoke went inside. The Cuban tile floor was streaked with dried mop marks. The old refrigerator ticked away with a double beat, like two overheated engines after the ignition had been turned off, and Hoke's heartbeats were not in sync with either beat. There were two open doors. One led into the kitchen; the other, into a long hallway to the living room. Two doors on the right side of the hallway were closed. Hoke could also get to the living room through the kitchen and then through the dining room. There was no woman in the kitchen, and from the mess no woman had been near the kitchen in weeks. The sink and counter were filled with dirty dishes, pots, and pans, and two brown grocery bags in the corner were overflowing with garbage. An aluminum coffeepot was on the stove. Hoke touched it, and it was still warm. Crouching to minimize the pain in his ribs, Hoke inched down the hallway instead of going through the kitchen. Before he reached the end of the hallway, he recognized Donahue's voice. Jesus! *Donahue* was on the tube from 9:00 until 10:00. It seemed as if he had been up forever, and it was only a little after 9:00 A.M.! The living room was comfortably furnished. There was a long davenport covered with black leather and several brightly cushioned Monterey chairs. The hide of a ten-foot alligator had been nailed to one wall above a four-drawer highboy, and an overhead fan whirled in the ceiling. The Prussian blue nylon carpet looked new, but several blue dust balls bounced about below the fan. The dining table, which Bock was obviously using as a desk, was piled high with ledgers, folders, and papers. There was a pen and pencil set with an onyx base and a file box covered with green leather. Four cushioned ladder-backed dining chairs were pushed up to the table. Tiny Bock, sitting in a deep pigskin chair, with his back toward Hoke, was watching Donahue on the tube. A white ceramic mug, with TINY baked into it in bold script, was on the glass-topped coffee table in front of him.

Hoke crossed the carpeted floor slowly, making no noise, and almost made it to the chair before Donahue said, "We'll be right back." A commercial for Colgate's toothpaste replaced him. Several workmen in hard hats were plastering plaque on the inside of a set of giant teeth. Bock got to his feet, stretched out his arms, and yawned audibly. He must have sensed Hoke's presence. He couldn't have heard him over the noisy commercial, but he turned around. His jaw dropped slightly as he saw Hoke, naked except for his high-topped shoes and belted makeshift pad, only three feet away from him. Bock's arms were still in the air as Hoke stepped forward and brought the business end of the heavy wrench down across the big man's nose. The nose cracked, and blood spurted from it. But Bock turned immediately toward the front door.

"I've got a gun!" Hoke said. "Open the door and you're dead!"

Bock paused in midstep, raising his hands level with his shoulders. He then put his right hand to his bleeding nose. Hoke moved in swiftly, clipped Bock behind his right ear with the wrench, and the man toppled over. Bock was down, but not out. Hoke hit him again, aiming for the same spot, and then Bock was unconscious, with bright red blood staining his blue carpet.

Donahue returned, and Hoke switched off the set. He wanted to sit down. He wanted to lie down, but there was no time for that. Except for his broken nose, Bock wasn't hurt too badly, and he would come around soon. There was a Mercer 12-gauge shotgun, an over-and-under, together with a Winchester 30-30 rifle, in a gun rack on the wall beside the front door. Two canes and a blue-and-white golf umbrella were in a large brass stand beneath the rack. Hoke selected the shotgun and broke it open. It wasn't loaded. Hoke crossed to the sideboard that was half in and half out of the dining room and opened four drawers before he found a box of double-aught shells. He loaded the shotgun, closed and cocked it. Before sitting down, Hoke took a long swig from an opened bottle of Jack Daniel's black label that was on top of the sideboard. The whiskey helped. Hoke didn't want to get up from the comfortable chair, but he forced himself to get to his feet. Bock was already making sounds deep in his throat. Hoke took the cable box from the top of the TV set, jerked the long cord loose from the back of the set, and wrapped the cord around

Bock's ankles. There was plenty of cord. After encircling the ankles and making square knots, he wrapped the extra cable around Bock's legs to the knees, and then wedged the box with its twelve push bars under Bock's belt at the back. That would give Hoke a few more minutes to look around. Even if Bock regained consciousness, he wouldn't be able to run.

Hoke went back down the hallway and entered the first door on his left. This was a bedroom. The double bed was unmade, but the sheets were clean. Hoke got a clean, long-sleeved sport shirt and a pair of blue serge suit pants from the closet. The pants were much too large for him at the waist; Bock outweighed him by at least fifty pounds, so Hoke didn't try on any of Bock's underwear. He slipped into the trousers, removed his belt, dropped his jeans-pad to the floor, and threaded his belt through the loops. He rolled the trousers up a turn at the cuffs and slipped his wallet into the right rear pocket. The shirt was an extra large, with square shirttails, and Hoke had to turn the cuffs back two inches.

Hoke entered the bathroom and opened the opposite door, which led to a smaller bedroom. Both bedrooms, then, had hall doors. The smaller room, Hoke supposed, was Chico's. There was a single metal cot, and the bed was neatly made, with hospital corners on the tucked-in Navaho blanket. Hoke returned to the bathroom and looked through the medicine chest and found a partially used roll of adhesive tape. He lifted his shirt and wrapped the tape around his waist as tightly as he could. He used all of the tape. He would have preferred to have the tape tighter than it was, but that was the best he could do, and it relieved the pain in his side much better than the improvised belt pad had.

Hoke returned to the living room. As he reached the end of the hallway, he heard the report and felt shards of plaster sting the back of his neck at the same time that Bock pulled the trigger on a .38-caliber pistol. Bock was sitting by the doorway, holding the pistol in front of his body with both hands. Hoke dropped flat to the floor and fired his shotgun as Bock shot a second time. Once again Bock's slug entered the wall instead of Hoke, and it went into the wall at least four feet above his prone body. Bock was trying to lower the pistol awkwardly as Hoke fired the second time. Bock dropped the pistol and fell over. At this distance, less than fifteen feet, almost all the shotgun pellets of Hoke's second shot had gone into Bock's upper chest. Hoke crawled toward the man on his knees and brushed the pistol away. He felt Bock's pulse. There was no pulse. Bock was dead, and there was no one left to answer his questions.

Hoke picked up the .38 pistol and shoved it behind the waistband of his trousers in the back. The pistol hadn't been in the sideboard, and Bock hadn't been armed when Hoke wrapped his legs with the cord. Bock had probably kept the pistol hidden in the bottom of the umbrella stand near the door. Hoke had another drink from the bottle of Jack Daniel's and then took the bottle over to the dining table and sat down. Both these deaths could have been avoided, Hoke reflected, if Brownley had let him keep his pistol. If he had only had his weapon, both these men—bastards that they were—would still be alive. Both deaths were justified, of course. He had had to kill the Mexican after he blinded him; blind, the man wouldn't have been able to find any work. The Mexican hadn't learned anything from the loss of his first eye, apparently, or he wouldn't have attacked Hoke in the first place. And Bock, of course, had fired at Hoke first. Twice, in fact. Hoke shuddered. He was lucky to be alive.

Hoke took another drink from the bottle, a shorter one this time. He put the cap back on the bottle. He couldn't feel the drinks, but it would be best to stop before he did. He went to the front window and peered through the venetian blinds. The door to the middle trailer was still closed. Hoke couldn't understand it. The five Haitians were still inside, or perhaps they all had fled when the shooting began. He decided to go through Bock's papers first and check on the Haitians later. If they had run away (American blacks would have started running at the sound of the first shot and would have disappeared forever, but he didn't know how Haitians would react), fine. If they were gone, they were gone; if not, he would decide what to do with them, but at the moment he wanted to sit down and rest. Hoke wasn't in bad physical shape, but he wasn't in good shape either. He spent too much time sitting at a desk writing reports. When he got back to Miami, he would talk Bill Henderson into playing a little handball a couple of times a week the way they used to when they were partners. Hoke hadn't been to the gym in more than six months, but a couple of years back he and Henderson had managed to squeeze in some handball once or twice a week.

Hoke looked through the papers and the ledgers on the table. There was a check for $1,700 made out to Bock Enterprises on top of the pile. It was signed by the treasurer of Gaitlin Bros., Ft. Myers, Florida. This was probably the check for this morning's truckload of watermelons. Most of the papers were bills, many of them second and third notices of overdue bills. Hoke went through the ledger, beginning with the first page. Not only was Bock broke, but he was heavily in debt, and there was a second mortgage on his farmhouse and on another four hundred acres of land he held in Collier County. The man had been land-poor, and during the last four years he had purchased more land than he could either farm or pay for; and on top of all that, he hadn't paid out any wages to anyone. Not a dime. If he had, there was no evidence in the ledger. Perhaps he had paid off his labor in cash. Even so, there should have been a record of the payouts somewhere.

Hoke went over to the body and took Bock's wallet out of the hip pocket. It contained $103, a VISA card, three gas credit cards, and the registration for the Ford half-ton truck. There were some business cards in the wallet as well. The keys to the Ford and the keys to the semi were in Bock's right front pocket. Hoke pocketed the money, the registration slip, and the keys and dropped the wallet on the floor.

Hoke reloaded the shotgun, stepped over Bock's body, and opened the front door. The two pit dogs were whining and sniffing, smelling the blood, and they were at the ends of their chains. Both dogs were only two feet away from him. Hoke killed them both with the shotgun, stepped over their bodies, and crossed the yard to the trailers beneath the trees. The first trailer was empty, and so was the third, although there were signs that they had been occupied in the recent past. When Hoke looked at the closed door of the middle trailer, he solved the mystery. When the door had closed from inside, a flat metal bar on the outside, fixed with a spring at the top, dropped into a welded metal slot on the outside, and locked the men in. The bar could be raised and would stay put in its original position from the outside, but there was no way to lift it from inside the trailer.

Hoke raised the bar and opened the door. There was a brick on the floor to wedge the door open, and Hoke kicked it into place. The trailer was the same size as Elena's had been, but there was no furniture. Without moving away from the door, Hoke surveyed the interior. There was a stove and a counter, and a goat stew was cooking on the stove. The other half of a dressed kid was on the counter. The five men slept on the floor apparently. The stench from the overflowing toilet in the tiny bathroom was overpowering, and the bathroom door was missing. Four Haitians sat on the floor, their backs to the wall, and the fifth man was at the stove, holding a long-handled metal ladle. The five men looked at Hoke without moving; their eyes were wide, but their faces were expressionless. There was a stack of metal pie pans on the counter. The man with the ladle dropped his hands to his sides. The man sitting closest to the stove quivered like an Australian pine in a heavy wind and stared at Hoke's leveled shotgun. His bare black heels beat a tattoo on the metal floor.

"Who speaks English?"

"I speak a little," the man at the stove said.

"You ever hear of Delray Beach?"

He nodded. "I know Delray Beach."

Hoke took out the bills he had taken from Bock's wallet and handed each man twenty dollars. He put the remaining three dollars into his pocket. He gave the man at the stove the keys to the Ford pickup and the folded yellow registration slip.

"There're about ten thousand Haitians in Delray Beach," Hoke said. "Go to Delray, and join them. There's no more work for you here, or in Immokalee either. So take the black truck and drive to Delray Beach. You got a driver's license?"

"No, sir."

"A green card?"

"No, sir."

"D'you know how to drive?"

"I drove a taxi in Port-au-Prince."

"If you're stopped, this registration won't do you any good, but maybe one of the Haitians in Delray will know what to do with it. Don't take the Tamiami Trail into Miami. Take Alligator Alley instead and then the Sunshine Parkway to Delray. Do you understand me?"

The man nodded and put the keys into his pocket. "I know Delray Beach."

"The smart thing to do is to abandon—I mean, just *leave* the truck on the street somewhere after you get to Delray. And forget that you ever worked here for Mr. Bock. Understand?"

"Yes, sir." He nodded and licked his lips.

"All right. Tell the others."

The man said something to the others in Creole. Hoke watched them as they nodded their heads. They all had broken into smiles when he had given them money, but their faces were solemn again now. Hoke left the trailer and its stench and waited in the yard until the men came out. They all had small bundles and blankets; one man had a faded quilt. The tall man also brought the pot of steaming goat stew, and they had their tin plates and spoons. The short, quivering man carried the other half of the dressed kid and had an OD army blanket rolled up and over one shoulder. Helping each other, they climbed into the pickup, two in front and three in back. Hoke waited until the truck was well down the graveled road before he returned to the house.

If they didn't speed, the chances were fairly good that the pickup would make it safely to Delray, with its huge Haitian colony alongside the railroad tracks. Trucks and old buses filled with laborers were plentiful on the Alligator Alley route to the Sunshine Parkway, and if a trooper did stop them, he would turn them over to the INS. The INS would, in turn, take them to the Krome Detention Center, but all the illegal Haitians knew by now to say that they came to America to escape political persecution. Now that Duvalier had been deposed, the persecution gambit didn't work any longer, but there were still enough immigration shysters in Miami to keep them in the States for months, sometimes years. And if they could contact a relative of any kind here in the U.S. who had somehow obtained a green card, a lawyer could get them paroled. Once paroled, they disappeared again, either to New York or to New Jersey. They wouldn't be able to explain how they got the truck if they were stopped, but Bock would never report the truck stolen.

There were additional papers and letters in the sideboard and in the highboy as well. From these, Hoke discovered that Bock had a married daughter living in Fitzgerald, Georgia. He also found the death certificate for Bock's wife in a drawer.

The Mexican hadn't owned much of anything. He had a yellow linen suit in his closet, fresh from the cleaners and encased in plastic, and a pair of polished cordovan loafers. But there was no correspondence from anyone, either in Spanish or English, or any personal papers. There was a coiled leather whip and a P-38 in a bottom dresser drawer, and Hoke left them there. The other drawers held underwear, T-shirts, and a half dozen pairs of argyle socks—none of them worn.

Hoke left the house and looked inside the utility shed outside the house. There was a generator in the shed, to be used for emergency power, Hoke surmised. It was an old Sears generator and hadn't been used for some time. There were four five-gallon jerricans in the shed, and two of them were filled with gasoline. There were two aluminum tanks in one corner. DANGER! VIKANE was stenciled in red paint on both tanks. Hoke took the two filled cans of gas back to the house. He put them down in the kitchen and went into the bathroom to take a leak. When he looked at his face in the mirror, he shuddered. His face was haggard, and his eyes were red. Bits of oatmeal were lodged in his beard. He looked at least ten years older than he should look, even without his teeth. He swallowed three aspirin with water and then shaved off his beard, using a new Bic razor he found in the medicine cabinet. He put a Band-Aid over the puncture wound in his chin. He felt better, even if he didn't look a lot better.

Hoke poured a half can of gasoline over Bock's body and then splashed the rest of the gas throughout the living room. With the last of the gas, he made a wide line to the doorway and out onto the veranda. He lit the gas with his lighter, and the fire snaked across the porch. It blazed fiercely when it reached Bock's body.

Taking the second can with him, Hoke got into the semi cab, made a wide turn in the yard, and drove it into the barn as far as it would go. He poured half the can over the Mexican, more on the pile of loose boards, and splashed the remainder on the engine of the truck. He found his straw hat and put it on. He lit the gas from outside the barn and walked down the gravel road toward the highway. He looked over his shoulder but kept walking. The house and the barn both were on fire. In the middle of the yard the nanny goat, bleating, stood on her milking box.

When Hoke reached the highway, almost a mile away from the farm, he could still see black smoke from the two fires. No one driving down the highway, either way, would pay any attention to the smoke, and the farm itself was shielded by the palmetto trees on both sides of the gravel road. Farmers set fire to their fields to clear them all year round.

No one stopped to give Hoke a ride, and it took him almost four hours to walk the nine and a half miles back to Immokalee.

CHAPTER 12

*T*HERE WERE A GOOD MANY THINGS TO THINK ABOUT ON his walk back to Immokalee, and Hoke had to sit down frequently to rest. During his rest periods he picked out most of the splinters embedded in his hands. His tailbone hurt with every jarring step, especially when he stumbled slightly, and his arms felt heavy and sore. Swinging that two-by-four had been like two hours of batting practice, and his muscles weren't used to being stretched.

Hoke hadn't spent any time looking around the farm for any buried bodies. Beyond the farm and the field of Brussels sprouts, the Everglades began, stretching to the horizon. If Bock and Chico had buried any bodies, they would have driven them to the sea of grass and dumped them into some deep water-filled sinkhole where the alligators would eat them. There was no way to prove it now, but Hoke had no doubt that Tiny Bock had killed his Haitian workers when they finished their jobs instead of paying them. All Bock had to do, when it came to payoff time, was to lock the men in their trailers, attach the Vikane gas tanks to the copper tubes that were used for propane cooking gas for the stove, and turn them on. Bock and Chico could then throw the bodies into the truck and drive through the fields to the water-soaked Glades and dump them. That still didn't account for the dead Haitian found behind the billboard on the road to Bonita Springs. With a hundred square miles of swamp in his backyard to dump bodies, why would Bock and Chico bury a dead Haitian behind a billboard on a fairly busy state road? It didn't make sense, because the body was bound to be found. Someday, perhaps, an illegal hunter might find a skull out in the middle of the Glades, but an illegal hunter wouldn't report a find like that; he would take it home and put it on his mantel as a *memento mori*. Someone else, other than Bock, must have buried the dead Haitian behind the billboard. After all, Bock wasn't the only grower going broke in Immokalee or in the so-called green belt surrounding Lake Okeechobee. In recent years many farmers had given up agriculture altogether and started catfish farming instead. And they were prospering. Five years ago catfish were hard to find in Miami, but now a man could get fried catfish in every seafood restaurant in South Florida, and it didn't have the muddy taste of wild catfish either.

BY THE TIME HOKE REACHED THE OUTSKIRTS OF IMMOKALEE he was depressed. Part of his depression was caused, he knew, by the unnecessary killing of Bock and Chico, but mandatory under the circumstances. If Bock hadn't been groggy from the blows to his head, he certainly would have killed Hoke with his first shot. He must have had double vision to miss at such short range.

There weren't many people on the dusty streets. A few Mexicans lingered beneath the pepper tree, and there was the same mix of homeless white winos and blacks in the

parking lot of the Cafeteria, but the other townspeople—
those with shelter—stayed inside during the middle of
the day. Immokalee did not as yet have an enclosed air-
conditioned mall, so many townspeople—those with cars,
anyway—were probably shopping in Naples or Fort Myers.
Local shop owners stayed inside their air-conditioned stores.
There were workers in the row of packinghouses, of course,
and huge sixteen-wheelers, both loaded and unloaded, rum-
bled through the streets; but there was a dead, lethargic
feel to the town.

Hoke passed Myrtle's discount drugstore, stopped, and
then went back to the store. He bought a roll of three-inch
adhesive tape, the widest she had on hand, and a small box
of extra-strength Tylenol, but decided against cigarettes. It
hurt his side every time he took a shallow breath, so he
would have to give up smoking for a few days whether he
wanted to or not. He went past the 66 gas station on the
next corner. Noseworthy's Guesthouse sign was on the following corner, as Mel Peoples had told him. The guesthouse
was two blocks east, right next to an empty lot that had
been used as a dump. The lot was littered with piles of
bottles and tin cans and the burned-out wreck of an auto-
mobile. The twisted mass of metal was so black Hoke
couldn't determine the make of the car.

The guesthouse, however, a two-story wooden structure
with a sloping cedar-shingled roof, had been painted recently—a shiny off gray, with white trim on the windows.
All the windows, upstairs and down, had slanting wooden
Bahama blinds on the outside. The house would be dark
inside, but the slotted blinds would make it cooler. The
small front yard was covered with gravel instead of grass
and was surrounded by a low rock wall about two feet high.
Such walls were common in the Bahamas, where homeowners always marked their boundaries with rock walls, but

they were rare in Florida. There were some hanging plants on the porch, and three wicker rockers painted a glaring white. The guesthouse sign,

NOSEWORTHY'S
GUESTHOUSE
(est. 1983)

in black lettering on a white board, had been tacked above the front door. The upper half of the front door was glass but was curtained with white draperies, so Hoke couldn't see inside. A smaller sign beside the bell read "Ring and Enter." Hoke rang the bell and opened the door. There was a maple costumer and an elephant-foot umbrella stand in the foyer. Straight ahead, to the left of the stairs, were a table and a chair. There was a sign-in book and a silver bowl containing jelly beans on the table. The living room, on Hoke's right, was crowded with mid-Victorian chairs and spindly-legged walnut tables, short and tall, either beside or in front of each chair. There was a brick fireplace containing a large bowl of daisies and a tall glass-fronted bookcase beside it. The walls were covered with old and faded pink wallpaper and cluttered with watercolors, photos, mirrors, mounted birds and small animals. Beyond the living room, a step up, was the dining area—a bare buffet table against the wall. A long mirror on the wall behind the table reflected the living room and made the crowded interior appear larger. There was a swinging door with a beveled glass window that opened to the kitchen beyond the dining area.

A tall black man came swiftly through the swinging door, and he crossed the room, dodging the chairs and wine tables, swiveling his hips like a broken-field runner. He wore a wide white smile and a black linen suit with a white shirt and a pearl gray necktie. There was a hand-painted picture of a dog's head on the tie, either a collie or a wolfhound. Hoke wasn't sure. The man held out his hand, so Hoke shook it.

"Welcome to our guesthouse, sir."

"You must be Mr. Noseworthy."

"At your service, sir." The smile didn't leave his dark face, but his eyes took in Hoke's drooping shirttails and baggage—a small brown paper sack from Myrtle's discount drugstore.

"Can anyone overhear us?" Hoke pointed toward the kitchen door.

"Mrs. Noseworthy's out back, but she's ironing on the back porch."

"Any other guests?"

"Do I have a room, d'you mean? I have rooms, yes, but you must pay in advance. Usually reservations are requested well ahead of arrival, and I always require the first day's rent in advance on mail reservations—"

"Are there any other guests?" Hoke repeated.

"Yes. A Mrs. Peterson. But she's not here at present. She was going to visit the Corkscrew Swamp Sanctuary today, she said. Where did you park your car, Mr.—?"

"Let's cut the shit, Noseworthy. Mel Peoples told me to contact you. My name's Adam Jinks. Or did Mel give you a different name?"

"Jinks is correct, yes, sir, but I didn't expect you so soon. What happened to your chin?"

"A shaving nick. Can you contact Mel for me?"

Noseworthy shook his head. "Not right away. Mr. Peoples called me from the airport—Fort Myers—yesterday. He had to fly up to a conference in Tallahassee for three days. Of course, if he calls from Tallahassee, I can put you on the phone, but I don't know his number up there or where he's staying. I'll just have to give you a room, and you'll have to wait till he gets back or phones."

"Terrific. Give me a room with a tub bath, if you've got one."

"Our rates are sixty dollars a day, and that's with breakfast, of course. We have wine and cheese in the living room every evening between five and six—"

"I don't care what it costs. It all goes on Mel Peoples's tab, so give me the best room you've got."

"He didn't say anything about that." Noseworthy licked his lips.

"He didn't tell me he was going to Tallahassee either. What part of the Bahamas are you from?"

"Abaco. You may not know where that is—"

"But I do. We have something in common. That's the island my ancestors came from. They sat out the Revolutionary War in Abaco and moved back to Florida when the war was over. They were Loyalists, you see."

"Have you ever been there? To Abaco?"

"No, I plan to fly over sometime, just to see it, but I've been busy. I also need a bath. Perhaps you can show me my room now, and we can talk about the islands later."

"Sign in, please." Noseworthy went behind the table, and handed Hoke a ballpoint. Hoke signed the register, "Adam Jinks, Abaco, Bahamas," and returned the pen to the innkeeper.

"I'm sorry you had to sign in." Noseworthy shrugged. "But they check on me sometimes, because of the tax, you know."

"I understand. You aren't doing too well, are you?"

"Not yet, but word is getting around. I really don't understand it. There are many interesting places to sight-see, all within easy driving distance of Immokalee, as I was telling Mrs. Peterson this morning."

"Maybe you ought to put in a pool. It's ninety degrees out there, and eighty degrees in here."

"We don't cater to that kind of clientele. Tourists who want a pool can stay at the Day's Inn or a Howard Johnson's. A guesthouse is for people who want a quiet atmosphere with homelike surroundings."

"Yeah. Most people have stuffed squirrels and owls in their living rooms, so they'll feel right at home here."

"It's upstairs. Follow me."

Hoke's room was in the front of the house upstairs, and it had a large bathroom. The Bahama blinds shielded the window to the street, so there was no view, but there was nothing he wanted to see in Immokalee anyway. Noseworthy handed him the key. There was a brass tag on it with the name LeRoy Collins intaglioed onto the tag.

"The downstairs door is locked at ten, but your room key fits the front door as well, in case you go out."

"Did Governor Collins ever stay in this room?"

"No, sir, but all the rooms are named for former Florida governors. Mrs. Peterson is down the hall, in Governor Kirk's room."

"A good idea, Mr. Noseworthy. And educational, too. If Mel phones, come and get me right away—even if I'm still in the tub."

"Don't worry, Mr. Jinks, I will." He closed the door behind him as he left.

There was a full-length mirror on a wooden wardrobe next to the double bed, and Hoke caught a glimpse of himself. No wonder Noseworthy had given him such a cool greeting. His serge suit pants, rolled up at the cuffs, were dusty, and the sport shirt was far too big for him. Hoke had rolled up the sleeves and had left the long square tails out to cover the pistol stuffed behind his waistband. Hoke turned on the hot water in the tub and undressed. A bruise the size of an orange was on his stomach, where Chico had hit him with his fist. It looked very dark against his white hairy stomach. The tub had claws for feet, and each claw clutched a large round marble ball. There was a framed sepia-toned photo of Queen Victoria on the wall, which was hardly appropriate for LeRoy Collins's room, Florida's former liberal and best governor ever. Hoke turned off the hot water and then ran enough cold to cool it so he could barely stand it. He eased his aching body into the steaming water. He soaked for about an hour, running the hot water again as the tub cooled, before he soaped himself and rinsed off.

He removed the wet tape and almost fell asleep before he decided to get out. He washed his white socks in the tub before he pulled the plug. He dried off and put fresh tape around his cracked ribs. He dressed again, putting his shoes on without socks. He felt refreshed, but his neck was still sore and tender to the touch. He was also hungry.

Hoke put the pistol under his pillow and went downstairs, leaving his room key in the door. Noseworthy wasn't in the living room, so Hoke pushed through the door and went into the kitchen. A woman, about thirty-eight or forty, with curly lion-colored hair, was sitting on a stool at the worktable, snapping pole beans into a green bowl. She was a handsome woman, even without makeup, and she looked at Hoke with cool blue eyes.

"May I help you? Mr. Noseworthy went to the post office."

"Are you Mrs. Noseworthy?"

"I'm Mrs. Noseworthy, yes," she said, lifting her chin.

"Yes, ma'am. I'd like to get something to eat."

She shook her head. "We don't serve meals except for

breakfast, and that's from seven-thirty till ten. Eleven is checkout time, you see. But we serve wine and cheese from five to six."

Hoke nodded. "Mr. Noseworthy told me, but I missed breakfast."

"I can give you a half-off coupon for the Cafeteria downtown."

"I guess your husband hasn't told you anything about me. You'd better talk to him. I'm also expecting an important call."

"He told me."

"So I can't leave the house. If I have to wait till five for a piece of cheese, I'll starve."

"I guess I could scramble you an egg."

"If you're too busy, I can do it myself."

"I'll bring a tray up to your room." She bent over her bowl again, dismissing him.

"Thanks. By the way, Mrs. Noseworthy, there's no Gideon Bible in my room. I checked."

She lifted her head and stared for a moment. "There's a bookcase in the living room for guests. But I don't think you'll find one there either."

Hoke grinned as he climbed the stairs to his room. Mrs. Noseworthy, whether she was actually married to the innkeeper or not, explained a few things that had bothered him. Here in Immokalee, on an unpaved side street, was the worst location possible for a guesthouse. The room, without a phone, radio, or television, was way overpriced, and there wasn't even a pool. But it was a safe place for a white woman married to a black man. No one would bother the couple here, and the social stigma, in a backwater like Immokalee, would be minimal at best. There would always be some guests for their seven rooms. Even one guest at sixty bucks a day would provide a living for two people. The guesthouse would also serve as a safe house, a secure hideout for someone who wanted to cool off for a couple of weeks. Because of the recent drug wars in the Bahamas, particularly in Nassau, on New Providence, there was a real need for a quiet hideout like this one. And for his hot guests, Noseworthy would charge a lot more than sixty a day. Hoke looked forward to meeting Mrs. Peterson, wondering how she happened to be staying here. He shook his head. He still had his own problems to solve. Instead of being curious about the Noseworthys and Mrs. Peterson, he should be making up some kind of story to tell Mel Peoples.

On the long walk from the farm to town he had decided to tell Peoples the truth about what had happened. But after reflection, now that he had relaxed a little and was feeling better, he suspected that the truth would terrify a bureaucrat like Mel Peoples. If he told Peoples and Major Brownley the truth, he could get into a little trouble, perhaps a lot of trouble— There was a knock at the door.

Hoke got up from the bed, where he had been lying and staring at the photograph of Booker T. Washington on the wall. It hurt to move, and he groaned when he got to his feet. He crossed the room and opened the door. Mrs. Noseworthy had put the tray on the floor outside the door and gone back downstairs.

There was a one-egg omelet on the large white plate, and a piece of white bread, skimpily spread with margarine. A small dish contained three prunes, and there was a six-ounce glass of skimmed milk—the kind his father called "blue john." As he put the tray on the bedside table, he regretted making the comment about the Gideon Bible. Hoke ate slowly, taking his time to make the meager meal last. Except for wine and cheese later, this would be the last meal he would get until breakfast. He would have to stay put in the house until he heard from Peoples.

There was a battery-powered digital alarm clock on the bedside table, but no phone. He could call Brownley in Miami on the downstairs phone and ask Brownley to come and get him, but that wasn't a good idea. When the fire at the farm was discovered, if it hadn't been already, there would be a sheriff's investigation, and Brownley should avoid this area altogether. He would just have to wait.

At five Hoke took his tray downstairs to the kitchen and put it on the counter by the sink before going into the living room. There were wrapped singles of Velveeta cheese food on a large platter arranged in an overlapping pattern. The center of the plate held an unwrapped waxed-paper square of unsalted soda crackers. There was also an opened half gallon jug of burgundy on the buffet table. Hoke poured a plastic glass with wine but skipped the cheese and crackers.

He was on his third glass of wine when Mrs. Peterson came downstairs. She introduced herself, and told him she was a retired history teacher from Rome, Georgia. She was driving around the state by herself, sight-seeing, and staying at guesthouses. She loved out-of-the-way places, she said, and met very interesting people at the guesthouses. At first, she said, when she left Rome, she had stayed at motels. But they all were alike, and she hadn't met anyone. Then she got a list of Florida guesthouses from a travel agent in St. Augustine, and it became a different trip altogether. She was in her early sixties, Hoke figured, wearing khaki culottes and a short-sleeved blouse, and she seemed to be a nice, pleasant woman. When she left Immokalee, she said, she was going to skip Miami and drive directly to Key West, where she had reservations for a week at the Cabin Boy Inn. Hoke knew that the Cabin Boy Inn catered primarily to gay couples on vacation from New York and New Jersey.

"You'll meet some interesting people there, I'm sure," he told her.

She didn't ask Hoke a single question but rambled on about her afternoon at the Corkscrew Swamp Sanctuary. Mr. Noseworthy had poked his head through the swinging door a couple of times, but neither he nor his wife joined them in the parlor. Mrs. Peterson told him in some detail about the birds she had seen and ate a half dozen slices of cheese. Hoke finally excused himself, poured another glass of wine, and took it upstairs to his room to get away from her.

Hoke undressed and went to bed and was asleep by seven-thirty. The house was quiet, and he didn't awaken until seven the next morning. He was still stiff and sore. He took a short tub bath before going downstairs for breakfast. He drank two cups of coffee from the Mr. Coffee machine and ate a bowl of Cheerios, pouring them from the opened box on the buffet table. There was milk in a glass pitcher. There were only two slices of cantaloupe on a plate, so Hoke only ate one slice, figuring that the second slice was Mrs. Peterson's. Mrs. Peterson, on her retirement vacation, was still asleep.

After his frugal breakfast Hoke looked in the bookcase. Most of the books were paperbacks or *Reader's Digest* condensed books in hard cover, but there were a few interesting hardbacks, with dust jackets missing. Hoke took a copy of Sabatini's *Scaramouche* out of the bookcase and opened it to the first page. "He was born with the gift of laughter, and the knowledge that the world was mad."

Hooked, Hoke took the book back upstairs to his room and read until noon.

CHAPTER 13

THE FOLLOWING DAY AT 1:00 P.M. NOSEWORTHY CAME UP to Hoke's room and got him. Mel Peoples was on the line from Tallahassee. Noseworthy went into the kitchen, and Hoke picked up the phone.

"Moseley, here."

"What in the hell happened out there, Sergeant?" Peoples began, and his voice was higher than Hoke had remembered. "I just talked to Sheriff Boggis awhile ago on the phone, and he said the house and barn were burnt down."

"I imagine they are, because they were burning when I saw them. I spent my first night here in town and hitch-hiked out to the farm the next morning. An old couple driving to Miami picked me up and dropped me by the gate. It was almost a mile out to the farm itself, but I didn't go all the way. As soon as I saw that the house and the barn were on fire, I walked back here to Immokalee. And I had to walk all the way, too. You should've left a number here for me to call you. I wasn't about to call Boggis or anyone else about the fire."

"I realize that now, and I'm sorry. But I wasn't sure where I'd be staying. I guess I should've called Noseworthy last night to let you know. But what do you s'pose happened out there? There were no aliens on the farm, and Bock's half-ton is missing, Boggis said."

"I have no idea what happened. As I told you, as soon as I saw the fire, I took off. With no official ID, I couldn't've explained what I was doing out there. You and Brownley already said you couldn't cover me. Did you tell the sheriff anything about me?"

"Of course not! He'd go through the roof if he knew a Miami cop was working in his county."

"Well, don't let him find out, or both of our asses will be in trouble."

"What've you been doing since?"

"Sleeping, reading, and eating skimpy meals here at the guesthouse. How do I get back to Miami?"

"Let me think a minute."

Hoke waited, although he could have suggested several methods.

"Hello? Are you still there?"

"Still here."

"Tell Noseworthy to drive you to Four Corners in Bonita Springs. Trailways stops there, and you can catch the bus back to Miami. He can advance you the money, and I'll pay him back later."

"I'll call him to the phone, and you tell him, Mel. Coming from you, he'll feel better about it. He's already worried about my tab here, even though I told him you'd take care of it."

"Don't worry about the tab—"

"I don't. But Noseworthy does, I suspect."

"Okay, put him on then. And thanks for your efforts, Sergeant. Tell Willie, when you get back, that we're 'kits' now."

"It was nothing, Mel. I got there too late to check into anything. How's your meeting going in Tallahassee?"

"It's a mess so far. Advance planning for the new immigration law. Mostly appointing new committees for studying the possible effects. It's too soon to actually write any state regs, and there are all sorts of loopholes in the law. For example, they're only going to fine an employer who knowingly hires more than twenty illegal aliens, which doesn't make good sense. How do you interpret something like that if he only hires nineteen at a time?"

"I'm sure you'll work something out, Mel. I'll get Noseworthy."

Hoke went into the kitchen and got the innkeeper. Noseworthy was whispering something to his wife. As Noseworthy left to talk to Peoples, she looked at Hoke with her bold blue eyes and pushed a strand of hair away from her forehead. "Is that the call you've been expecting, Mr. Jinks?"

"Yes, ma'am. I'm afraid I'm going to have to leave now. But I've enjoyed my stay, especially the little trays you fixed for me. Be sure you add the meals to my tab."

"I intend to, although, as I told you, we aren't set up for meals other than breakfast. To run a restaurant or a boardinghouse, another license is required. We aren't used to having people stay in their rooms all day either."

"Well, I don't have a car." Hoke shrugged. "And it's too hot to walk around town in the sun."

"So now you're leaving."

"Yes, ma'am. And thanks again. And add a fifteen percent tip on my bill—for the meals, I mean."

"I don't accept tips." Her cheeks colored.

"Why not? My friend will be happy to pay for the extra service." Hoke left the kitchen.

Noseworthy was sitting at the check-in table; his fingers were still touching the phone when Hoke joined him.

"Melvin said I was to drive you to Bonita Springs and buy you a bus ticket to Miami."

"No, Mr. Noseworthy." Hoke shook his head. "He didn't say that. What he said was that you're to drive me to Bonita Springs and advance me money for my trip. I'll buy my own ticket, and I'll need another twenty bucks for essentials."

"What kind of essentials d'you need for a bus ride?"

"Several things, and perhaps a pint of bourbon. I'll get my stuff." Hoke started for the stairs.

"What stuff?"

"Didn't your wife tell you? She cleaned my room. I've got some adhesive tape and a few Tylenols left. And my pistol, of course. I'll be right down."

NOSEWORTHY HAD A THREE-YEAR-OLD CHEVY STATION WAGON. It was in excellent condition, with only twenty-five thousand miles on the odometer. He didn't turn on the radio, but he occasionally rolled his eyes toward Hoke and looked as if he wanted to ask some questions.

"How much," Hoke said, "did Mel Peoples tell you about me?"

"He didn't tell me anything. He just asked me to take care of you if you showed up at the house. But the way he said it, I didn't think you'd come. At least that was my impression at the time. If you called instead of coming to the guesthouse, he said to phone him right away and get your number."

"Is that all?"

"That's all. But I can't say I'm not curious."

"What do you want to know?"

"I've known Mel Peoples for three years. He's never mentioned you before, and I don't see how a man like you and Mel Peoples ever became friends. No offense, but—"

"None taken, Mr. Noseworthy. But that's easy. I knew Mel up in Tallahassee. He was going to A and M and I was in FSU. I used to get student tickets to the FSU football games, and he scalped them for me. We split the profits sixty-forty. Those were halcyon days, Mr. Noseworthy. We were young, carefree, and we both had brilliant futures. Ask Mel to tell you about his ticket scalping days sometime."

"He did tell me about that. What do you do now?"

"I'm a retired teacher from Rome, Georgia. I just travel around the state, visiting guesthouses and seeing the sights."

Noseworthy frowned. "If you don't want to tell me, don't tell me."

While Noseworthy sulked, Hoke looked incuriously at the gray-green flatlands of Lee County. A lot of the land near the state road had been cleared for cultivation, and they occasionally passed small herds of Black Angus cattle in fenced fields. There were also developers' billboards as they got closer to Four Corners, advertising low preconstruction prices for new condo complexes that were still in the planning stages. When they passed the billboard advertising the Bonita Springs dog track, the sign where the dead Haitian's body was purportedly discovered, Hoke shook his head with sudden insight. The mystery of the "dead" Haitian behind the billboard was now explained to his satisfaction, but he still didn't know why Mel Peoples and Willie Brownley had lied to him about it. He would find out, however, when he got back to Miami and talked to Willie, even if he had to twist Willie's arm.

There was no bus station at Four Corners, but there was a fifteen-minute rest stop for passengers at the restaurant, and Hoke could buy his ticket from the cashier. Noseworthy gave him money for the fare and an extra twenty dollars, but he handed the money over reluctantly. He shook hands with Hoke, however, and wished him luck before heading back to Immokalee.

Hoke ordered a breakfast of poached eggs, grits, and milk toast and drank three cups of coffee. He had to wait four hours before the bus for Miami pulled into the lot. He could smoke again, if he didn't inhale too deeply, and he smoked ten Kools while he waited for the bus. He was puzzled by Mel Peoples's sudden departure for Tallahassee and Noseworthy's intuitive feeling that he didn't think that any man named Adam Jinks would show up at his guesthouse. It looked as if Mel had been covering for himself, in case anything happened at Bock's farm, by being four hundred miles away from the area.

HOKE CALLED HIS HOUSE FROM A PAY PHONE IN THE MIAMI bus station. He let the phone ring ten times before he hung up. It was after 9:00 P.M., so someone should have been home. Hoke dialed again, thinking he had inadvertently dialed the wrong number. But no one answered the second time either. No one was home. Not one of the three females in his house would be able to let the phone ring ten times without answering it. As a general rule, one of the girls picked up the receiver by the second or third ring.

Hoke walked to the police station, a dozen blocks away. He took the elevator up to the Homicide Division; but his office was locked, and he didn't have his keys. Captain Slater was night duty officer in charge. Slater wore a black silk suit, a navy blue shirt, and a striped blue and white necktie. His pale, pockmarked face, because of his dark clothes, made him look as if he were recovering from a serious illness, but he always looked this way. Slater looked Hoke up and down, and gave him a lipless smile.

"Back from vacation already? Where'd you go, anyway?" Hoke's right sleeve was scorched slightly, his oversize rolled-up trousers were baggy at the knees, and he needed a shave again.

"Just working around the house, Captain. Is González around?"

"He's still on days. I haven't seen him for a week or so. Half the time I don't even know what you cold case people are working on."

"That's up to Major Brownley. I report directly to him, as you know, but I'll get permission from him to fill you in if you want me to."

"Never mind. I don't want to know. I've got enough on my plate already. You hear about Rodrígues and Quintero?"

"What about 'em?"

"Arrested. Both of them. They're both in jail on a hundred-and-fifty-thousand-dollar bond. It should be in the papers tomorrow."

"What happened? They're on your night shift, aren't they?"

Slater nodded. "They held up a crack house in Liberty City. It wasn't the first time, either, but this time IA undercovers were planted and arrested them with their hands out."

"That's hard to believe." Hoke shook his head. "These guys've been in plain clothes for five or six years, and they're both married, with families."

"It's a fucking shame, Hoke. But the money's too easy to get, and there's too much of it out there. And these are Homicide cops. God only knows what the Vice cops are stealing."

"I blame Internal Affairs, Captain. Lieutenant Norbert sits on his ass over there, and he doesn't know half the things that are going on in the department. They should send Norbert back to Traffic, where he belongs."

Slater pulled his thin lips back again. "He managed to get Rodríguez and Quintero. They've been suspended, of course, and that leaves me four detectives short on my night shift. Smitty resigned yesterday, without being asked, and Reynaldo's on a six-month psychiatric leave. He'll never return to duty either. He was cleared at the hearing, but both those boys he shot were under sixteen, and the new chief won't take him back."

"He can fight that with the PBA." Hoke shrugged. "Both those boys he killed had pistols."

"Oh, I don't blame Reynaldo, Sergeant. I would've shot them myself in the same situation, but that makes six he's killed in five years. Six, as you know, is beyond chance. They'll give him a psychiatric disability pension, and he'll be fixed for life. What the hell, Hoke, Reynaldo's got sixteen years in. You take his pension fund money for sixteen years, and add a disability on top of that, and he'll make more retirement money than he would if he stayed for twenty."

"I guess you're right, Captain."

"I know damned well I'm right. I worked out the figures on my calculator."

Hoke shrugged and took out his cigarettes. "Reynaldo's always been a little flaky, if you ask me, but—"

"You can't smoke out here in the bull pen."

Hoke put his pack away. "But Quintero and Rodríguez were good cops."

"'Were' is the word. Can I help you with anything, Hoke?"

"No, sir. I was just looking for González, is all. I'm still on vacation. I'll just leave a message in his box and tell him to call me at home tomorrow."

"Okay. I happen to see him, I'll tell him to call you."

Before going downstairs, Hoke put a message in González's box. He checked an unmarked Plymouth out of the motor pool and drove home to Green Lakes. He turned on the radio. Miles Davis was playing "In a Silent Way." Miles Davis hated white people so much he always played with his back to his audiences. But he took their money; he let them buy his records. Hoke switched to a Spanish station. An unhappy baritone was singing about his *corazón*. The Latins all had heart trouble, Hoke thought. He switched off the radio and drove the rest of the way home in silence.

No one was home, the house was dark, and Hoke didn't have his keys. Hoke's Pontiac Le Mans was parked behind Ellita's Honda Civic, and Sue Ellen's motorcycle was chained to the carport support column. He rang the bell several times, but no one answered.

Hoke went next door to Mr. Sussman's house. Hoke hadn't talked to Mr. Sussman for more than a month and wasn't eager to see him now; but Hoke kept an extra set of house keys at the Sussmans', and Sussman had left a set of his at Hoke's for emergency purposes. Mr. Sussman was religious and wore a crocheted yarmulke at all times, even when he was inside his house. The old man had berated Sue Ellen one afternoon for revving up her motorcycle in the yard, and she had told him to go fuck himself. Hoke had talked to him about it and then had to persuade Sue Ellen to apologize. The two families weren't close; but Mrs. Sussman was a nice old lady who made over Pepe whenever she saw the baby with Ellita, and Hoke didn't want to have a feud going with his neighbors.

Mr. Sussman, wearing his skullcap, answered the door when Hoke knocked and peered at him with watery blue eyes. He had a pointed chin, and his cropped gray beard made him look like a billy goat. He took off his reading glasses but didn't invite Hoke inside.

"I don't have my keys with me, Mr. Sussman, and no one seems to be home."

"They all left, that's why. I'll see if I can find your keys." He closed the door, and Hoke waited on the porch. Hoke lighted a cigarette and smoked while he waited. Sussman came back with the keys, unlocked the screen door, and handed them to the detective.

"What do you mean they all left? Both cars are still there."

"They left with that man who moved in across the street. About ten this morning. They were all dressed up, and they had suitcases and the baby, too. They got into this stretch limousine—a big blue Lincoln—and drove away."

"The man across the street, too?"

"That's what I said. There was a man driving the limo, and he was wearing a dark suit, but if he was a chauffeur, he didn't wear a cap. Sarah and me both watched 'em leave from the yard. I'd been on the phone for an hour or so, lining up volunteers for Super Sunday—that's for Federation, you see—and Sarah'd just got back from the store with Bumble Bee."

"Bumble Bee?"

"That's white tuna. That's what Sarah always calls it. When she sends me to the store for tuna, she always writes down 'Bumble Bee' so I don't get a different kind by mistake. Anyway, as I was saying, most people on the block, those that were home, came out to take a look at that stretch Lincoln. You could almost put my little Escort in the back seat."

"They didn't say where they were going?"

"It only took 'em a minute. They seemed to be in a big

rush, although I thought your daughter, Sue Ellen, said something or other to me when she got into the car. I don't know what it was, but I can make a pretty good guess."

"That's all over with, Mr. Sussman. Sue Ellen apologized to you for the last time, and she told me she was sorry, too. I won't bother you again this evening, Mr. Sussman. I'll just hang on to these keys for now and bring 'em back to you tomorrow sometime."

"Suit yourself."

Hoke let himself in to the house and looked on the refrigerator door for a note from Ellita. There was no note under the pizza magnet or anywhere else in the house. His car and house keys were on top of his dresser, however, and that would have been a logical place to leave a message. But he couldn't find any notes, and he looked in the girls' room as well. Clothes were scattered about in Ellita's bedroom and the girls' room, but then, they always were—most of the time anyway. Both of Ellita's suitcases, the big bag and her expensive camelskin airplane carry-on, were missing. Pepe's blue nylon diaper bag was missing, too, but Ellita would need that if she were going to be away for only a couple of hours. Still, it was past ten now, and if they had left at ten this morning, they had been gone for twelve hours!

Hoke called the Sánchez house, hoping he would get the old lady instead of Ellita's father. Her English was better than the old man's, and when she had lived with Hoke for a month right after Ellita came home from the hospital with the baby, the two of them had got along fairly well. She was a good cook, and Hoke had praised her meals. She had certainly been a big help to Ellita during her postpartum periods of depression. For a couple of weeks, when she first came home with Pepe, Ellita had cried a lot for no apparent reason, and Hoke didn't know what was the matter with her. "Don't worry," Mrs. Sánchez had said, raising her gray eyebrows. "We all do that. She'll quit after two or three more weeks. She'd cry even more if she'd had a girl."

On the fourth ring Mrs. Sánchez answered the phone.

"It's me, Hoke," Hoke said quickly. "Sergeant Moseley. Don't hang up."

"I didn't see you leave the party."

Hoke had already forgotten about the party. "I thought I said good-bye to you, Mrs. Sánchez. I had to go to work. An emergency. I know I said good-bye to Uncle Arnoldo. How is Tío Arnoldo, by the way?"

"He has cancer. There's a tumor in his bowels."

"I'm sorry to hear that."

"He bleeds down there. He has to wear a pad. Like a woman."

"That's too bad."

"He's at Jackson now, but they're sending him home from the hospital to die in two days."

"Back to Cuba?"

"No, here, at my house. He will die here in America, a free man, as soon as we get the Medicaid papers signed."

"I'm sure you'll keep him comfortable, Mrs. Sánchez. Is Ellita there? At your house?"

"No. I haven't seen her since the party. If she doesn't want to talk to her mother, she should at least call her father."

"You don't know where she is then?"

"She hasn't called me since the party. If she doesn't want to talk to me, tell her to call her father. He is very sad about Tío Arnoldo."

"Of course. Tell Tío Arnoldo I'll come by and visit him after he gets home. I don't like to bother people when they're still in the hospital."

"I'll tell him. He will be pleased. And tell Ellita to call her father."

"I'll tell her."

After he put the phone down, Hoke undressed and went into the bathroom to shave and shower. He pulled off the Band-Aid preparatory to shaving, and found that the puncture wound in his chin was festering. He cleaned out the yellow pus with a Q-tip dipped in iodine and shaved carefully with a new Bic throwaway razor. He plastered another Band-Aid over the wound before he took his shower. He slipped into a pair of khaki slacks, a light blue sport shirt, clean white socks, and the Nikes he wore when he went to the gym to play handball. His black, high-topped shoes were dirty, and damp inside, so he put them outside the door to the girls' room so Aileen could clean and polish them when she came home. When she came home? Where in the hell would Aileen, Sue Ellen, and Ellita go with a creep like Donald Hutton? That is, if they'd gone willingly. Mr. Sussman said that Sue Ellen had said something or other he couldn't hear when she climbed into the limo. Were they being kidnapped? That seemed unlikely, but on the other hand, if Hutton had a weapon, they would do what he told them, including packing their bags. One way or another Hutton would get his revenge, and a good way to do it was by doing something evil to Ellita and the girls. But Hoke couldn't entertain this thought seriously. If Hutton were going to kidnap Ellita and the girls, he would do it surreptitiously, not in broad daylight with a chauffeured limo.

There was plenty of food in the refrigerator. Hoke made a tomato and cream cheese sandwich on white bread and drank an Old Style with it. He had to make his report to Major Brownley, and he couldn't decide how much or how little to tell him. Brownley still had his badge, weapon, and teeth. Despite the hour, Hoke decided to drive to the major's house instead of phoning.

He threw the .38 pistol he had taken from Bock's house into the bottom drawer of his dresser and covered it with T-shirts. It might be useful as a throw-down weapon someday. He drove the unmarked police car he had checked out instead of taking his Pontiac. Brownley lived in the middle-class section of Liberty City, but to get there, Hoke had to drive through some mean black streets where kids often threw rocks at cars with white drivers. If rocks were thrown, let them throw at a department car instead of his Le Mans.

Hoke hadn't been to the major's house in more than two years. He had forgotten the address but knew where it was and how to get there. On Hoke's last visit Brownley, when he had been promoted to major, had thrown a backyard barbecue for all the off-duty detectives in the Homicide Division. Only five of them, including Hoke and Bill Henderson, had shown up. Ellita had been there, too, but the other detectives hadn't brought their wives. Mrs. Henderson came along, of course, because Bill made her. It would have looked bad for him as the executive officer if he hadn't brought his wife. There was a full keg of draft beer and enough pork barbecue and baked beans for at least forty people. Brownley's three sons wore white shirts, red bow ties, and white pants, and his two daughters wore white party dresses with red sashes. It had been an embarrassing evening for the Brownleys, and Hoke thought at the time those kids would be eating barbecue for a week afterward. After that the major hadn't given any more parties for the detectives in his division.

Brownley had a four-bedroom ranch-style house, and it was surrounded by an eight-foot unpainted board fence.

There was a kidney-shaped pool in the backyard. Three cars were parked on the circular asphalt driveway in front of the house. Hoke parked in the street and pushed through the gate, ignoring the Bad Dog sign. Brownley's dog, a fifteen-year-old poodle bitch named Mary, was half blind and too feeble to bark.

One of Brownley's sons, a boy of fifteen or so, let Hoke into the house and asked him to sit in the living room. This was a room rarely used, except for company, and it smelled strongly of Lemon Pledge. Hoke could hear talking and the sounds of the television coming from the Florida room in the back of the house. Willie Brownley, wearing plaid Bermudas, slippers, and a striped Saint Laurent shaving robe, joined Hoke within minutes. Hoke stood up. Brownley waved him back down and sat in a tapestry-cushioned straight chair across from him.

"I know it's late—" Hoke said.

"When did you get back?"

"This evening. I rode the bus from Bonita and checked a car out of the motor pool at the station."

"Mel's pretty upset, Hoke. He's called me twice now, both times with new information. He's sorry as hell now, he said, that he asked me for help, and he's afraid I'll tell somebody. Apparently he's up for a big civil service promotion, and he doesn't want any word of your investigation to get out."

"There's no investigation to talk about, Willie. Mel told me to tell you that you were 'kits' now—I guess he meant 'quits'—but all I can tell you is what I told him. I went out there all right, but when I saw the house and barn on fire, I took off in a hurry."

"Did you see any Haitians out there?"

"I didn't see anyone, and no one saw me. The farm's

186

almost a mile from the highway, and I couldn't see the fire till I walked down the gravel road to the farm. I could see smoke, but I thought at first they were just burning a field. There's a heavily wooded hammock between the highway and the farm, and the highway along there's bordered by palmettos."

"The sheriff found two dead bodies, Hoke. Mr. Bock was inside the house, and his foreman was in the barn. Bock's chest cavity was filled with shotgun pellets, and the Mexican's skull had been crushed with a blunt instrument."

"No shit?"

"That's right. What do you suppose happened?"

Hoke shrugged. "What about the workers?"

"He had some Haitians working out there, but no one seems to know how many there were. But they've all disappeared, and his truck's gone, too."

Hoke nodded reflectively and touched his sore chin.

"What happened to your chin?"

"Cut it shaving, and it's infected, I think. Maybe his workers revolted, killed Bock and the foreman, and then took off. Perhaps they got word or found out that he's been killing Haitians instead of paying them, so they beat him to the punch."

"I don't think so. Haitians are a pretty docile lot, and the illegals are afraid of getting picked up and deported back to Haiti. They're the most law-abiding noncitizens we have in Miami."

"Ordinarily, yes. But maybe Bock threatened to turn them in to the INS. Besides, Haitians aren't all that docile. Their ancestors were warriors back in Africa, and they beat the French Army to get their independence."

"I know a few things about Haiti, Hoke. We studied some about Haiti in my black history courses. They fought the French in the early eighteen-hundreds, but since then they've been kept down by one tyrant after another. Haitians don't have much fight left in them by now."

"That's a generality, Willie. A few men, afraid for their lives, might act differently."

A skinny black girl, about twelve or thirteen, with her hair in tight cornrows and wearing jeans, sneakers, and a Miami Dolphins T-shirt, brought in a tray holding two frosted steins of beer. She offered one to Hoke before taking the other to her father.

"Thanks," Hoke said. "What's your name?"

"Lily."

"Her name's Lillith," Brownley said, "but we call her Lily for short."

"That's a nice name, Lily," Hoke said, taking a sip of beer.

The girl looked at her father. He tilted his head, and she left the room.

"What did you tell Ellita about me? To explain my absence?"

"Well . . ." Brownley took a long swig of beer, swallowed. "I didn't talk to her personally, Hoke. I had a patrolman drive your car over to your house, and I told him to tell Elitta you'd be out of town on a special assignment for a few days. Because of the nature of the assignment, you couldn't contact her, and she shouldn't try to get in touch with you. I left it at that. I figured if she got worried after a couple of days and called me, I'd make up something else to tell her. But she never called."

"And she swallowed all that? Without any questions?"

"Why wouldn't she? She used to be a police officer, and it isn't unusual for a detective to go undercover. But you're holding something back, Hoke. What really happened over there?"

188

"Nothing. I've been on a vacation for a few days, that's all. I was on unofficial business, private business, and I didn't have my badge, weapon, or even my teeth. So whatever happened over there is none of your fucking business!"

"There's no need to—"

"That's right. There's no need for you to know anything. What you don't know can't hurt you. As you told me in the first place, if I got into any trouble, you couldn't back me up."

"Mel said the two pit dogs were killed, too. Shot."

"That couldn't have been me, Willie. You had my pistol. When I saw the fire, I also thought about the dogs. A fire like that can make dogs crazy, so they're another reason I left in a hurry. I know you told me how to catch 'em by the front legs and break them off, but without any practice I didn't want to try it. So I left before they could sniff me out."

"Okay, let's forget about it. I'll get your stuff."

Hoke finished his beer. He looked around but couldn't see a place to put down the stein without leaving a ring on the polished tables. He took the empty mug into the foyer and put it on the floor. Brownley returned and handed Hoke a brown grocery sack. Hoke shoved his holstered weapon beneath his belt at the back and pocketed his badge case and wallet. He looked at the floor for a moment.

"Ellita and the girls aren't home, Willie. Do you know where they are?"

"What d'you mean, aren't home? They might be at a movie."

Hoke shook his head. "I stopped at the house before driving over here, Willie. They're gone, and they left with packed bags. According to my next-door neighbor, they left in a stretch Lincoln with Donald Hutton. There was no note, but if you told Ellita not to contact me, that explains why she didn't leave one. That is, if she was able to write one. I can't think of anyplace Ellita and the girls would go with Donald Hutton. But my neighbor said they left the house at ten this morning."

"That's strange, but I don't know anything about it. She didn't call me."

"Hutton promised he'd get revenge on me, Willie. So if Ellita told him I'd be away for a few days, maybe he decided to kidnap them."

"Not at ten, in broad daylight. There's probably some simple explanation."

"They took their clothes along. They're on a trip of some kind, Willie."

"In that case you haven't got anything to worry about. School's out, so maybe he took 'em down to the Keys. Why not call Ellita's mother? She'd know."

"I did. She hasn't heard from Ellita since the party for her uncle."

"Maybe she'll send you a postcard. I wouldn't worry about it if I were you."

"Thanks, Willie. But if you were me, you'd worry about it."

Brownley shook his head and smiled. "If it was someone else other than Ellita, I might worry. But she's a match for any man, in my opinion."

"I guess you're right. She still carries her pistol, and there's probably a simple explanation."

"See what I mean? Hutton's got lots of money. Maybe he took them for a drive—up to Palm Beach or maybe on a boat ride."

"Sure. Can you let me have Mel Peoples's phone number?"

"No. He doesn't want to talk to you again, Hoke. He wants all this shit to blow over."

"Okay. Can you call him for me?"

"I guess so."

"There's a woman in Immokalee, living in the Lucky Star Trailer Park. Her name's Elena Osborne, and she's got a retarded son about three years old. Tell Mel to get that kid away from her and put it in a state institution somewhere."

"He's on the State Agricultural Commission, Hoke. He doesn't have any authority for something like that."

"I didn't have any authority in Immokalee either. He owes me a favor for my investigation, and he knows the people over there who can do something."

"What's your interest in this woman, Hoke?"

"Elena Osborne. Mrs. Elena Osborne. None at all. The kid is ruining the woman's life, that's all. So tell Mel to get the welfare people to commit that kid. If he doesn't, I'm going to phone Boggis and tell him the whole story."

"You'd be in trouble, not Mel."

"I don't give a shit. If Mel's up for a promotion, he'll do it. If Bock and his foreman are dead, Mel can't afford to get his name in the papers, even though he meant well."

"All right. I'll call him tonight. What's the woman's name again?"

"Osborne. Mrs. Elena Osborne. The Lucky Star Trailer Park. And when you call him, tell him I'm going to check on this matter later, after things have cooled down over there in Immokalee."

"I believe I can persuade him, Hoke."

"Thanks, Willie, this is important to me. I'd like to see something positive come out of this fiasco."

"I wouldn't call it that."

"You wouldn't? What are my chances of getting a look at the autopsy report?" Hoke got to his feet and felt for a cigarette. He lit a Kool and put his lighter away. "The dead Haitian. The one you said was buried behind the billboard."

"Not a chance." Brownley shook his head.

"That's what I figured. There isn't any dead Haitian, and there never was, right?"

"The dead Haitian was Mel's idea, Hoke, not mine. There are Haitians missing, that's true enough, but we haven't found any of them yet. But Mel thought that if we told you we had a dead one, it would be easier to get you to check out Bock's farm. How'd you find out?"

Hoke shrugged. "The innkeeper in Immokalee drove me to Four Corners in Bonita Springs. Along the way we passed the billboard advertising the dog track. The billboard's in Lee County, not Collier County, so if you found a dead man buried behind it, the Lee County sheriff would've been called, not Sheriff Boggis. What the hell is going on, Major?"

"I can't tell you, Hoke. I'd like to, but I can't."

"Okay. I'll accept that. But you owe me a big debt, Willie."

"And you will be paid, Sergeant. That's a promise."

Hoke drove home and went to bed. He was too exhausted to think about the matter. Just before he fell asleep, he decided that he would call the limousine services first thing in the morning and go on from there. That is, if Ellita didn't call him or return home by morning.

CHAPTER 14

THE NEXT MORNING HOKE PARKED THE UNMARKED PLYM-outh in the police lot. As he got out of the car, he flipped his cigarette on the ground and stepped on it. Three cars away, Captain Slater was just getting into his Lincoln Continental. He held up a hand and walked toward Hoke. His shoulders were straight, and his back was stiff, as if someone held a gun to his spine.

"Were you smoking in the car, Sergeant Moseley?"

Hoke nodded.

"That's a twenty-five-dollar fine."

"Jesus, Captain Slater, I was alone in the car. My smoke didn't bother anyone."

"It bothers the new chief. The rule's been posted, D-T-one-oh-seven, and that means unmarked cars as well as patrol vehicles. I'll have to put you down for a fine. Commander Henderson will have it deducted from your next paycheck. You're a sergeant, and you're supposed to set an example for the younger officers."

"I forgot about the damned rule."

"That's tough shit. Next time the fine'll make you remember it."

Slater walked toward his car without looking back. Hoke checked the Plymouth in with the dispatcher, signing his name and time on the clipboard. From now on, he thought, when he smoked in an unmarked car, he would have to remember to sneak it.

Teodoro González, wearing a white linen jacket with the sleeves rolled up to the elbows, was already in the office.

"I called you at home," he said, "soon's I got your note, but no one answered so I figured you'd already left."

Hoke nodded and pulled the two telephone books over to his side of the desk. He was going to look up limousines. The books were bulky, and this year the phone company had divided them so that half of the Yellow Pages were in A–K and the other half were in L–Z. This made it equally inconvenient to look up private numbers and commercial Yellow Page numbers.

González clasped his hands together and smiled expectantly across the desk. As Hoke looked at González's young, vacant face, freshly shaved and stinking of Brut, he wondered what would have happened to the young detective if Brownley had sent him to Immokalee. He would be one dead Cuban-American. For the first time since they had been working together, Hoke felt sorry for González.

"Report," Hoke said, without opening the L–Z book.

"Report?"

"Report."

"Oh, sure, now I know what you mean. I swallowed that peanut butter ball, just like Major Brownley told me to do, but I really didn't need to. I wasn't X-rayed, so it didn't make any difference. I made the appointment with Dr. Schwartz, and I spent the first hour in his reception room filling in a medical history form before he saw me. By the way, what's enuresis? I didn't know what it was, so I put down I never had it."

"I'm willing to bet good money you did. It means wetting the bed."

"Oh, sure, I had that, until I was eleven or twelve. How'd you know?"

"Basic deduction, Teddy. What happened with Dr. Schwartz?"

"He took my blood pressure, listened to my chest and back with his stethoscope, and asked me if I ever coughed up any blood. I said no, and then he asked me if I had a stressful job. I started to say yes, but I'd already put down on my form that I was a tennis instructor, so I had to say no again."

"Tennis instructor? When did you start playing tennis?"

"I don't, but I had to put down an occupation that would let me get away for two hours in the morning to see a doctor. There aren't many jobs where they'll let you off to sit in a doctor's office."

"Okay. Was he wearing the ring?"

González nodded, and plucked at his lower lip. "He was wearing an onyx ring with a diamond in it. But I can't say for sure it was the same ring Dr. Russell was wearing. Those rings are seen a lot around town, especially at the dog tracks. He was wearing a gold Rolex, too. But that may not have been Dr. Russell's watch either."

"What makes you say that?"

"On my way out of the office I saw Dr. Schwartz's partner, Dr. Farris. He was talking to the nurse, and he was wearing a gold Rolex. Once you start looking, you see 'em everywhere. Even Captain Slater's got one."

"Captain Slater's a prick, Teddy, but he isn't a suspect. And neither are the one hundred and one drug dealers and lawyers who wear gold Rolexes. I'm glad you spotted the watch on Dr. Farris, but now we have two suspects instead of one."

González shook his head. "Max Farris operated for Dr. Russell that morning. After Sergeant Quevedo called the clinic, the nurse called Dr. Schwartz first and then Dr. Farris to perform the operation. Isn't that right?"

"Farris had enough time, and so did Schwartz. Russell was dead for about fifteen minutes when the deliveryman found him. That's the estimate, but it could've been longer. He had to go to a neighbor's to call nine-one-one. Then it took the police car about five or six minutes to get there after that. That's at least twenty-five. So Dr. Farris had plenty of time to shoot Dr. Russell and get back home before anybody called."

"These are all approximate times."

"But underestimated, not overestimated. Besides, it seems unlikely to me that either one of these doctors would do the actual shooting himself. I mean improbable, not unlikely. They both profited by Russell's death. The only reason Dr. Schwartz is the prime suspect is that he profited most. He got Russell's house and wife, in addition to half the clinic. We're going to have to flush these fuckers out. One or the other or both."

"What about my money?"

"What money?"

"I couldn't use my insurance because I had to use an assumed name when I saw the doctor. José Smith. The nurse gave me a little lecture, too, about not having any medical insurance. Then I had to pay one hundred bucks in cash. I had the money, knowing I'd have to pay something, but I didn't think I'd have to pay a hundred bucks just to be told to take Maalox. I talked to Commander Henderson afterward about getting my refund, and he said I couldn't get any refund without a legitimate bill from the doctor. My receipt, you see, was made out to José Smith."

"How about department funds?"

"The undercover wasn't authorized in advance, Henderson said."

"Jesus Christ. The undercover was tacitly authorized by Major Brownley when he explained the peanut butter ball to you. Did you tell Bill that?"

"I tried to, but I didn't have anything on *paper* in advance. So he said he couldn't do anything for me."

"You still got your receipt from Dr. Schwartz?"

"From his nurse, yes. Right here."

"Okay, give it to me. I'll type a backdated okay of one hundred bucks in undercover expenditures and get Major Brownley to sign it. Then I'll give it to Bill and get your money for you. This is something you should've done yourself, Teddy. Paperwork isn't just a part of this job, it's ninety percent of it."

González handed over the receipt. "I'm sorry. But I really can't afford to lose that much dough, Sergeant."

"Can you afford coffee and doughnuts?"

González grinned and got to his feet. "Glazed?"

"One glazed and one burnt coconut."

Hoke put the receipt into his in-box, as González left, and then walked his fingers through the Yellow Pages to limousines. There were more than fifty limousine services listed, to his surprise, not counting the large display ads that repeated some of the same numbers in larger type. Hoke chose the numbers from the display ads that advertised stretch Lincolns first and narrowed his search down to a half dozen. He wrote the numbers on a legal pad and started from the top. On the fifth call he got lucky. The dispatcher said that a Mr. Hutton and party had been picked up the day before in Green Lakes and had been driven to the Port of Miami. They were dropped off at Slip Three, for the *Caribbean Princess*. This ship visited Nassau, in the Bahamas, and the limousine was scheduled to pick up Mr. Hutton and his party again when the boat docked at 10:00 A.M. on Sunday. "Actually," the dispatcher said, "the boat's there by nine, but it takes customs about an hour on the boat to check out the crew and aliens first. Passengers start to disembark around ten. Then they get their luggage on the dock and go through a customs check. It all goes pretty fast, once it gets started, but it's usually eleven by the time they're ready to leave. But our man'll be there at ten because that's the official disembarking time."

"How much do you charge an hour?"

"It all depends, Sergeant. Usually it's seventy-five an hour for a stretch Lincoln, but if you want the car and driver for three or four days, we work out a much lower rate."

"But if your driver's at the dock by ten, you gain an extra hour, don't you?"

"Well, I guess so, but it's our experience that it's better to be early than late. People who rent limos don't like to wait."

"Is the driver there?"

"No, sir, he isn't. He's home today."

"Can you have him call me here at the police station?"

"If he's home, I'll tell him."

Hoke gave the dispatcher his extension, thanked him, and racked the phone. He felt relieved but angered as well. He was relieved to know that Ellita and the girls hadn't been kidnapped or made to go with Hutton against their will, but he was angry because they had gone with Hutton and made him worry about them.

González came in with the coffee and two doughnuts and put the Styrofoam cup on the desk. The doughnuts were on a paper plate and covered with waxed paper. Hoke wadded the waxed paper into a ball and threw it at González, missing by two feet.

"What took you so long?"

"While I was down there, I decided to have a little breakfast. I thought—you know—while I was in the cafeteria, I might as well. It saved two trips, bring you the doughnuts and coffee, and then go back down again—"

"You thought wrong. Take the Russell file, and find the home addresses of Dr. Schwartz and Dr. Farris, and then go downstairs and find out from the desk sergeant who patrols the neighborhoods where they live. I want to see if they're patrolled in the daytime as well as at night."

"What's this for, Sergeant Moseley?"

"I'll explain when you get back."

HOKE ATE HIS DOUGHNUTS AND FINISHED HIS COFFEE BEFORE he left his office to talk to Bill Henderson. Henderson was on the phone, and Hoke waited out of earshot until he finished talking and racked the receiver.

"Bill," he said, handing him the receipt from Dr. Schwartz's bill, "González needs his hundred bucks back."

"Not a chance." Henderson shook his head. "I already talked to him about it."

"I know you did, but there's a way around it. Put his name on the insurance form, and then type 'José Smith' in parentheses after his name. That'll make it a legitimate bill, and the insurance will pay eighty percent. González'll lose twenty bucks, but at least he won't be out the entire amount."

"I don't know if that'll work, Hoke."

"Sure it will. They do this over in Vice all the time when they check out doctor suspects, to see who's writing phony scripts for H. You can't expect undercovers to pay phony doctor bills, but most doctors want cash in advance before they'll even talk to a patient. I know they do it this way because Marcia in Vice told me so."

"Okay, I'll send it in, but González'll still be stuck for twenty bucks. If you backdated a request for department funds and could get Major Brownley to sign it, he could get the entire amount."

"I was going to do it that way, but I changed my mind. If González loses twenty bucks, next time he'll fill out his request in advance. I wasn't here to hold his hand, or this wouldn't've happened."

"Okay. Have a good time on vacation?"

"Terrific."

When González came back with the patrol schedules, Hoke went downstairs to Traffic and talked to Lieutenant Vitale, explaining what he wanted the patrol cars to do. "The people who live at these addresses are witnesses in a cold case, Lieutenant. All I want the night patrolmen to do is stop for three or four minutes outside the house, put the spot on the address numbers or a front window, and then drive away. If they drive by two or three times a night and do this, they might look for any signs of departure. I mean, they can see if the occupants are getting ready to leave."

"Won't this make the occupants suspicious?"

"Yes, sir. That's the idea. On the day patrols, when the officers take their breaks, I'd like to have them park in front of these houses for ten minutes or so. If anyone comes out of the house to ask what they're doing, just tell 'em to drive away without answering."

"What are they looking for?"

"A U-Haul trailer, suitcases, whatever."

Vitale frowned. "This is all aboveboard, isn't it, Sergeant?"

"Yes, sir. I don't know about you, but I'm always happy to see a patrol car in my neighborhood. I like to know they're out there. Of course, if I was running a crack house, I wouldn't like to see one."

"Are these suspected crack houses?"

"No, sir. The important thing is, I want the cars and the uniforms seen, but I don't want the officers to talk to the occupants."

"Who lives here? In these houses?"

"You don't need to know. If you did, I'd tell you. But if the guy we're looking for is hiding out in either place, seeing blue-and-whites might flush him out."

"I see. Now I see what you're after." Vitale nodded. "Why didn't you say so? How long should my men do this?"

"Two or three days and two or three nights. I appreciate this, Lieutenant."

"No problem." Vitale grinned, clasped his hands behind his head, and sat back in his swivel chair. "I thought you came down to bitch about the fine you got for smoking in an unmarked car."

HOKE WENT BACK TO HIS OFFICE. "DO YOU STILL HAVE FAR-ris's and Schwartz's addresses in your notebook?" he asked González.

"Sure."

"Here's what I want you to do. First, go to Dr. Farris's house. If the maid answers the door, flash your badge, tell her you're from Homicide, and ask her how long she's been working for Dr. Farris. Just that, and nothing more. When you get the information, leave. Don't answer any of her questions. Just leave. If Mrs. Farris, instead of the maid, answers the door, ask her if you can talk to her maid. Show Mrs. Farris your badge, and be polite, but don't answer any of her questions either—if she has any. She'll get you the maid. Ask her then how long she's been working there, and write down her answer in your notebook. Then leave. Think you can do that?"

González nodded. "Sure."

"Then drive to Dr. Schwartz's house and do the same thing. Ask her maid the same question, and then come back here to the station. If I'm not here, wait for me. I want you to drive me home tonight."

González nodded. "I heard you got caught by Captain Slater smoking in an unmarked car this morning."

"Who told you that?"

"A guy from the motor pool, while I was having breakfast."

"I did. Sometimes the rumors you pick up in the building are true. Do you understand what I want you to do?"

"Sure, but we don't need this information. It's all in the file, I'm sure."

"Three years is a long time. They both may have new maids. And maids, sometimes, overhear a lot of conversations, whether they want to or not."

"But if they're new, the information won't help our case any."

"These doctors don't know that. Just do what I tell you to do."

"I was showing some initiative. You're always telling me I don't show any initiative."

"Okay, you've shown it. Now you can go."

After González left, Hoke studied the Russell file for about ten minutes before the phone rang. It was the limousine driver, a man named Raúl Goya y Goya. "I've had my chauffeur's license two years now," Goya y Goya said, after identifying himself, "and I've never had a ticket."

"I'm not interested in your driving record, Raúl. You

aren't in any trouble with the police. I just wanted to ask you a few questions about the passengers you picked up yesterday in Green Lakes."

"Mr. Hutton and party?"

"That's right. Did you overhear them saying anything that seemed a little funny or strange?"

"I don't listen in to passengers' conversation, Sergeant. I just go where they tell me, that's all. If I started listening in to what was being said in the back, I wouldn't've lasted this long. I've seen some weird stuff going on back there, but I've never been asked to do nothing wrong, like make an illegal U-turn or—"

"I realize you're a good driver, Raúl. I just wondered if you overheard them talking about the purpose of the cruise —why they were going, anything like that?"

"The two teenagers were excited, that's all. They'd never been on a cruise before, and they were asking Mr. Hutton if they could play the slot machines, and like that. He also explained roulette to them, I believe, but as I say, I wasn't listening. The only thing that struck me funny was the lady. She was nursing the baby, and you don't see things like that much anymore. Not in the car, I mean. The windows are tinted some, but not real dark, and people can still see in at stoplights, you know. So when she started nursing the baby, I hung back a little so I wouldn't get stopped at the lights, and I concentrated on my driving."

"Okay then. And you'll pick them up again Sunday morning?"

"I hope so. I asked for the run, but I may not get it. Mr. Hutton tipped me a twenty. What's this all about, Sergeant? This was just a happy family, going on a cruise. I don't know what else I can tell you."

"You've been very helpful, Raúl. And incidentally, you speak English very well."

"I should hope so. I was born and raised in Springfield, Ohio."

"Is that right? Well, if it'll help you any, tell the dispatcher I'd like you to do the pickup Sunday."

"It'll help a lot. Thanks, Sergeant."

Hoke hung up, satisfied, now that he had talked with the driver and knew that his daughters were okay. In the last few months Sue Ellen had saved a good deal of her money. He hoped that she hadn't taken all of it along to gamble away on the cruise ship. He knew she shot craps with the boys at the car wash, and she had been lucky a few times. But she wouldn't have a chance, shooting craps on the ship or at the Paradise Beach Casino in Nassau. What if she did lose it all? She had worked for it, so he hoped Sue Ellen and Aileen were having a good time. If Hutton thought he was getting even with him by taking his daughters on a free cruise, he was nuts. Let the bastard spend his money on Ellita and the girls. Why should he care?

Hoke signed out, took the same unmarked Plymouth out of the police lot, and stopped for lunch at the Saigon Café in the Bayside Shopping Center. He liked the lemon grass soup served there, and the sole with hot chiles. The manager knew Hoke was a cop, and when he was there, he tore up Hoke's check, and all Hoke had to leave was a tip for the waitress. Hoke enjoyed the meal; it was nice to have his teeth again. After eating, he drank two bottles of Corona beer and smoked three Kools. The clinic was closed between twelve-thirty and one-thirty for lunch, and he had to wait for it to open. The café manager wasn't in, so Hoke paid his tab with his VISA card.

Hoke parked in the clinic's lot at one thirty-five. Three elderly patients were waiting in the reception room. One old man was reading *Modern Maturity*, and two old women were staring at two parrot fish swimming around in the saltwater aquarium. There was an aluminum toy diver in the bottom of the tank, with bubbles coming out of the top of his helmet. Someone had painted "Mel Fisher" in white paint across the diver's chest. Hoke pushed the bell, and the glass window slid back.

"Mrs. Burger?" Hoke said, showing the nurse his badge. "I'm Sergeant Moseley, Miami Homicide."

Mrs. Burger was in her late fifties, with razor blue hair in tight curls, and she wore gold-rimmed aviation glasses. She wore a pink nurse's uniform, but no cap, and she became flustered when she saw Hoke's badge. Her lipstick almost matched her uniform, and her two prominent upper front teeth had made little dents in her full lower lip.

"Did you have an appointment?" She looked at her clipboard.

"No, ma'am." Hoke lowered his voice to a stage whisper. "I'd like to talk to you, Mrs. Burger, for a few minutes. Outside, if you don't mind."

"I don't know. We just opened—and—"

"It'll only take a few minutes. Get someone to take over for you. I'll be outside."

Hoke left the waiting room and waited on the brick sidewalk. He lighted a cigarette, and a minute later Mrs. Burger came through the door. She was carrying her purse, a brown alligator bag with several gold buckles. Not all the buckles were functional, Hoke noted. Women always brought their handbags, Hoke reflected, even if they were only going to the bathroom.

Hoke took her arm. "It's pretty hot out here in the sun. Let's sit in my car, and I'll turn on the air-conditioning."

"This isn't going to take very long, is it? I've got—"

"Just a few minutes."

They got into the car, and Hoke turned on the engine

and then the air-conditioning. He took out his pack of Kools.

"Would you like a cigarette?"

"I'd love one. We can't smoke in the office, you know. I've got my own." She opened her bag and took a long black More out of her pack. Hoke lit it for her and put his lighter away. He took out his notebook and ballpoint.

"What's this all about, Sergeant . . . ?"

"Moseley. Dr. Russell. You remember Dr. Russell's murder?"

"Of course. I've been with the clinic for more than ten years. But I thought that investigation was closed."

Hoke smiled. "A murder case is never closed, Mrs. Burger. The sergeant you talked to three years ago is no longer on the case, but it's never been closed. What I'm doing, I'm rechecking a few things. How well did you know Dr. Russell?"

"Well, I knew him in the office, but not socially or anything like that. And I was shocked by the way he was killed. He didn't have any enemies, and I don't see how he could have. He worked all the time."

"Did you like him? As a person, I mean."

"Yes, I did. He was a little brisk sometimes, but I respected him and liked him. When he thought about it, he could be very kind. He wasn't very religious, and neither is Dr. Schwartz. What I mean is, neither one of them took Yom Kippur off. But I wanted off, and Dr. Farris didn't want me to have it. He's a Methodist, you see, and because we close on Christmas Day, he thought I was trying to sneak in an extra holiday. Dr. Russell stood up for me on that. There are eleven Jewish holidays altogether, but all I ever asked for was Yom Kippur, and Dr. Farris didn't even want me to have that. I told him—Dr. Farris—that he could dock me a day's pay if he wanted to, but I still wanted the day off. Dr. Russell let me have it, and he didn't dock my pay either."

"They can't dock your pay for a religious holiday, Mrs. Burger. Have you had any trouble about that since Dr. Russell was killed?"

"No, but I lost Christmas. I have to come in Christmas Day and answer the phone, even though the clinic's closed."

"You don't care much for Dr. Farris, do you?"

"I didn't say that. I work for both doctors, and I get along well with both of them. This is a good job, Sergeant. I used to be in OR, and I don't want to go back to that again, ever."

"OR?"

"Operating room. I was in OR at St. Catherine's for three years, and then Dr. Russell offered me a job here. We're open on Saturdays, but we close Wednesday afternoons, and the hours are regular."

"I see." Hoke made some notes in his book.

"I told the other detective the same things. I don't have anything new to tell you."

"When you learned that Dr. Russell was shot, aren't you the nurse who phoned Dr. Schwartz to take over Russell's scheduled operation?"

"Yes, sir." She butted her cigarette and took out another. Hoke lit it for her.

"He wasn't here at the clinic? He was at home?"

"He was still in bed, he said. But he was very upset about the news and said he'd call Dr. Farris to do the operation. We have an answering service when we're closed."

"Well, thank you very much, Mrs. Burger. You've helped me a lot."

"I told all this before. Why are you asking me these same things again?"

"You want Dr. Russell's killer caught, don't you?"

"Of course, but it all happened so long ago I thought you gave up on it."

"D'you know how to keep a secret, Mrs. Burger?"

"I certainly do. But I don't have any secrets if that's what you mean."

"I don't mean that. I'll tell you something in confidence then, but I don't want it to go any further. If I tell you, can you keep it to yourself? After all, Dr. Russell was your friend, and I'd like to tell you."

"I won't say anything."

"All right then. We know who killed Dr. Russell, and we've known for some time now. An arrest is imminent. I can't tell you who did it, of course, but you'll be surprised when you learn who killed him."

"Who did it?"

"I can't tell you any more than I have, and I shouldn't have told you that much. But keep what I told you to yourself. Don't tell anyone."

"I will. My husband's been dead for six years."

"In that case, you have no one else to tell. And thanks again for your help."

"This is very good news, Sergeant Moseley." Mrs. Burger butted her cigarette in the ashtray. She took a mint out of her purse and offered one to Hoke. He shook his head, got out of the car, and then circled the car to open the passenger door. He winked, placed a forefinger to his lips, and she smiled and waggled her fingers as she started back to the clinic.

As Hoke backed out of the parking lot, he wondered how long Mrs. Burger would be able to keep the "secret." One hour? Two? On the other hand, maybe she would keep it. Most nurses were privy to confidential information, and if they didn't tell their friends about their prominent patients who had doses of clap, maybe they wouldn't talk about murders either. But Hoke had dated nurses, and they had often talked about their patients to him. What else did nurses have to talk about?

Hoke drove to Dr. Schwartz's house on Poinciana and parked in the driveway. It was a large two-story house, and the brick façade had been painted white. Four Corinthian columns on the concrete front porch supported nothing. They were there just for decorative purposes. Mrs. Schwartz opened the door to his ring, and Hoke showed her his badge.

"Mrs. Schwartz? I'm Sergeant Moseley. Homicide."

Mrs. Schwartz, a matronly woman in her late forties, was wearing dark-green poplin Bermudas and a lettuce-green silk boat-necked top. Her pinkish hair, in a modified Afro, was obviously dyed. Her brown eyes were almost as dark as Hoke's, and her arched eyebrows were blackened half circles. Her upper lip was thin, but she had made it fuller by adding a rim of lipstick above the lip.

"Would you like to come in?"

"If I may," Hoke said, following her into the living room. "I won't be long." She sat on one end of the leather couch and indicated the other end for Hoke. He shook his head and remained standing.

"I've got some good news for you, Mrs. Schwartz. It'll only be a few more days, but we know who killed your husband—Dr. Russell. I wanted to prepare you for this because as soon as we announce the arrest, you'll have reporters coming around to see you, asking questions."

"I don't understand." She seemed genuinely puzzled. "What's this all about? Another detective was here this morning, and he talked to my maid. Right after he left, she told me she had to visit her aunt in Mexico City. I thought he was here to talk to her about her aunt—"

"Has she left yet?"

"About an hour ago."

"It doesn't matter. That must've been Detective González. He's also working on this case, and he wanted to see her to clarify a few things. How long was your maid with you, Mrs. Schwartz?"

"It's been almost five years now. She doesn't live in, but we treat her very well, and I thought I knew her—but I didn't even know she had an aunt in Mexico City. She was more like family than a maid, if you know what I mean."

Hoke shrugged. "It's a cultural thing, Mrs. Schwartz. I work with Latins in the department, but we rarely socialize after hours because we don't think alike. There's one more thing I'd like to ask you about, though. When your husband was shot, you were up in Orlando visiting your sister—"

"My half sister, Becky Freeman. My maiden name was Goldberg, but when my father died, my mother married a man named David Freeman. So Becky's my half sister."

"Does she ever come down here to visit you?"

Mrs. Schwartz shook her head. "We're not very close. I invited her to the wedding when Leo and I got married, but she couldn't come, she said."

"According to my notes in the file, you visited your sister—half sister—for the first time when Dr. Russell was killed. If you weren't close, as you say, what was the purpose of the visit?"

"I wasn't asked that by the first detective."

"I know. That's why I'm asking you now."

Mrs. Schwartz tried to smile, but the corners of her lips turned down. "Do you have to know?"

"Yes, I do. The man who shot your husband had to know you'd be out of town, you see."

"All right. I can tell you, and you can check it out easily enough. Becky was mixed up with a married man and got pregnant. She got an abortion, and she asked me to come and stay with her for a few days. Our parents are dead, and I'm the only family she has left. So I went up there. You can check the records at the Fernandez Planned Parenthood Clinic in Orlando if you like. But that's behind her now, and I'd rather let it be. I don't see how it can have any bearing on this case. I don't know why Paul was shot. Who did it, Sergeant?"

"I'll have to withhold that information for a few days, but you'll know soon enough, I promise. And I don't think there's any need to bother your half sister. If I do make inquiries, I'll be discreet. In a right-wing city like Orlando a schoolteacher could lose her job if the school board found out she had an abortion."

"They don't know. The only ones who know are you, Becky and me, and the staff of the clinic."

Hoke nodded. "Don't worry." Hoke grinned. "But I did think I should prepare you for the announcement of the arrest. I know how women are. When TV cameras are involved, women want to look their best, and you might want to make a beauty shop appointment, buy some new clothes, or something. Not that you don't look lovely now, of course."

"I see. Well, thank you. Could I get you something? A drink? Coffee?"

"No, thanks. I'm just glad I could finally bring you some good news. No need to get up. I can find my way out."

Mrs. Schwartz got up anyway and trailed Hoke to the door.

"It is good news," she said, taking his hand after he had opened the door. "But I don't know what else to say. It's been so long now I thought the police had given up and closed the case."

Hoke shook his head. "A murder case is never closed

until the killer is tried and put away. For the time being, Mrs. Schwartz, at least for a few days, please keep this information to yourself. Don't even tell your husband."

"I will. How long will it be? Before you make your arrest, I mean."

"Not long. Just a few more days, and that's a promise, Mrs. Schwartz."

Hoke got into his car, and the woman lingered in the doorway, watching him as he drove away.

Hoke was well pleased by the interrogation. It had gone more smoothly than he had thought it would. Before returning to the station, Hoke stopped at Larry's Hideaway for a shot of Early Times and a beer. Sergeant Armando Quevedo was sitting at the bar, and staring glumly into a seventeen-ounce strawberry margarita. A large strawberry floated on top of the drink. Hoke sat on the stool next to him and ordered a shot of Early Times and a Michelob draft.

"When did you start drinking that shit, Armando?" Hoke said.

Quevedo turned and grimaced. "It's pretty awful, but the doc said I'd have to give up boilermakers. So I figured if I stuck to this belly wash, I wouldn't overdo it. It's sweeter than hell. Are you off today?"

"No, I'm working. I just stopped for a quickie. Have you come up with any ideas for our Homicide Crack Committee Report?"

"Yeah, one." Quevedo laughed. "It came to me the other night. What we should do, you see, is take all of the confiscated crack, all we've got, and all the DEA's got in storage, and then stage a big smoke-in in the Orange Bowl. We invite all the crack abusers and tell 'em they can smoke all they want free. Inasmuch as they'll smoke it until they die, we should be able to kill them all off, or at least the two or three hundred who show up. We can have TV cameras there, Channels Four, Seven, and Ten, and they can shoot the whole scene live. Maybe we can get Geraldo Rivera to emcee the event, and it'll show what crack does to the abusers. We can have black body bags stacked up, too, you see, and the medical examiner. As the ME pronounces each person dead, we can put the body in the bag, and then stack the bags on trucks. What do you think?"

"Sounds like a good idea to me, Armando. You type up the report tonight, and I'll sign it."

"You talk as if you mean it, Hoke. I was only kidding."

"Why not? At least it's an idea. I haven't been able to think of anything, and it'll give Brownley something on paper to turn over to the new chief."

"If you really mean it, I'll type it up tonight when I go on shift. But you'll have to sign it. I sure as hell won't."

"I'll sign it. Hell, I'd like to watch something like that on TV myself. Bartender!" Hoke beckoned to the man behind the bar. "Give this gentleman a shot of Early Times and a beer, and dump this pink stuff in the sink."

Quevedo sighed. "I guess one shot won't hurt me." He pushed the strawberry margarita to one side.

"The key to drinking is moderation," Hoke said. He finished his beer, paid for the drinks, and drove toward the station. A block before he reached the station, Hoke stopped at the curb, emptied the car ashtray into the street, and then drove to the lot to turn in his unmarked car. Mrs. Burger's black More cigarette butts, if found in the ashtray, would have netted him another twenty-five-dollar fine.

CHAPTER 15

WHILE HOKE WAS WATCHING SATURDAY NIGHT LIVE ON the tube, the phone rang. Hoke cursed and turned the sound down before answering the phone in the kitchen.

"I'm sorry to disturb you this time of night at home, Sergeant Moseley, but I couldn't get ahold of Lieutenant Vitale. I'm Officer Clyde Brown, and my badge number, in case—"

"Never mind, Brown. You didn't wake me. What's up?"

"I'm on a one-man patrol, alone in the car, you see—out here at the airport. There's a redcap watching my car at departures, and I'm phoning here at Eastern from a pay phone. My instructions were to stop at Forty-one thirty-five Poinciana two or three times on my patrol and put the spot on the house number for a minute or so. I asked Vitale why, and he said the instructions came from you, and that was all I needed to know. I was only there, he said, to look for signs of departure."

"Did you see any?"

"That's why I'm calling, Sergeant. On my second pass

the house was dark. I didn't see anything unusual, but I noticed the white Mercedes in the driveway. I turned off the spot, and drove down to the next corner, and parked. I wanted a smoke, and you have to get out of the car to smoke. There's this new rule, you know about—"

"I know about the rule."

"Okay. Anyway, I lit a cigarette. My car lights were out, and then I saw this white Mercedes drive by and recognized the number. I got back in the car and tailed it out here to the airport. He parked in the Eastern garage, up on the third floor. The man had a suitcase, and when he headed for the elevator, I drove around here to the Eastern loading zone and parked. I told the redcap to watch my car and waited inside the terminal. The man bought a ticket at the Eastern counter and then left for the concourse. After he left, I asked the ticket seller about the ticket, and she said the man's name was L. Black, and he bought a one-way ticket to Seattle. Flight Eight Thirty-two. The plane doesn't leave till twelve forty-five, and I can still pick him up. But I don't have any orders for that or any probable cause. So when I couldn't get ahold of Lieutenant Vitale, I thought I'd better call you. Captain Slater in Homicide gave me your home number."

"How come you're in a one-man car, Brown?"

"It's part of the new austerity program, I guess. In quiet districts like mine a one-man car is all you need anyway. I can always call for backup. But I'm way the hell out of my district now, and I'm gonna have to get back. Unless you tell me to pick this guy up."

"No, let him go. You did the right thing by calling me. When you write your report, send a copy to me, and I'll write a commendation for your file. The man's a murder suspect, but I don't have enough evidence to get a warrant. The best thing I could hope for was to have him run. You'd better get back to your car before someone steals it—unless you tipped the redcap in advance. And thanks again for calling me. If you get any flak for leaving your district, I'll cover for you with Lieutenant Vitale."

Hoke turned off the TV set altogether, sat back in his recliner, and savored the report. There was no doubt in his mind now that Dr. Schwartz was the killer. If the frightened bastard had used his own name to fly out to Seattle, the doctor could have said later on that he was on a vacation or visiting a friend. But "L. Black," an unimaginative pseudonym for Leo Schwartz, was a dead giveaway.

Before dressing again, Hoke called González at home, and told him to meet him at Dr. Schwartz's house.

"Tonight?"

"That's what I said. If you get there before me, don't knock on the door. Just wait for me. We'll talk to Mrs. Schwartz together. Bring your notebook, and take down everything that's said."

"It'll take me about fifteen minutes or so to get there."

"I may be a little longer, but wait for me out front."

GONZÁLEZ'S SHINY BLACK MERCURY LYNX WAS PARKED IN front of the house at the curb when Hoke arrived. Hoke pulled into the empty driveway, and González joined him on the lawn. He was wearing a white shawl-collared tuxedo jacket, with a red-and-blue bow tie and cummerbund, black tuxedo trousers, and black patent leather shoes.

"Why the semiformal?"

"I had a date," González said. "I'd just got home when you called. If things had worked out the way I planned, I wouldn't't've been home to answer the damned phone."

"You have your notebook?"

"Right here. I've also got a minirecorder in my jacket pocket, but I haven't turned it on yet."

"That's even better. Turn it on now. You're beginning to show initiative after all."

"It's mine, not the department's."

"That doesn't matter, if it works."

The porch light was on, and there was a light in the back of the house. Hoke pressed the bell ring, holding his finger on the button, and listened as chimes clanged softly behind the heavy metal door. Lights came on in the living room, and a square of light appeared on the lawn as the window whitened behind lace curtains. Louise Schwartz opened the door. Her eyelids were red and sore-looking, as if she had been crying. She wore a rose-colored negligee over her white satin nightgown, and her slippers were pink rabbits, upside-down rabbits, including furry heads, bright button eyes, and floppy ears. Hoke had seen slippers like these on sale in department stores but thought that only teenage girls bought them. The long rabbit ears flipped up and down as she invited them in and retreated to the living room.

"If you've come to arrest my husband, Sergeant Moseley, you're too late. He's gone."

"I know that," Hoke said. "He's on his way to Seattle, but the sheriff'll meet the plane. We want to ask you a few questions, however—"

"I didn't know Leo did it—not until tonight, when he told me."

"That was one of my questions."

"When Leo came home this evening, he was irritable. Something was bothering him, and he could hardly eat dinner. Mrs. Burger, his nurse at the clinic, told him in confidence this afternoon that the police knew who the killer was and would soon be making an arrest. I told him the same thing, what you told me. I know you told me not to, but he knew already, so I went ahead and told him. All he said at dinner was that he wondered who it was. But

217

then he had three drinks after dinner. Brandy. He sometimes has one brandy, but when he poured the third one, I knew that he was worried about something. When I pointed out to him that this was his third drink, he got mad and said he didn't need a woman around to count his drinks for him. He went into his den and closed the door. I thought he'd be out in a few minutes to apologize, but then, when he didn't come out, I went upstairs and got ready for bed—" She smiled at González. "You look very nice, Lieutenant."

González smiled, looking up from his notebook. "I'm not a lieutenant. I'm just an investigator. Sergeant Mosely here is in charge."

"You still look very nice."

"Perhaps if we sat down . . ." Hoke suggested.

"I have coffee in the kitchen," Mrs. Schwartz said. "I could bring it out here, or we could go back to the breakfast room."

"Sure."

They followed her down the hallway to the kitchen, and she seated them in the breakfast room. One wall was open to the kitchen, and the other three walls, mostly glass jalousies, were surrounded by a patio. She switched on the lights outside. Hoke looked out and saw a leering stone gnome with a wooden wheelbarrow in the bushes encircling the patio. There was a large green metal frog inside the wheelbarrow. She brought cups and saucers to the table and poured the coffee before seating herself. Hoke put a half spoon of sugar into his coffee, and noticed that the creamer held real cream, not milk or half-and-half. He also realized that Mrs. Schwartz had used some delaying tactics, just as she had been about to tell all. But perhaps she was merely trying to organize her thoughts.

"How long have you known that Dr. Schwartz killed your husband?"

She studied the tablecloth for a moment and nibbled her thin lower lip. There was a triangle of flesh-colored adhesive tape plastered between her eyes. This patch was supposed to minimize or reduce frown lines between the twin arches of her eyebrows, but the frown lines were under the tape all the same, Hoke thought.

"Not till tonight," she said finally, with a shake of her head. "I'm still trying to take it all in, what Leo told me, and it seems unreal."

"Perhaps I can help you, Mrs. Schwartz. Were you and Leo having an affair before Dr. Russell was killed, or did it begin afterward?"

"Afterward. And it wasn't any *affair*, as you put it, because I was a widow then. I don't like the word *affair*. The implication in that word is that something sordid was going on, and that wasn't the case at all."

"I'm not implying anything. I need information. I'm trying to determine what Dr. Schwartz's motivation was, that's all. In their partnership arrangement Dr. Farris and Dr. Schwartz, after Dr. Russell's death, had a fifty-fifty split of the clinic, so it wasn't necessary for Leo Schwartz to marry you in order to profit."

"I also share in the profits, Sergeant. Not as much, but I still get a five percent profit until the clinic is sold or their partnership is dissolved. The thing is, as Leo told me, my husband was bringing in most of the money. He had the most patients, and he brought in more than half the money, and they were barely making up the second half. My husband, you see, had threatened to leave, to sell out his third interest to another doctor. If he'd done that, they would've been in trouble. That was Leo's motivation. It wasn't for me. I didn't know anything about the business side of the clinic. I got my insurance, of course, but then I turned to Leo for help. I didn't know how to invest my money or run my affairs, and he was very helpful. We saw a lot of each other, and then one thing led to another. It wasn't a mad love affair, and there was no triangle—I want you to understand that. We're mature people, and it seemed like a sensible arrangement to get married. It was easier for me, and it seemed foolish for Leo to keep a separate apartment when he was spending most of his nights here anyway." She sipped her coffee but held the cup with both hands. "But I didn't know that Leo had killed my husband. The idea never occurred to me. And I still can't believe it, even though he told me so tonight before he left. Taking lives is not something doctors do. They *save* lives, not take them, and Leo and Max Farris would still have made lots of money, even if my husband had sold out his third of the practice."

"Some people never have enough money, Mrs. Schwartz. Look at Ivan Boesky. Greed was Leo's motivation. This is not a community property state, so Dr. Schwartz also got you, your house, the white Mercedes, and Dr. Russell's ring. He also made a handsome profit, I suppose, when he sold his condo and moved in here with you. You'd better see a lawyer sometime tomorrow, Mrs. Schwartz, even though it's Sunday. Salvage as much as you can before we bring Dr. Schwartz back here for trial. Otherwise, he'll try to spend all your money, as well as his, for lawyer's fees. So get a good lawyer, and close your joint accounts."

"I still can't believe that Leo would do such a thing."

"He did it, all right. Detective González will be over here in the morning with a statement for you to sign. Try to get some sleep, and if you remember any pertinent details, give them to Detective González. The state's attorney will contact you by Monday or Tuesday."

"Will I have to testify against Leo in court? I thought a wife wasn't allowed to testify against her husband."

Hoke laughed. "That isn't true, although a lot of people think it is. In your case your testimony will be necessary for you to avoid being considered an accomplice, you see. You'll have to clear yourself, which will be easy enough because you were out of town at the time of the murder. You see what I mean?"

She nodded. "I guess so. Leo has a lawyer on retainer. Should I contact him or get another?"

"Get another. You can't ask Leo's lawyer to help you hide money and assets now, can you? I'm not allowed to recommend anyone, but call some of your women friends— preferably a woman who got a decent divorce settlement— and use her lawyer."

Hoke got to his feet, and so did González. Hoke took his cup and saucer over to the sink, but González didn't.

"I have one more question, Mrs. Schwartz," Hoke said as he turned at the sink. "How do you get your garage door open?"

"I—I just unlock it and lift it with one hand. Why?"

"You don't have electronic garage openers then?"

She nodded. "We have two. Leo keeps one in his car, but I leave the other one here in the house. I had to order replacements when you kept Paul's opener as evidence, but the new ones don't work very well at times. Is this important?"

Hoke shrugged. "Not any longer. Just a loose end. Let's go, González."

"Thanks for the coffee, Mrs. Schwartz," González said.

She led the way to the front door to let them out. She

opened the front door but blocked it with her body. "One more thing, Sergeant. Leo took his pistol with him. In his suitcase. I'm afraid he might do something foolish with it. He was very distraught when he left."

"Thanks for telling me this."

After she closed the door, Hoke told González to meet him back at the office.

"This is Sunday morning already," González protested. "I'm supposed to take my mom to the nine o'clock mass."

"If you get the statement typed, and then I edit it, and then you retype it without any mistakes, and then you get Mrs. Schwartz to sign it before nine, then you can go to mass. Otherwise, phone your mother and tell her to make other plans. Our work is just beginning on this case. Now get moving."

When he got back to the station, Hoke called the sheriff in Seattle and arranged for him to pick up Leo Schwartz, traveling under the name L. Black, when the plane landed at the airport.

"He'll have the murder weapon in his baggage, so it'll have to be returned as well. Even though he's a murder suspect, Schwartz isn't a dangerous man, and he likes high living. So if you can, Sheriff, make jail uncomfortable for him. Don't isolate him, but shove him into the drunk tank. I want him to suffer enough discomfort so he won't fight extradition."

"I know what you mean, Sergeant. Two deputies will meet him at the airport."

"It'll probably be Monday before I can wire you a confirmation order, but the weapon alone will be enough to hold him without bail till we get the extradition order."

"No problem. How's the weather down there in Miami?"

"It was about eighty-five today—maybe a little higher than that."

"It's cold and wet here. I've never been to Miami, but I'd like to come down there on a vacation sometime."

"If you ever do, call me, and I'll show you a few high spots."

"I might just take you up on that some day. How far's Miami from Disney World?"

"Hell, you don't want to go there, Sheriff. Orlando's a high-crime area, but if you come to Miami, I'll get you a permit to carry your weapon while you're here."

The sheriff laughed. "Okay, Sergeant Moseley. Leo Schwartz traveling as L. Black."

"Right."

IT WAS ALMOST 7:00 A.M. BEFORE GONZÁLEZ HAD A STATEMENT typed well enough to satisfy Hoke. Hoke made three photocopies and gave all four copies to González to take to Mrs. Schwartz to sign.

"She'll probably be asleep now," González said. "Perhaps if I went over after the nine o'clock mass, she'd be awake."

"You'll go now, before she changes her mind and before she talks to a lawyer who'll advise her not to sign anything. Then come back and put the statements in the safe. I'll probably still be here because I've got to write my notes for the file and a memo to Major Brownley. I want you to type up your notes, too, but you can come back and do it after you go to mass. I'll want to talk to Brownley first thing tomorrow to see how we should handle this thing with the state attorney. Here we are, with a solved case handed to us on a silver fucking platter, and all you can think about is taking your mother to mass."

After González left the office, Hoke typed a redline memo to Major Brownley and put it in his box. He tried to phone Lieutenant Vitale in Traffic but couldn't get a line on his whereabouts. He then typed another redline to Vitale, telling him to call off the surveillance and commending Officer Brown for his alertness and initiative. Then he drove home.

Hoke wanted to be awake when Ellita and the girls got home, so he didn't undress and go to bed. He removed his shoes and sat back in his recliner, so he would awaken when they came through the door. As soon as he levered the seat back, his mind began to race, thinking of all the things he still had to do. Then, with an effort, and using a trick that had worked for him before, he imagined a heavy black blind in his mind. His fingers grasped the pull cord, and he slowly lowered the black mental blind. When it was down, all the way down, and completely dark, he fell into a heavy sleep.

CHAPTER 16

HOKE AWOKE WITH A GROAN AT TEN-THIRTY. HIS NECK, still bruised and sore, had developed a crick in it from his position in the chair. Shooting pains pulsed tiny darts into the backs of his eyes. Hoke showered and shaved, scrubbed his teeth, and rinsed his dentures in Listerine before adjusting them in his mouth. He made coffee, took three Tylenol, and was on his third cup of coffee when the phone rang. It was Major Brownley.

"Did I wake you?" Brownley asked.

"No, I was awake. Did you read my redliner?"

"Yes, I'm in my office now. That's one of the things I want to talk about. I'm taking you off the Dr. Russell homicide. I gave it to Sergeant Quevedo to finish up."

"There's still a lot to do, Willie," Hoke protested. "I've got to interview Dr. Max Farris, and I want to talk to Mrs. Burger again at some length. I told her something in confidence, and she could hardly wait to pass it on to Schwartz. The nurse knows a lot more than she ever let on when I first talked to her. Then I—"

"Never mind, Hoke. Quevedo's taken over. I've already given him the file, and González can fill him in on any other stuff he needs to know."

"González doesn't know everything, Willie. He doesn't know about the garage door."

"What garage door?"

"Mrs. Schwartz's garage door. Sometimes it opens with the electronic opener, and sometimes it doesn't."

"Hell, they're all like that at times, Hoke. Mine doesn't always work either. I think it's the humidity. Why is it so important?"

Hoke thought for a moment and then laughed. "It isn't important, not any longer. It's just a loose end I wanted to tie up. If Dr. Schwartz still has the murder weapon, it won't be an issue."

"He's in jail now in Seattle, and the weapon—or *a* weapon—was recovered. I've already had word on that. Later on, Quevedo has a few questions, he can talk to you, but I don't think you'll have much time for him."

"Even if you take me off the case, I'll have to testify at the trial."

"That'll be two or three months from now. I'll say it slow: You are officially off the case."

"I don't understand this, Willie. What—"

"I'm trying to tell you. Do you know where Molly's Coffee Shop is, on the Trail?"

"Not exactly. Although I remember passing by it."

"It's at Eighth Street and Third Avenue. At the end of a new little shopping center there. Molly's the new chief's sister-in-law, so he likes to eat breakfast there two or three times a week. Anyway, you're to meet the new chief there tomorrow morning at eight o'clock."

"What about? This isn't another weird undercover job

like that Immokalee fiasco, is it? If it is, forget it. I'd rather go back into uniform and turn with the signals on Flagler."

"I can't tell you what it's about, Hoke. The new chief will do that. Just be at Molly's at eight. That's all I can tell you."

"Will you be there, Willie?"

"No. It'll just be you and the new chief."

"I'm not going to do any more undercover work, Willie."

"I wish I could tell you about it, Hoke, but I can't. I'll just say you'll be surprised. Pleasantly surprised. Okay?"

"I'll be there. One more thing, while we're on the phone. Let's do the division a favor and transfer González the hell out of Homicide. Ordinarily, when a man loses his ignorance, he doesn't regain it, but that doesn't hold true for González."

"We're short seven detectives already, Hoke, counting three on suspension."

"We can get a mutual. Do you know Murdock, over in Robbery?"

"I think so. What about Murdock?"

"I talked to him about a month ago, and he wants to get out of Robbery and into Homicide. He's been in plain-clothes for about six years or so, and maybe we could make a mutual transfer between him and González."

"No, we can't do that, Hoke, even if Robbery was willing to let Murdock go. It would throw off the ethnic balance. On a mutual transfer we'd have to have another Hispanic. But I'll check around, and if I can trade González for another Hispanic somewhere, I'll see what I can do."

"That doesn't make sense, Willie. Murdock's an experienced investigator, and González is good with figures and statistics. He'd fit in well over in Robbery. They could let him handle inventories and simple things like that."

"I know you're right, but Murdock's a WASP, and we can only make a mutual for another Hispanic."

"Forget it then. Anything else, Willie?"

"No . . . I don't think so. What've you heard from Ellita?"

"She's just fine. I'll tell her you sent your regards." Hoke hung up quickly before Brownley could ask any more questions.

A LONG BLUE STRETCH LINCOLN PULLED UP IN FRONT OF THE house at eleven-thirty. As Hoke watched from behind the screen door, Sue Ellen and Aileen got out, and the driver opened the trunk to get their luggage. The driver, a squat dark-faced man with short muscular arms, was probably Goya y Goya, Hoke thought. Hoke retreated to his bedroom instead of going outside to help the girls with their luggage and to avoid giving the chauffeur a tip. Ellita and Hutton—"Donnie"—were not in the car. When Hoke heard the girls talking in the living room, he walked back down the hall to greet them. Both girls were wearing straw hats, purchased from straw market vendors in Nassau, and their faces were bright with sunburn. Aileen ran to Hoke, hugged and kissed him. Sue Ellen, showing more restraint, kissed him on the cheek.

"How was Nassau, and where's Ellita?" Hoke said.

The two girls exchanged glances.

"I've got a present for you, Daddy," Sue Ellen said, opening her bag on the couch.

"Me, too," Aileen said, getting her bag.

Something is wrong, Hoke thought. So far neither one of the girls had looked him in the eye. Sue Ellen hadn't redyed her hair blue; it was now brown and curly, and she was wearing a new powder blue sundress. The skirt barely reached her bony knees. She handed him a gray T-shirt

They kissed him good night and went off to their respective rooms and closed the doors.

Hoke stayed up and drank a couple of beers while he watched the tube. But he couldn't get interested in anything and soon turned off the set. He wondered what the new chief wanted to see him about. The new chief of the Miami Police Department was always called the new chief because he was always a new chief. The average tenure for a new chief was about eighteen months. The average tenure for a city manager (who hired and fired the police chiefs) was also eighteen months. So every time the city commission fired a city manager and hired a new one, the new one soon found a reason to fire the new chief and put in a new chief of his own. Then the new new chief shook things up in the department, transferring and promoting people he thought would be loyal to him. The three assistant chiefs, all colonels, had all been demoted and promoted several times apiece. Survival at or near the top was a tough proposition, no doubt about it. And the three assistant chiefs had to be the right ethnic balance—one black, one Hispanic, and one white man (but the white man couldn't be a Catholic because the Hispanic was a Catholic).

The new new chief was moving cautiously so far—Hoke had to give him credit for that—although he had vowed, when he was sworn in, that he intended to modernize the department, whatever that meant. The city manager was new, and his new chief was new, so there probably wouldn't be any radical changes for at least another year or so, Hoke thought.

Hoke popped the top on another can of Old Style and went outside on the front lawn to drink it. The house across the street was dark, and most of the lights in the other houses on the block were turned out. Tomorrow was a

Monday, and people had to go to work again. They went to bed early in the Green Lakes subdivision on Sunday nights. Hoke returned to the kitchen, got an ice pick out of the utility drawer, and then crossed the street. He jabbed the point of the pick into the left front tire of Donald Hutton's Henry J. As the air hissed out, the sound seemed to direct him around the little car, and he punched through the other three tires. As the air hissed out, the little car sank perceptibly.

"There's a wedding present for you, you bastard," Hoke said softly. Then, feeling a little sheepish but happier, he returned to his house and put the ice pick back into the drawer. Hoke undressed and finished his beer while sitting on the edge of his army cot. His muscles were sore, his cracked ribs ached, and his head buzzed from the beers. He fell asleep as soon as his head hit the pillow.

CHAPTER 17

MOLLY'S COFFEE SHOP DIDN'T HAVE MUCH OF A BREAK-
fast crowd, Hoke thought, but when he examined the
menu, he could see why. There was no pass-through coffee
bar, and this was an anomaly for Little Havana. Most of
the Cuban restaurants on Eighth Street served a *desayuno
especial*—two fried eggs, ham or bacon, long slices of
margarined Cuban toast, and *cafe con leche*—for $1.49.
Molly's breakfast was standard American—two eggs (your
way), bacon, ham, or sausage, with grits or home fried
potatoes and white bread toast for $2.79. Coffee, at fifty
cents, was extra, and there were no free refills. Molly
probably made her money, if she made her nut at all, he
thought, with the white-collar lunch crowd, workers from
the office buildings over on Brickell Avenue. There were
several salads on the lunch menu and a few light lunch
items that would appeal to legal secretaries.

Hoke got a table by the window and ordered coffee. He
was early, and he had brought the sports section from the
Miami Herald along to read while he waited for the new

chief. He read a long interview with Vinny Testaverde, the Miami Hurricanes' hotshot quarterback, and then folded the paper and tossed it onto the empty table behind him. In another five years, Testaverde would be a multi-millionaire, Hoke thought, and he'd be trying to make ends meet on a pension of $734 a month, unless, of course, he stayed on the force and tried for thirty years. He shuddered at the prospect.

Hoke signaled the waiter, a sullen-faced Iranian, and asked for another cup of coffee. The new chief came in and joined Hoke at the window table at eight-fifteen. Hoke had talked to the new chief only a couple of times, but then the man had had his job for only three months and hadn't settled in. Hoke hadn't made up his mind about him yet. The old new chief had always worn his uniform, one he had designed himself, complete with four stars on each collar and four more on each epaulet. His cap bill was loaded with gold scrambled eggs. He had been a reserve major in the U.S. Marines, and by giving himself four stars to wear, he had achieved his lifetime ambition to become a general. And like most generals in the army and marines, he had delegated everything, including some important decisions he should have made himself. When a few scandals broke, he didn't know whom to blame, so he had been fired.

The new chief never wore a uniform and probably didn't have one. He wore tailored tropical suits, complete with vests—even when the temperature soared into the nineties. And when he left the station in his Lincoln town car, he wore a white Panama hat with a one-inch black silk hat-band. He had had a few years' experience as a police chief in Lawrence, Kansas, but he had spent most of his adult life in college classrooms, lecturing students on sociology and juvenile delinquency. He was purportedly an authority on juvenile delinquency and had written two books on the subject that were used as texts in a dozen colleges. At least he wrote clearly, compared with the old new chief's memos and written directives. The ex-marine new chief had been semiliterate, and Bill Henderson used to circle all his sentence fragments and misspelled words with a red grease pencil before posting his memos on the bulletin board.

The new chief placed his Panama carefully on an empty chair, smiled at Hoke, and said: "It's nice of you to join me here, Sergeant Moseley, and I appreciate it." The new chief was in his early forties, and the pale skin beneath his blue eyes was puffy. His black hair was quite full, with a widow's peak, and two locks were curled on each side of his forehead like commas. Either his wife cut his hair, Hoke thought, or he paid at least thirty bucks for his haircuts.

"I didn't have a hell of a lot of choice."

"Did you order yet?"

"No, sir, I was waiting for you."

"I'm sorry I held you up, but I had a phone call just as I was leaving my apartment. My sister-in-law owns this place, and I hope she can make a go of it. She and my brother were divorced three years ago, and if she can make a decent living here, he'll be able to ease up on some of his alimony payments."

"I know what you mean, Chief, but it doesn't work out that way. My ex-wife married a ballplayer who makes three hundred and twenty-five thousand a year, and I still have to pay alimony. It was in the settlement, you see, when we got our no-fault, and I was dumb enough at the time to sign it."

"Perhaps if you petitioned the judge?"

Hoke shrugged. "I could do that, I suppose. The kids live with me now, as you probably know, and they didn't when we got our divorce. What I do now is send her a check when I have some money left over and skip it when I don't. And about two weeks after a skipped check I get a nasty call from her bitchy lawyer."

The Iranian came over and took their order. The new chief ordered two three-minute eggs in a cup, one slice of dry toast, and a small glass of orange juice. Hoke ordered a Belgian waffle with sausage links and told the waiter to have the cook heat the syrup.

"I always try to eat a light breakfast," the new chief explained. "I drink coffee all day long in the office, and Mrs. Sincavage, my secretary, always has a box of Dunkin' Donuts on her desk. About ten or ten-thirty I usually succumb and take one."

"My father does that," Hoke said, smiling. "He loves jelly doughnuts."

"How is your father?"

"He's in fine shape for his age. He plans on living forever, and I think he'll make it, too." Hoke lighted a Kool, and the new chief frowned.

"You're still smoking?"

"Yes, sir. It's an acquired habit."

"Have you tried to quit yet?"

"I'm not ready to quit yet."

"You can do it if you want to badly enough. I smoked two packs a day, and I managed to quit."

"Is that why we met this morning, sir, to discuss my smoking?"

The new chief exposed a row of tiny blackened lower teeth. "I'm sorry. Ex-smokers, like ex-drinkers, have a tendency to preach the good word. No, that isn't why I asked you here. Ahh—here's breakfast."

The waiter placed the plates on the table. Hoke tested the syrup in the small white porcelain pitcher with his forefinger. "It isn't heated. Take it back to the chef and have him warm it up." The waiter shrugged and left with the little pitcher.

The new chief crumbled his slice of toast into his runny eggs and stirred the mess with his spoon. Hoke buttered his waffle, cut it into bite-size pieces, and then cut up his three link sausages. The waiter returned with a steaming little pitcher of syrup.

Hoke dribbled some of the syrup onto his chopped-up waffle and dug into his breakfast. They ate silently. The new chief shot quick glances at Hoke occasionally, but he didn't say anything until he finished eating his eggs and drained the four-ounce juice glass.

"We've got some problems in the department, Moseley, as you are well aware." He took out a round tin of Copenhagen snuff and removed the lid. The lid was of silver, made to fit the regular container of Copenhagen, and an eagle was engraved on it. He put a small pinch of snuff behind his lower lip, replaced the lid, and put the can back into his jacket pocket. "Eight cops are now waiting trial for murder, and three cops are in jail waiting trial on home-invasion charges. It's bad enough to invade a home, terrorize the residents, and rob them, as these men did. On the murders the men killed were all drug dealers, so there's no loss there, but they weren't killed in a legitimate raid—they were killed during a drug rip-off. At least three of these cops'll be exonerated, but it looks bad for the department when you have that many cops being tried for murder. And when it looks bad for the department, it makes me look bad."

"It not only looks bad, it is bad, Chief, but it's the money. When a patrolman's only making twenty thousand a year or so and can make ten in only two hours on a drug deal, it's hard for him to turn down. Especially if he's married and has a family."

"Would you risk your career and take a chance on going to prison for ten thousand bucks?"

"Not a chance, Chief. But my background's different from these younger cops. Besides, my father's rich and in his late seventies. When he dies, I'll get a good chunk of cash, even though his new wife'll get most of it. In addition to that, I have only five years to go for retirement."

"I know this, Moseley. Major Brownley and I have gone over your jacket and records, and we know more about you than you do because you've forgotten a lot of it. Major Brownley recommended you for promotion, and I concurred. In two more days, Wednesday at ten, I'll swear you in as a lieutenant in your new office."

"Can't I think this over, Chief? I like working on the cold cases, and so far I've been doing a fair job. I know I took the exam and all, but that's because I didn't think I'd get promoted."

"No, you don't have a choice. You're going to head Internal Affairs. What you'll have to do, and you'll report directly to me, is get rid of our bad cops before they've had a chance to become bad cops. I want you to begin with the new graduating class at the academy. Check their jackets, interview each man personally, and if you have any doubts about any one of them, check his name off the graduation list. They've all been tested for drug use and had a battery of psychological tests, but that isn't good enough. If you don't want a man to graduate, you don't have to give a reason. Just scratch his name off the list. There are also some pending suspensions to investigate, but you'll know how to handle these without any trouble. Later on, maybe by next Friday, we'll get together in my office and discuss further probes. I'll have Mrs. Sincavage call you and set up a time."

"This is a big responsibility, Chief. What about Lieutenant Norbert? I don't respect him, and I don't think I can work with an asshole like him."

"You're Norbert's replacement. He's retiring. He's got twenty-four years in, and I persuaded him to put in his papers. He retires Wednesday, and you'll take over the office. There'll be a little ceremony for both of you in the office when he retires and you're sworn in. The press'll be there because I want the change to be known by everyone as soon as possible."

"I'd still like some time to think this over, Chief."

"There's nothing to think over. The decision's been made, Lieutenant. Incidently, Moseley, Sheriff Boggis, over in Collier County, was mighty grateful about the way you took care of the little problem he had. And that's good for us, too, to have a friend of the department over in Collier County. Don't look so surprised. I had Brownley set this up to see how well you could work on a secret assignment, and you came through beautifully, just as Brownley told me you would."

The new chief got to his feet and waved to the waiter. "Put these breakfasts on my tab, son," he said when the waiter came over, "and add a fifteen percent tip for yourself. And be sure to tell Molly, when she comes in this morning, that I was here for breakfast."

The waiter nodded, picked up two empty plates, and turned away.

Hoke started to rise, but the new chief put a restraining hand on his shoulder. "Stay and finish your coffee, Lieutenant. Take some time off, and I'll see you Wednesday morning at ten. Till then clear out your desk, do some shopping. Buy a new suit perhaps."

The new chief left abruptly, departing through the front door without looking back.

Hoke sat still for a moment, benumbed, and then leaped

up from the table. He stumbled slightly as he rushed through the empty tables to the men's room at the end of the short hallway. When he started to remove his teeth in the men's room, he noticed he was still clutching his coffee cup. He put the cup into the sink, removed his teeth, and then vomited into the toilet bowl. It all came up: sausage, waffle, warm syrup, coffee. Hoke flushed the toilet. He washed his face at the sink, let the cold water flow over his wrists, and then put his teeth back in.

Major Brownley and the new chief, with an assist from Mel Peoples, had set him up. Hoke had suspected something that morning at Monroe Station, when he had asked the major if this was a test of some kind, but he hadn't suspected anything so deviously Byzantine. The new chief had come up with this weird plan to make sure that he would have something on him; it was a way to ensure that Hoke would be his man. But it wasn't blackmail; it was a stalemate, a Mexican standoff. There was no way that the new chief could use this knowledge without implicating himself, Brownley, and Mel Peoples. If Hoke didn't like it, he could resign from the department, and they wouldn't do anything to prevent that. But if he did resign, he would lose everything—his occupation and his pension. A man is defined by his job, by his work, and if he weren't a detective, he would be nothing. Nothing.

Hoke rinsed his cup at the sink, returned to his table, and ordered fresh coffee. He was calmer now and could think a little more clearly. Deep down he had wanted to be promoted to lieutenant, but it had seemed so far away in the future he hadn't let himself think about it. Looking for dirty cops was a rotten job, and even the straight cops— the majority of the department—resented the men in IA. But a good man was needed for the job, and he knew that he could handle it. Norbert, ever since he got his twenty years in, had been coasting, and there was a lot of work to be done to clean up the department. Now that he thought it over, he realized that the new chief, with Brownley's recommendation, had picked the best man for the appointment. Not only did he know where a lot of bodies were buried, but he now had the shovel to dig them up. He had no intention of confining himself to investigating cadets.

He was feeling better about his new promotion and appointment already. But first things first. He'd order a new tailored uniform, and buy two new black suits like the ones Captain Slater usually wore, black silk, with a little shine to the material. The new chief had wanted his own man in the office, but he would learn, in time, that Hoke Moseley was nobody's man but his own.

Hoke finished his coffee, dropped a crumpled dollar bill on the table, drove home, and phoned his father in Riviera Beach to tell him about his promotion to lieutenant.

CHAPTER 18

*T*HREE WEEKS LATER, ON A SUNDAY AFTERNOON, HOKE WAS
fixing sandwiches in the dining room. He had a plate of
assorted cold cuts, a loaf of rye bread, and some freshly
picked beefsteak tomatoes he had purchased that afternoon from a stand on Krome Avenue. Aileen sat across
the table from him, watching, and Sue Ellen was making
potato salad in the kitchen.

Evening meals were rather casual now that Ellita had
gone away. They rarely ate together in the evenings, except
on Sunday, although Hoke had taken the girls out to dinner
at Burger King a few times.

The Huttons, Donald, Ellita and Pepe, lived in a new
two-bedroom condominium apartment Hutton had bought
in Hallandale. Hutton wanted to be near the track, he told
Ellita, but Hoke knew that Hutton hadn't liked the girls
coming across the street all the time to see Ellita and the
baby. Hutton had also sold his Henry J by putting a classi-
fied ad in both daily papers. Before they had moved out
of the house across the street, a man had come by for it

with a tow truck. Ellita still had her little Honda Civic, but Hutton had bought a new Mercury Lynx station wagon to haul the baby's stuff around with them when they went out together.

Except for wishing Ellita good luck, when she returned from Nassau with a gold band on her ring finger, Hoke hadn't spoken to her again. When Hutton came over for her furniture and other belongings, Hoke had gone to Larry's Hideaway and stayed there until everything was moved.

"What do you want on your sandwich? Mustard or mayonnaise?"

"Mayonnaise," Aileen said.

Sue Ellen came in from the kitchen with a bowl of potato salad and placed it on the table. "Help yourself to potato salad. I still have to sugar the tea."

"D'you want mustard or mayonnaise on your sandwich?"

"Both." Sue Ellen returned to the kitchen.

"Daddy," Aileen said, "don't you ever miss Ellita?"

Hoke shook his head. "Did you ever watch Ellita eat a Cuban sandwich? First, she'd nibble the bread all the way around, and then she'd take off the top slice. She'd eat all the ham with her fingers, and then she'd put the top slice back on the cheese and pork. After the ham was gone, she no longer had a Cuban sandwich, for Christ's sake, she had a pork and cheese sandwich. If she wanted a pork and cheese sandwich, why didn't she order one in the first place instead of asking for a Cuban sandwich? Hell, why would I miss a woman who ate a sandwich like that?"

Suddenly, Aileen began to cry. Tears, unchecked, streamed down her cheeks.

"What's the matter? Why are you crying?"

"Be-because," she said, finally, still sobbing, "because you can't!"

ABOUT THE AUTHOR

CHARLES WILLEFORD has been a professional soldier, boxer, radio announcer, and painter. A former Californian, he lives in South Miami, where he reviews suspense and mystery novels for the *Miami Herald*. His novels include *The Burnt Orange Heresy*, *Cockfighter*, *Miami Blues*, *New Hope for the Dead*, and *Sideswipe*.